GODSWAR

MAGITECH CHRONICLES BOOK 7

CHRIS FOX

CHRIS FOX WRITES LLC

For Lisa.
The last time I dedicated a book to you we were dating. Now you are my wife, and the most fantastic editor an author could wish for. Thank you for everything you do.

CAST OF CHARACTERS

The Magitech Chronicles are vast, and we now have a dizzying array of gods, demigods, drifters, Shayans, planets, and other stuff. Below you'll find a mostly complete list to remind you who's what.

If you find anything missing, please shoot me an email at chris@chrisfoxwrites.com and I'll get it added!

Gods, Wyrms, & Demigods

Arkelion- Son of Drakkon.

Drakkon- The Guardian of Marid. Dwells on the world of the same name.

The Earthmother- A Wyrm of tremendous power. Sibling to Virkonna and Inura. Killed by Krox during the godswar.

Inura- The undisputed master of *air* in the sector. Inura was the chief architect of the *Spellship*. Sibling to Virkonna and the Earthmother.

Krox- One of the most ancient gods in the sector. Nebiat is in control of Krox.

Malila- The guardian of Xal, a demon queen who rules the Skull of Xal.

Marid- Wyrm mother of the water flight. Devoured by the Ternus ships that formed Nefarius.

Nefarius- Nefarius is a Void Wyrm of immense power who ascended to godhood in the earliest days of the godswar.

Neith- The first arachnidrake, and the eldest of the draconic siblings. Sister to Virkonna, Inura, and the Earthmother, but much, much older.

Shaya- A mortal raised to godhood by Inura in order to defend her people. Died doing exactly that. Now entombed under the great tree on the planet Shaya.

Talifax- Guardian of Nefarius. Talifax's age and race are unknown, but he is rumored to be nearly as old as Xal.

Virkonna- The Wyrm of *air*, sister of Inura, Neith, and the Earthmother. Virkonna is known as the mother of the last dragonflight and helped Inura build the first *Spellship*.

Xal- One of the eldest gods in the sector, and also one of the largest repositories of *void* magic. Xal allowed himself to be killed by a pantheon including most of the other gods on the list, because he knew eventually that would allow for his return. Best known now as the Skull of Xal.

Inurans

Jolene- A powerful Inuran matriarch. Mother to Kazon and Voria.

Kazon- Brother to Voria, son of Jolene. Kazon was mind-wiped alongside Aran.

Skare- A powerful Inuran patriarch, who worked with Talifax to raise their dark goddess.

The Krox

Frit- Frit is an escaped Shayan slave, one of the Ifrit, who were molded by Shayan slavers into beautiful women made completely of flame.

Kahotep- Son of Nebiat, grandson of Teodros. Kahotep, or Kaho for short, is Nebiat's last surviving son. He is a powerful true mage and master scholar.

Nebiat- Daughter of Teodros, granddaughter of Krox, mother of Kahotep. Nebiat is a centuries-old Wyrm, and one of the most powerful true mages in the sector. Her hatred of Voria borders on irrational.

Teodros- Son of Krox, father of Nebiat. Teodros was a hatchling during the last godswar, and played no notable role. However, he's spent the intervening millennia gathering strength, and building his people into a military powerhouse. Teodros orchestrated the rise of Krox, but did not live to see his work completed.

Shayans & Drifters

Bord- Bord is a lower-class Shayan born in the dims at the feet of the great tree. He was conscripted into the Confederate Marines just before the Battle of Starn, and has been cracking bad jokes ever since. Kezia's boyfriend.

Ducius- Thalas's father. Ducius has been a Caretaker of Shaya for many years, one of the most powerful political positions, second only to the Tender. After Eros's death, Ducius took up the role of Tender, and is currently the leader of the Shayan people. However, he is Tender in name only and lacks the divine infusion that both Eros and Aurelia had.

Ducius hates Voria. Kind of a lot.

Eros- Eros was the head of the Temple of Enlightenment on Shaya, and Voria's original master. Eros became Tender of Shaya when Aurelia died. Eros died shortly thereafter fighting Teodros in the Chamber of the First.

Kezia- Kezia is a blonde, curly-haired tech mage drifter born in the dims, not far from where Bord was raised. She was conscripted in the same wave, and went through basic training beside him. Bord's girlfriend.

Thalas- Son of Ducius. Thalas was Voria's second in command for several years. He was executed by Voria for insubordination during the Battle of Marid.

Voria- Daughter of Jolene and Dirk. Sister of Kazon. Voria served as a major in the confederate military, and commanded the *Wyrm Hunter* until she acquired the mythical *Spellship*. She now commands the Shayan defense against Krox's inevitable invasion.

Ternus

Governor Austin- Austin is a young, ambitious politician in the wrong place at the wrong time. He is woefully unprepared to lead his people during a time of war, and is desperate for allies that can help his people survive. Seriously distrusts magic.

Fleet Admiral Kerr- Commander of the Ternus fleet during the Battle for Marid, and subsequently promoted to Fleet Admiral and placed in charge of all Ternus fleets.

Nara- Former space pirate, now powerful true mage. Nara was mindwiped by Voria, and conscripted into the Confederate Marines. She's fought alongside Aran, Crewes, Bord, Kez, and Voria ever since.

Pickus- Pickus is a freckle-faced grease monkey turned tech mage who has somehow found himself as Voria's right-hand man.

Virkonans

Aran- Born on Virkon. Manipulated by Neith into being mindwiped in preparation to forge him into a tool to kill Krox and Nefarius. Aran is currently the Captain of Aran's Outriders, a mercenary unit based out of the *Talon*.

Kheross- Father of Rhea. An ancient Wyrm from an alternate timeline where Virkonna was overcome by a sea of blood. Kheross was corrupted by Nefarius, and despite being cleansed on Shaya, still bears the mark. He's currently allied with Aran's Outriders, but Aran doesn't trust him, and Kheross knows it.

Rhea- Daughter of Kheross. Rhea is an unknown quantity. She believes herself to be a human Outrider, but is in fact a Void Wyrm. She is a powerful war mage, with limited true magic. Until recently she was held on Yanthara, in the custody of the Temple of Shi.

After Crewes freed her, she joined the Outriders with the rank of lieutenant, and has become a devoted member of the company.

Yantharans

Marcelus Crewes- Brother of Sergeant Crewes. Marcelus is a prosecutor living on Shaya. He prosecuted Voria during her trial.

Sergeant Crewes- Brother of Marcelus Crewes. Sergeant Crewes was born on Yanthara. He voluntarily joined the Confederate Marines, and was quickly assigned to the *Wyrm Hunter*. He is one of the strongest tech mages in the sector, and his mastery of *fire* is unrivaled.

Sarala- Priestess of Shi, and former girlfriend of Sergeant Crewes. Sarala is the head of the Temple of Shi, and is responsible for guiding new members to the Catalyst. She dated Crewes briefly in secondary school, but that ended when Crewes enlisted in the Confederate Marines.

PREVIOUSLY ON

You guys all know the drill by now. The *Previously On* is where I get to snarkily relate the previous book, and is always my favorite part to write. That said, having recaps for every book is getting longer and longer, and we're reaching a point where it is no longer feasible.

You can check out all the recaps at magitechchronicles.-com/previously-on. Just as a heads up, this is the last book in the main series. There will be spin-off series!

One last thing before I let you get to the recap. **We've begun play testing the Magitech Chronicles pen and paper RPG**, so if that's something you're interested in, sign up to the mailing list at magitechchronicles.com and I'll get you some details.

The first ever game was run at the 20BooksTo50k convention. I played with five science fiction authors, several of whom I'm betting you'd recognize. By this fall I'm hoping you'll be playing too.

Okay, enough about me. Let's get to the recap.

Last time, on The Magitech Chronicles…

Nefarius opened with the *Talon* being ambushed by a fleet of black ships as they enter the Umbral Depths at Shaya. I decided to write the ambush because if I don't open with some action I'll get hate mail, but also because it needed to underscore something you'd see repeatedly throughout the book.

Talifax and his minions are everywhere. They have thought of every eventuality. They've carefully manipulated the Krox and the Confederacy into &*%-punching each other for decades, so they'd be both weak and dependent on the Inurans. It worked smashingly well, and neither side has ever suspected a thing.

Anyway, Aran and the company win the engagement, but Aran does so by draining magic from the Inuran flagship in the same way the black ships do. This terrifies the crew, especially Crewes, because draining magic is what demons do.

That gives Aran a lot to think about as they fly to Neith's world. Aran is hoping to find some answers there. Who is Xal? What is Aran's connection to him, and does Nara share that connection?

Aran meets with Neith, who answers some of his questions. She confirms that a Hound of Xal exists to devour magic, and then to return it to their master. Since his master is dead, Aran will simply have to use the magic to resurrect him.

She asks Aran why Xal allowed himself to be killed. Surely he must have had a plan. Aran still isn't sure what that is, but the idea that it involves him coming back seems likely. Spoilers, that shit is going down, yo.

Anyway, Neith confirms that Nefarius is a way worse

threat than Krox, and that Aran should start with that. She also suggests Aran head back to Virkon, both because the author needed an excuse to write about samurai-dragon people again, and because it is time to wake Virkonna and get her in on the war.

Meanwhile, Voria says goodbye to Ducius, and we see that Shaya is recovering, but severely underpopulated after the devastating war.

We flip over to Nebiat, who is trying to get information out of Krox on how she can directly interact with the universe. Krox recommends that she create a guardian. They are powerful agents, and can go many places a god would fear to send an avatar directly.

Nebiat approaches her son Kaho, who is still aboard the *Spellship*. He tells her to screw off, because she's Nebiat and he's seen her screw overly literally everyone she's ever talked to. Okay, not literally, but pretty close.

Next Nebiat tries Frit, who also tells her to screw off. But by this point the reader has also seen that Frit is terribly unhappy. Nara doesn't have time for her, and she's lonely... and vulnerable.

We swap to Voria and Nara who have a plan to maybe save Ternus. It's convoluted, so we know right off the bat it's going to fail. Voria grabs another habitable planet in the system, and moves it into synchronous orbit with Ternus.

She tries to move the last surviving refugees off, about two million of them, but Talifax totally trolls her and disintegrates the planet. Worse, he does it in a way to make it look like Voria did it. Ternus exiles her, and every news cycle is devoted to how terrible she is.

Talifax sits behind it all, laughing. He's very good at that. He meets with Skare and we get a "is production on schedule" trope, where the reader realizes that the ritual to resurrect Nefarius is being prepared. The cover sort of gives that away, though, to be fair.

We complete our bad guy interlude chapters with Skare and Governor Austin meeting. Skare offers vague assurances that they can fix their planet if they had the right magic. And, even if they don't want to use it, they should deny it to their enemies.

The people of Ternus are angry, and swallow this line, empowering Austin to get the fleet built and strengthened in time for the *dun dun dun* dark ritual.

We flash to the Ternus fleet over Marid, and they just wreck Drakkon and his children. He calls Voria for help, and she comes to save him...in full view of the Ternus cameras. This cements their view of her as a traitor since she's helping a dragon they claim is a menace.

She retreats to Virkon, where Aran is already chilling. Speaking of....

Aran arrives on Virkon, and Cerberus, the giant door dog/dragon who guards Virkon, is excited to see him. Aran lands and heads to the council chamber where he had an audience with the Wyrms before.

They give him some lip, which he's over, so he uses *void* to smack their emissary around. This gets exactly the type of attention he's after, which is the fastest way to wake Virkonna.

Afterwards Astria, Aran's sister, approaches and asks if Aran will be a spokesperson for Please Don't Treat Outriders Like Crap. She says that he can change the way dragons view humans, and urges him to help.

He refuses the call, but don't worry, he'll get forced into it later.

Meanwhile, Voria is officially welcomed to Virkon at a party, where Voria catches her up on the Krox/Nefarius situation. Voria is frustrated, because she wants to deal with Nebiat and Krox but feels like her hands are tied.

We flash back to Frit, who is feeling increasingly isolated, and we already know what's going to happen. She accepts Nebiat's offer of having a real home and power. Nebiat convinces her that she's changed, and we, the readers, gave a collective eye roll, 'cause...Nebiat.

Meanwhile, Aran and Nara reach the Crucible, where they find Inura and Kazon hard at work building a giant golden mech, because why doesn't this series already have mechs? Anyway, after our reunion, Inura gives them the middle finger and says that Voria can handle waking Virkonna, and to stop interrupting his work.

Voria performs the ritual, and Virkonna wakes. In the process, she rips free of the planet and kills tens of thousands of citizens. Aran is horrified, and finally sees that his sister is right. The humans need a champion.

After Virkonna wakes, she starts taking job applications for guardian. Much to our shock (we're not shocked), Aran kicks the crap out of all of them. It was one of the most fun scenes I've ever written, with Virkonna constructing a mini "system" and them having to protect a replica of a planet.

Prior to the fight, we had a montage scene with Aran and his company training under Drakkon, so we expected some badassery.

After the fight, Virkonna offers to make Aran guardian and he refuses. He takes her to task for killing her own Outriders during her rise. She makes him guardian anyway, and gives him a bunch more *air* magic, because Aran totally didn't have enough power.

Meanwhile, Frit finally agrees to take Nebiat's offer. Nebiat gives her a MASSIVE amount of *fire* magic. She doesn't just make her a guardian. She turns Frit into a full goddess. Krox is utterly pissed, but Nebiat maintains that it was the right decision. We get that she has some secret plan, but not what it is.

Frit goes to the world Nebiat, which of course she named after herself. Nebiat's children are thriving and building a culture. Frit loves it, and loves that she gets to be a part of it. Nebiat's bait is perfect, because now Frit has something to protect.

Frit does return to the *Spellship* one last time to say goodbye to Nara, and to get a vital piece of information. Nebiat has commanded her to find Neith, despite not even knowing the spider-goddess's name.

Frit realizes that the coordinates to Neith's world must be in the *Old Texas*'s computers. If she can scry that moment, then maybe she can find the world. She tries, and it is a good plan, but Neith's geas (super powerful spell) fights her. The resulting explosion destroys the Mirror of Shaya.

Voria is not happy. She and Frit get into a divine battle, which stops only because neither wants to destroy the *Spellship*. Voria banishes Frit and says they are enemies now. Frit leaves and her face is all =(.

We flip over to Talifax, who is overseeing the ritual of resurrection at the Fist of Trakalon. For those keeping score, Trakalon was a titan, one of the eldest gods. His fist is the magic that will fuel Nefarius's ascension, if our heroes can't stop it.

During the conversation we see that Skare has some new super armor that absorbs all magic, and makes him effectively invincible against mages. Totally not going to have to fight that at the end, of course.

Meanwhile, Frit finally makes it to Neith's world, and Neith offers to make her an apprentice. Thanks to Nebiat, Frit is one of the finest fire dreamers in existence, or will be once she's trained. Frit is incredibly gifted at scrying and divination, which will be very important in Godswar.

Frit returns to Nebiat, and pleads with her to work with Voria against Nefarius and Krox. There is no need to be at war. Nebiat laughs, and tells Frit that, like it or not, they are at war. There can be no peace.

Annddd we're back to Aran, Nara, and Crewes. The *Talon* is ready. We're going to ride on the Fist and stop Talifax and Skare! There's just one more problem.

It turns out Virkonna has a lot of pride. She tries to get Voria to fall in line, and we all know Voria. That's not happening, especially not after Virkonna casually killed thousands of her own people.

So Virkonna puts Voria on time out and says she can't come to the battle of the Fist. Voria reluctantly translocates to Drifter Rock, because who wouldn't need a beer after dealing with Virkonna?

Virkonna rallies the rest of her troops and attacks Skare at the Fist. Any guesses on how this plays out? Yeah, not good for the heroes. Skare has a massive fleet of black ships waiting. Most of those ships are involved in the ritual, but enough are left over to hold off the heroes.

Virkonna tries to push to the fist, but Talifax executes a vicious spell and hits Inura with about 50 disintegrates through a series of opening and closing Fissures. Drakkon gets geeked too. Our heroes are losing. A powerful life goddess sure would come in handy.

Aran pulls off some crazy stuff with the *Talon*, and they blow up a bunch of ships, but it isn't slowing down the ritual. He crashes the *Talon* through the rear of the *Dragon Skull*, the flagship of the Inuran fleet.

They slog their way through the Inuran's new cyborgs, and eventually get into a boss fight with Skare in his new suit of super-spellarmor. During the fight the company suffers their first real casualty, which caught a lot of readers by surprise.

Skare kills Kezia, though the company quickly claims vengeance. They trash the inside of the *Dragon Skull*, but fall back when they get word that the ritual is happening.

All the magic of the Fist is consumed in one spell, and the black ships pull together into the skeletal outline of a dragon. Muscles, bone, scales, and sinew grow over the metal body like a straight Terminator dragon god chick. Thing.

Anyway, Nefarius is reborn and she starts going PEW PEW. RAWR. She crushes everyone. She badly wounds Virkonna. Aran takes his best shot, and fails. We're losing and losing badly.

Nefarius is about to swoop in, kill Inura, and gain his *life* magic, so Aran takes him out with a preemptive disintegrate. Nefarius is piissssssed. She had big plans for that magic.

Then our heroes translocate back to Virkon to lick their wounds, while Nefarius vaccu-sucks up all the bodies to eat their magic.

Right after they appear on Virkon, Frit shows up. She apologies and says she is an emissary. She's come to broker an alliance against Nefarius.

Voria, Virkonna, and Frit start to argue.

Nebiat translocates into the system, grabs the *Spellship* in orbit, shoves it down her pants, and yells, "See ya!" No one is in any shape to chase her, and she gets away...but poor Frit is left high and dry.

The very last chapter shows Shinura (the shade of Inura) revealing something to Kazon. Inura knew he was going to die, so he updated his shade with the latest OS, and gave that shade half his magic. The whole sector thinks he is dead, because he died. But he cheated and Shinura exists as a perfect copy, complete with up-to-date memories.

Which brings us to...Godswar. The end of the series. Not the end of the Magitech Chronicles, mind you. I'm already plotting the *Dying World* series to go with the first RPG adventure path. If that piques your interest, shoot me an email at chris@chrisfoxwrites.com and I'll get you some details.

In the meantime...enjoy the conclusion. =D

-Chris

PROLOGUE

Nebiat waved one of Krox's cosmic hands, and the sector's largest void pocket sprang open over the dark side of her world. She reached inside and carefully withdrew the *Spellship*, the ancient vessel still shrouded beneath the layer of wards she'd created to keep the people trapped within, unable to even send a missive, much less escape.

She inspected the vessel, and hesitated. Perhaps before she dealt with this task it would be prudent to inspect the new body she'd ordered her followers to construct. That effigy was critical, and if the tiniest flaw slipped by...well, she'd seen what tiny flaws could do when her father had been devoured by Krox.

Prevarication is unlike you. It appears driven by cognitive dissonance completely unrelated to your current thought processes, Krox rumbled. *You fear meeting your son. You fear his rejection. The possibility that he will not conform to the role you wish of him. Yet you have it in your power to ensure that he does.*

Nebiat stifled an acidic response, as it would only

confirm Krox's words. The god was right, much as she hated to admit it. She'd been putting this off.

There would be little point to enslaving his will, as the role I have for him requires his cooperation, Nebiat finally explained. *The reason you have failed over and over is that you've always stood alone. I wish to strengthen my people so that they will outlive me. Even gods can be killed, and one day I will be gone. I wish to leave a legacy. Once you said we are our own legacies, and now more than ever I know that is a mistake.*

Krox pulsed thoughtfully, but did not reply.

Once the conversation ended, Nebiat had no choice but to tend to the task at hand. She detached herself from Krox, and manifested within the *Spellship* in the same human form she'd always worn when visiting Shaya.

It wasn't flesh and blood, of course, but she still felt more like her old self than she had at any point since her ascension.

She appeared outside the ship's library, which was positively cavernous. Level after level rose up into the distance, until finally disappearing out of sight. Every last part of that library was filled with shelves, each containing hundreds of knowledge scales.

It was no doubt a pale shadow of the fabled library where Voria and her blasted minions had acquired this ship, but it was certainly the finest collection Nebiat had ever seen. Even her father would have been impressed, she'd wager.

Nebiat strode into the library as if she had every right to be there, and cut a bold path through clusters of scholars, most of whom didn't even look up as she passed.

A few did, though, and one or two seemed puzzled by her appearance. Not a single one recognized her, though. How odd. She'd bedeviled their worlds, and scorched their confederacy, but they didn't even recognize her face? No wonder they'd lost.

She made her way to the largest cluster of scholars, who stood in small groups around a hatchling that towered over them. Nebiat puffed up instinctively at the sight of her son, and smiled proudly as she watched him lead their discussion.

"We have no idea where here even is," he explained, fixing a human elder with his slitted eye. "It's possible we're in the Umbral Depths, and simply hampered by the cocoon of wards created by Krox."

Even her own son didn't use her name. Did no one understand the role she played in all of this? It was her that they should be frightened of. Not Krox.

"Ah hem," Nebiat said loudly.

No one looked in her direction. Conversation continued. Her hands balled into fists, and she fought the rising tide of anger. This was not how she wanted her son to see her. She would not lose her composure in front of him. Not ever.

She reached back into Krox's vast sea of magic, and drew enough *spirit* to send a tendril to each of the people standing between her and her son. For a single breath she controlled their actions, and they parted before her like the legendary ocean before Bekel.

"My son," she called, not loudly, but with enough volume to catch his attention. "We need to speak. In private, or with your advisors if you wish."

A hush descended over the library. Not just around their little gathering, but throughout this floor, and then others. One by one, every scholar with a whit of perception noticed, and Nebiat became the focal point of their attention. As it should be.

"Hello, mother." Kaho folded his arms, and his tail lashed behind him in irritation.

His dark scales gave him a dangerous look under the magical light, a menacing look, one she'd observed much more often in Kaho's brother, before Aran had slain him. She rather liked it. He'd grown so much.

"Why have you come?" Kaho prompted. That was it. No sullen words. No attacks. None of the rancor she'd come to expect from him whenever they met.

"To take you home," she answered simply. Nebiat threaded a path through the scholars to her son, though her feet made no noise on the soft carpet, as they were ethereal. "You may bring your followers, if you wish. Or you may stay here, and guide them from this ship."

"I do not lead this vessel, much less her people." Kaho unfolded his arms, and pointed at a mousy-looking human with fiery-red hair, and a smattering of freckles across both cheeks. He wore a simple black uniform, though she noticed an official-looking patch she didn't recognize on the shoulder. "This is Administrator Pickus, Voria's, ah, high priest, if you will."

"Pleasure, ma'am." The mousy man inclined his head slightly, and then approached. He had manners, at least. "We were just trying to figure out where you stuck us. This is a giant void pocket, ain't it?"

Nebiat gave a delighted laugh, "Indeed. When one wields the level of power I do, such magic is trivial."

"Mother." There it was. Kaho's exasperated tone spoke volumes. "Why did you steal this vessel? Nefarius is ravaging our sector. Inura is dead, and Nefarius is stronger for it. Virkonna will be next, but as soon as she's done killing her sister, Aunt Nefarius will come for us."

"I am well aware." She nodded gravely, giving weight to

his words. "Which is why I borrowed the *Spellship*. I needed it for a ritual, one that will free me from Krox. I can become a goddess in my own right without being shackled to that...thing."

"I see." Kaho cocked his head, and his expression softened. "You knew there was no way Voria would allow you to use the *Spellship*, so you seized it. What is your plan when she comes to take it back? Or if Nefarius comes to take it?"

Nebiat waved dismissively, then rolled her eyes for added effect. "By the time Voria and Frit arrive I'll already be a goddess, in a new body. I will be a Wyrm again, and more powerful than ever. I'll simply return the ship to Voria, and apologize. She is a weak-willed simpleton willing to forgive, well, pretty much any transgression. She needs me to defeat Nefarius, after all."

The mousy man began to laugh. Not a nervous titter, but the kind of obnoxious braying that made her eye twitch. Metaphorically, at least, as she no longer had eyes in the traditional sense.

"Ma'am," the mousy man began with a buck-toothed grin, "you ain't got no idea what you're in for. You killed Tender Aurelia, right in front of Voria. Your dad killed Eros. Then you came back and torched her planet. You blew up her tree and killed her people. Even after all that, Voria might have been willing to come to the table. But what's the first thing you did?"

The mousy man paused. Was she supposed to answer?

"You betrayed us. You stole the ship that was left for Voria by an elder god." Pickus folded his arms, and eyed her with clear contempt. The humor was gone now. "When the Lady of Light arrives she's going to kill you, and take back this ship. She ain't stupid, Nebiat. She'll bring enough juice to kill you; you can count on that. You ain't getting out of this alive."

It was Nebiat's turn to laugh. She reveled in it, her scorn making many of the observers wince. "Voria doesn't have it in her. But even if you are right it will not save you or your people. Ah...yes, I thought that might get your attention."

Nebiat winked at the suddenly terrified little man, then she gave a friendly smile. "We don't have to be enemies. In fact, I'd prefer we not be. So I'm going to give you a very simple ultimatum. You need to get these people, every last one, to participate in my ritual of ascension."

"And why would we do that? You'll just kill us after. Or worse." Pickus spat on the deck near Nebiat's feet.

"Because." Nebiat's smile never slipped, and she kept her tone just as light. "If you don't, then I will devour you all, and repopulate this ship with Wyrms and Ifrit. I don't care who fuels the ritual. It can be you or it can be my children. If it's you, then you get to live, and I can give you back to Voria when you've completed the task. I'll give you a few hours to think it over, and then we'll start the ritual. Make sure your people are ready, Administrator."

All blood drained from the man's face, underscoring all those freckles. He nodded once.

"Mother," Kaho growled, "I know that you think you are clever, but please, be careful." His eyes narrowed dangerously. "You are not nearly so clever as you think."

1

THAT SIMPLE

Nefarius allowed her awareness to flow through her new body, and was pleased by what she discovered. The humans, with their limited lifespans, had invented things that not even gods had fully achieved.

Her body was comprised of two parts, a union of magic and technology that eclipsed her natural body by an order of magnitude. Like her previous incarnation, one body was tiny, roughly the size she'd been as a hatchling—what was often referred to as an avatar. The other was titanic, on a planet-shattering scale.

She dwelt in both at once, her consciousness split seamlessly between them, even as she surfed the digital corridors of the Quantum network the humans had created.

They'd stored vast quantities of data, and a dizzying array of sensors across trillions of devices, and she had access to them all. Unfortunately, that taxed her consciousness, and thus far she'd avoided delving too deeply into the network.

First, she had important business to attend to. Then she could indulge in a little exploration.

Nefarius translocated from the wreckage-strewn battlefield at the site of her rebirth, and appeared at the world the humans had designated Colony 3. It was the most populous of their remaining worlds, and the site of their world's new government.

Curiously, their people had chosen to disallow any association between their religions and their governing body. That independence would be one of the first things she would eradicate.

A tiny, pathetic fleet lay strewn around an equally pathetic station, the technology a sharp contrast to that utilized in the construction of her body.

That station represented the last vestiges of the human government, one that would soon be stripped by their own people. When that happened, Nefarius would be there to fill the vacuum, and she would offer the people hope and power.

In exchange they would fuel her with enough worship to devour the entire sector. Only when that had been accomplished would she finally be able to focus on the true threat. She needed to remove their spies. They had agents everywhere, but if everyone were dead, well, then there couldn't be any spies. It really was that simple.

"Time to introduce myself," Nefarius murmured into the void. She shifted her focus from the titanic Wyrm down into the mortal-sized android avatar.

She still found that metal body alien, its smooth curves completely unlike the flesh and blood form she'd once worn. It was more than that, though. She was used to being a dragon. Her body looked...human. But flawed.

The face was too dark to be a real skin tone, and the hair

a series of fiber cables to enhance the transmission of data. The skin was smooth, unbroken by scales, or even pores. The curved limbs were clearly human, though thankfully a pair of metallic wings extended up from her back.

She even had a tail, which was capable of delivering spells, and possessed a surprising amount of strength. Her whole body did. It was a magnificent creation worthy of her brother Inura, and he'd clearly had some hand in its creation, or his children had at least.

A brief whiff of sadness bubbled up around her, but she suppressed it. Her little brother could have worked for *them*, and even if he hadn't, he would have eventually. What she'd done had been a mercy, and in the end it hadn't been her. This Outrider had killed her brother, not her.

Nefarius tapped into the communications array in the back of her neck, and overrode the security protocols around the humans' Quantum network. She projected an image of her avatar, majestic and powerful, to every surviving comm device, terminal, and holobank. Her voice echoed across a dozen worlds, all at once, without the need for magic.

"Hello, citizens of Ternus. My name is NEF-1, and I have been created to protect you." Her voice carried a faint drawl, the kind rural citizens tended toward. She summoned up memories of the battle at the Fist of Trakalon, and broadcast that for all to see. "A few days ago you witnessed my triumph against the monsters and demons plaguing this sector. Everywhere we turn there are monsters. Well, I am the monster sent to slay the other monsters. I am your vengeance and your shield."

She paused and let the footage play for a moment. It showed Inura's death and Drakkon's. It showed their hero, the Hound of Xal, this legendary Aran, attempting to slay her...and failing. It showed her triumph, and her enemies translocating away until she was the only god left in the sector.

"Our enemies attempted to stop my birth," she explained, stifling the urge to say 'rebirth'. "They failed. I am here now. My mission is clear, delivered to me not only by Governor Austin, but also by the mandate created when these monsters slaughtered our people. Every son, every daughter. Every mother, every father. They will all be avenged. One by one I will kill these false gods. I will slaughter the demons. I will scourge the Wyrms. Anything that poses a threat to humanity will be eradicated, until every last one of our colonies is safe."

She paused, and eyed the camera drone plaintively. "I can't do it alone. I need your help. I know it sounds strange, but belief matters. Faith matters. If you believe I can save you, that I'm powerful enough to stop all the monsters, well, then I am that powerful. So I'm calling on every man, woman, and child. Pray for deliverance. Pray to NEF-1, and I will offer deliverance. Thank you, citizens of Ternus. I will keep you apprised of my victories."

She let the broadcast end, and settled back to listen to their social media as generals and politicians and common folk chimed in with their opinions. The seed had been planted, and they'd begun to believe. But if she was going to secure their worship, she needed to deliver them exactly the kind of victory she'd promised.

"What will you do now, Mistress?" Talifax rumbled, appearing just as suddenly as he'd always done, next to the reactor, which spread pulses of glorious magic throughout her magnificent body.

She stifled the urge to destroy the sorcerer. He was almost certainly one of *their* agents, the prime spy they'd sent to prepare the way for them. But she needed him still. His ability to perceive possibilities was second only to Neith, and there was no way her sister would help her. Not after Nefarius had slain their mother.

"I will do exactly as promised." She turned to face Talifax, the lenses in her eyes whirring as they focused on his bulky black armor, as featureless and unassuming as her servant could manage. The optics delivered a dizzying array of metrics about that armor, more than she could have gotten from magic alone. Talifax was nervous. Terrified, but hiding it well. What secret did he fear that she might discover? She would ferret it out in time. "I will deliver vengeance upon their enemies."

"And you believe this will win their hearts? That they will worship? They are not a devout people," the sorcerer pointed out. He moved to stand near her, in a subservient position, as always.

"I would disagree," Nefarius countered, her metallic face simulating a smile. "I'd argue that they number among the most devout societies I have ever encountered. They merely worship different gods. These people love technology. They believe it can do anything, and because they believe it can... it does."

She knew that Talifax badly wanted to ask her where she intended to go. Everyone would expect her to kill Virkonna, both because of the power and because of their longstanding rivalry to be the best blade master.

But Nefarius had made her name into a word for treachery by always doing the very last thing her enemies expected.

She would deal with Virkonna in time. For now, she had another target in mind.

2

GAME PLAN

Aran rested his hand on Narlifex's hilt, and translocated to the Crucible. It still awed him that he could envision a place, and then alter reality so that he was there. It was a truly divine act, and forced one to examine the whole "I'm a god" thing.

He appeared in the fantastically advanced workshop he'd last seen, where Kazon and Inura had been constructing the golden mecha. That armor was still there, though Inura was gone of course. Killed by Aran, while denying his magic to their enemies.

But the mecha was still being worked on. Kazon's bushy black beard boiled out from around some sort of welding mask, and he dangled from a harness affixed to the mech's shoulder. He was perched next to an open panel on the mech's otherwise smooth hide, near the right hip.

"Ahh, brother," Kazon called without looking up from his work. "Thank you for coming. The others are here and tensions are, ah, quite high, as you will see."

Kazon finished his weld, then closed the panel and raised his dark goggles. He smiled down at Aran. "We'd best get in there before Frit and Voria tear each other apart. I'm not sure why that hasn't happened yet judging from the way they talk to each other."

Aran braced himself for what was about to come. He was damned tired of being the conciliator, especially since that was normally the role Voria took on. Of course, he couldn't blame Voria in the slightest. Frit was hard to trust.

"All right, let's get this over with." Aran waited for Kazon to lower himself with the harness, resisting the urge to assist with gravity magic. "You know you could hold yourself aloft with *void*."

"I could." Kazon nodded. "But *void* is dark magic, Aran. It is Nefarius's strength. I do not like it. Once you have tasted of *life*, well, *void* is a lot less appetizing."

Aran nodded as if he understood, but of course he couldn't since he didn't possess *life*. The implications were disturbing, though. *Void* was perceived as being dark magic, though Aran still had no idea if there was any substance to that. If there was, then the sector was in a whole lot of trouble, because he and Nara were carrying around a big chunk of it.

They walked down a wide corridor, past a few intersections, and finally entered what appeared to be a conference room. There were currently two camps, one around Voria at one end of the room, and the other around Frit at the extreme opposite side.

Voria sat with Crewes, Rhea, and Bord, while Frit sat with Nara. It was an antagonistic stance, and Aran didn't love that there were already clear divisions in their ranks. That was going to make what followed all that much harder.

"Morning, all." Aran strode into the room with Kazon. His company snapped to attention, while Voria and Nara both offered nods. Frit didn't even offer that much.

"Where is Virkonna?" Aran demanded, looking around. "Are we seriously going to discuss the fate of her world, and she can't even clear a spot in her schedule for that?"

"She is playing Kem'hedj," Voria explained with no small amount of distaste. The goddess grimaced as if she'd swallowed something sour. "I cannot condone her shirking her responsibilities, but there is a spot of good news. Her constant partner in the game is a friend. Kheross survived the Fist."

"My father?" Rhea spoke up suddenly, blinking. She clutched her spellrifle a bit closer to her chest, but then all emotion vanished and the wall was back. "It's good that he lives, and that he's still serving our lady. But he has to know what that means and...well, he's as good as dead if he stays, so I suppose I shouldn't stop mourning him."

That smacked Aran hard. His people had given up. They knew Nefarius was coming, and that anyone left here was going to die.

Crewes gave a snort. "Maybe. I'll believe scaly's dead when someone shows me the body. If he survived the Fist of Trakalon, he'll survive this."

Bord said nothing. The quips were gone, and his expression was sober and unsmiling, as always since Kez's death. The curly locks had been shaved down to a smooth military cut, which he tended to daily, just like Crewes.

Aran left it alone, though sooner or later he was going to have to reach the specialist. Bord was in a dark place.

"Let's focus on what we can control," Aran suggested, loudly enough to get everyone's attention. "Where do we stand on locating the *Spellship*, and on repairing Ikadra?"

Frit rose slowly from her chair, flames rising from her smoldering skin, though it did nothing to diminish her beauty. "I've confirmed that Krox is still in the Nebiat system, and yes, that's what we're calling it. I don't know what her plan is yet, but she's there, and waiting for us."

"Which means it is almost certainly a trap," Voria offered. She too rose from her chair, mirroring Frit's stance. "I believe we need to spring that trap. Come with force, and see if we can bring Nebiat back to the table. I cannot imagine she wants a war, though I have no idea why she thought the *Spellship* important enough to steal."

"Because it can raise a god?" Nara said, joining the conversation at last. She rose, and looked around the room. "I don't know how she'll use that power, but if the ship raised Voria then who knows what it can do for her."

"Very little without the key," Kazon pointed out. "And we have that, broken though it may be." He nodded sadly at the staff propped against the wall behind Nara.

It wounded Aran to see the darkened sapphire, and the wide crack spiderwebbing down the center. Ikadra had given his life, nontraditional though it might have been, to help them fight. He hoped there was some way to restore the wisecracking artifact.

"With Inura gone, can we ask Shinura for help?" Nara asked. She plucked Ikadra from the wall, and held the staff in both hands. "Maybe he can guide us through the ritual."

"I am afraid that is not possible," Kazon protested, his face going stony. "Shinura has...departed. We are on our own, for good or ill. But I have all the tools we need to repair Ikadra. Come. I have prepared a workshop. I cannot do the work myself, but if we have potent *life* magic, and potent *air* magic, then there is no reason we cannot restore the staff today. Right now."

Aran relaxed into a smile for the first time all day. "Voria, if you can supply *life*, then I can supply the *air*."

"I can guide the ritual, if needed," Nara offered, also

smiling. The shift in mood was instant and powerful. "Before we do so, though, Frit, could I speak to you in private?"

Aran considered asking Nara to share it with everyone, but she glanced in his direction and seemed to sense what he was thinking.

"I have a plan to stop Talifax," Nara explained, "but it's a long shot. I just wanted Frit to scry some stuff for me. I'll let you know if anything pans out."

"Thanks." He squared his shoulders. It felt good to be doing something positive, even if he was only indirectly involved. He turned back to Kazon. "How about we get Ikadra back?"

"Yes!" Kazon gave a broad grin. "Let me show you what this place can do."

3

NEBIAT'S BODY

Nebiat experienced uncharacteristic unease as she slipped the *Spellship* back into the void pocket and closed it. All void pockets needed an anchor, and the caster usually chose a set of armor or clothing that they wore regularly. In her case, she'd chosen a fixed point in space, near the planet's nadir.

You fear this human speaks the truth, and that your foes will slay you, rather than seek an accord. There was no smugness in Krox's tone, but then there never was. She added that part herself.

True, she admitted. *That fear is there, though I don't lend it much credence. Voria is the great conciliator. She will see reason, particularly if I capitulate before her.*

That is dangerous, Krox cautioned, his voice echoing in her mind. *If you abase yourself before another god, and do it in full view of your worshipers, then that worship will go to another. Careful, lest you empower your enemy.*

That hadn't occurred to her, but it made sense. And it complicated things. She'd have to get Voria to see reason, without showing weakness. Fortunately, that was exactly the kind of challenge she thrived on.

In the meantime, though, she needed to ready the ritual that would finally free her. Nebiat's astral form swelled as she descended toward the planet, and by the time she'd reached the ritual site she was a magnificent spectral Wyrm, still roughly Drakkon sized.

A vast swamp spread before her, low and murky, and filled with scrabbly trees on the few islands that broke the placid waters. The only feature of note in that swamp was the titanic dragon's claw stabbing up into the sky, as high as any mountain.

That claw had belonged to the Earthmother, once. Perhaps the most powerful of the Wyrm gods, from the measure of pure quantity of magic. And power still lingered within her skeleton, the last vestige of her body that had survived when Nebiat had empowered her children.

The claw no longer resembled a dragon claw, though. Her followers had diligently shaped and molded it, carving with exquisite care until they'd created an exact replica of Nebiat's true body in life.

Majestic wings spread outward behind powerful shoulders, and her ebony scales gleamed even in the wan sunlight.

You are certain this will work? she prompted, though logically she already knew the answer. It bothered her that she felt the need to seek validation, but Krox did have access to vast repository of information.

The Spellship *is but a piece of the required whole. You will need their belief as well, but if you possess both, then this is a suitable repository for divine energy. Your new body will be strong, though as I have warned you numerous times, its existence also means that, like Inura, you can be slain much more easily than an entity such as myself.*

Yes, yes, Nebiat prompted. *I understand that you think physical bodies are a weakness. But they are also a powerful tool, and unlike you I am a warrior-god. I need a vessel with which to combat my enemies, one that I can make ever stronger as the centuries pass.*

So countless gods have said before you. They are dead. I am alive. Soon, you will be dead, and I will tell the next foolish mortal who happens into divinity your sorry tale.

Nebiat ignored the jab and instead focused on the effigy her people were creating. A dozen Wyrms and twice as many Ifrit were working on it now, each a master craftsman in their own right.

All glanced up at her arrival, but none offered a greeting or reacted to her presence in any way. In this instance, because she'd told them to do precisely that— ignore her. She'd had to, because otherwise the Wyrms insisted on performing their dance of worship, which took hours, when all she really wanted was a status report.

Being a goddess was proving less empowering than she'd have expected. Thus far all it had really given her was a larger hammer with which to smash problems.

It is not power that makes a god, which is why I say you are no true god, Krox rumbled. *It is context. Perspective. The ability to understand myriad contradicting possibilities all at once. It is this understanding that affords true divinity, because you can literally shape reality to your will. You? You have to put your followers on time out. You are no god.*

Nebiat resisted the urge to break something. She forced a deep, calming breath, and continued to survey her effigy. *Perhaps you are right, and I am no god. But I am the master, and you the slave. If you are a god, and have the benefit of all this context, then how did you end up enslaved to my will?*

There was no answer. Nebiat allowed a self-satisfied smile. She channeled a whiff of *fire* magic to carry her voice across the continent where her worshipers had gathered.

"My children," she began, drifting into the air, a radiant dragon comprised of magic, translucent and pure. "Today is a momentous day. Today, I consecrate the vessel you have long labored to create. Today, I ascend and become a goddess in my own right. No longer will I be shackled to the traitorous god Krox. I will be free to guide you. Free to lead you into the next era. The era of the dragonflights has come once more, and we will see it together my children. Pray. Pray for our collective strength, and for my ascension."

Her speech delivered, Nebiat fell silent and observed her children's reaction. All over her world there were nods, or groups chanting her name. She was well loved here, the opposite of her reputation throughout the system. She'd seen how love served Voria, and wanted the same benefits from her followers.

And, in a way, was she really any different from Voria? She too cared for her people. She was just a tad more ruthless in how she went about protecting them.

Nebiat glanced up at the sky, where the void pocket's anchor lay. The few hours she'd offered Pickus had elapsed. It was time to retrieve the vessel and begin the ritual. If he cooperated she could be done in a matter of minutes, a deceptively short requirement for such an immense ritual.

If he resisted, though? Well, she'd do as she promised. She'd slaughter them all, even her son if he stood with them, and then her children would take control of Voria's blasted vessel.

That would make a truce impossible, but Nebiat was

prepared for that eventuality. She'd seen precisely how powerful Voria was, and had crafted a body that would allow her to best Voria. She'd specifically crafted it with killing her rival in mind.

If it came to it, then Nebiat would happily devour every scrap of Voria's magic.

4

STAND

Nebiat appeared in the *Spellship*'s library once more, though this time she materialized in the air above the table where Pickus and Kaho had been sitting. As expected, both stood in roughly the same position, holding court for their followers.

"—And I think," Kaho was saying, "That if we do not do as she says, then we are all dead. My mother will absolutely make good on this threat. I am, frankly, more than a little shocked that she is willing to let us live and work with her. I know it pains you, but if we don't do this, then all of us die. Not only does that cost us personally, but Voria will have no chance of reconciliation then. If we work with Nebiat, then maybe the two of them can—"

"No." Pickus wore a frown, which seemed out of place on a face made more for smiles. The mousy man nodded up in Nebiat's direction, his gaze touching hers to indicate that he'd seen her. "I've seen what happens to those who work with Nebiat. I considered Frit a friend, and I know you considered her a good deal more. Where is she now? Nebiat left her to die back on Virkon. She got what she wanted, and betrayed an ally. Again. Working with her is suicide, and if we're going to die either way, then I'm going to die for the principles I believe in. I will not pray to another god. I follow Voria."

"I'm disappointed to hear that." Nebiat extended her arms to encompass all the people standing around the administrator. "And is that the final answer for everyone? You are condemning them all to death? But I thought you believed in democratic process. Shouldn't anyone who wants to live be able to? Who are you to force them all to go to their deaths rather than perform a simple spell before being dutifully returned to their goddess?"

"If I believed a word that came out of your mouth I'd agree in a second," Pickus allowed. He took a step closer to Nebiat, and stabbed up with an accusing finger. "You are a serpent, lady. You've betrayed anyone and everyone you've ever worked with, up to and including your father, the way I hear it. There's no way you're on the level. We do what you ask, and then you tell us that you just need one more thing done. One more favor. You get us to get used to agreeing with you, and one by one you convert our people. You steal them from Voria. Slowly. Reasonably. Well, I won't have it. I see you for what you are, snake."

The little man was quaking with rage. Normally that might have amused her, as she enjoyed causing such a reaction, but this time it worried her. All around her, onlookers adopted his same body language. His anger and his indignation spread out in a wave, washing over the crowd.

"I respect your decision," she allowed, and meant it. A little bit anyway. "You will go to your deaths as honored enemies, but as Nefarius swallows the sector while Voria and I attack each other...I hope your lingering spirit realizes that you had the power to change this. To build instead of destroy."

FLEE. FLEE NOW, Krox rumbled, his voice drowning out everything else, louder than it had ever been. If she didn't know better she'd say it was infused with panic. *Nefarius comes. If we are here when she arrives, then we will die alongside this world you value so much. Translocate. Immediately.*

"I will give you once last chance, Administrator Pickus." Though it was difficult, Nebiat forced her speech to be slow and stately. "You may have one more day to decide. After which, I request that you allow any who disagree with you to stay and aid us, rather than be murdered for your principles. Have we an accord?"

The fiery-haired human frowned up at her. "We do, though I fully expect you to betray it somehow."

Nebiat withdrew her consciousness from the *Spellship*, and quickly snapped the void pocket shut. She had no idea if something so basic would fool a god of Nefarius's strength, but then, what did she care? If Nefarius was free to take the *Spellship*, it meant Nebiat was already dead.

She shot back into Krox's body, and quickly inhabited it so she could respond to attacks if necessary. There was no immediate sign of any danger, not that Nebiat could see. *You interrupted my ritual for this?*

YOU FOOL, Krox thundered. *Nefarius comes. I once told you that when one elder god assaults another it is nearly impossible to hide. This possibility was well hidden indeed, but now it can be hidden no longer. Our enemy comes, and if we are still here when she arrives none of your scheming will matter, ever again.*

How is this possible? Nebiat demanded. She extended one of Krox's four cosmic arms, and opened the void pocket she'd anchored to Krox. This one contained something far more valuable than the *Spellship*, in the coming battle at least. She wrapped a continent-sized hand around the great spear Worldender, and withdrew it from the void pocket. She seized the weapon with two of her arms, then swam away from her world, into the void.

If Nefarius truly was coming, she didn't want her world damaged in the coming battle. She admitted that she knew little of gods battling, and had no idea how she would fare against Nefarius. But there was no way she was going to abandon her world, not on the eve of her own ascension. Where would she even run?

I will not scurry and hide. We have a world full of worshipers, a god-killing artifact spear that you claim is older than creation, and the might of all the magic we have devoured. We will never have a better chance at victory.

You risk much, Krox cautioned, his tone more moderate now. *If you are wrong, we both die, and not even a memory will survive. Nefarius will be unstoppable if she is able to devour my mind. She will know everything. See everything. And she will control everyone. Fleeing denies her that strength, and while it will not save your world it is the only way you can spite her.*

No. Nebiat tightened her grip on the spear. *We will stand, and fight, and die if we have to.*

5

FIGHT

Nefarius was beyond shocked when she arrived in Krox's home system to find the god girded for war. So total was her surprise that she hovered there in space, staring at her enemy.

The main body was familiar, though diminished, an orb of pearly white broken here and there by whorls of red belonging to the heart of flame. But Krox had arms, four of them, and a torso now. He'd given himself a body, and that body clutched one of the few weapons that could evoke fear in a god of her age and power.

Worldender.

The great spear preceded this universe, and perhaps the Great Cycle itself. Yet the weapon, as powerful as it was, could only disrupt magic it came into contact with. If she avoided being hit, then the weapon was worthless to Krox.

But that was thinking prematurely. If Krox were going to flee, he'd be long gone, but that didn't mean he wasn't open to speaking before combat began. She had so many questions.

"Tell me, Krox," she rumbled, the magic in her words

bypassing the laws of physics and carrying her words to all on the world below. Let them hear her, and tremble. "When did you discard your cowardly strategy of hiding behind pawns? You enslave. You manipulate. You do not fight."

"I am not Krox," a deep voice rumbled back. "I enslaved Krox. I am Nebiat, daughter of the Earthmother."

Now that was truly surprising. Nefarius had eradicated her sister's people not long after slaying her and devouring her mind. She glided a bit closer to Krox, but not in a hostile way. Krox did not react.

"I am pleased to see that my sister's progeny have finally turned the tables on their captor." And Nefarius meant those words. The idea of Krox enslaving Wyrms could not be borne. "That would explain the new body, and the fact that you are not running. Tell me, Nebiat, my niece, have you stayed to offer worship? Are you presenting Krox to me as a gift, then?"

Krox's posture shifted, and he wrapped a third hand around the spear. Nefarius could feel the magic growing within the elder god, though she sensed no spell as of yet.

Finally, Krox spoke. "This is my world, Nefarius. There is nothing for you here. If you wish, I will make a gift of Worldender to you, and you can use it to kill Virkonna, and Voria, and any other god you wish. Or, you can try to take it from me, and I can use it to kill you."

"Is that so?" Nefarius mused, amusement growing within her. She'd missed petty games and simple politics. Both were hallmarks of younger gods. "Krox, if you are in there somewhere, I hope you are horrified. I hope this child-god's ignorance is the last thing you feel before I devour your mind."

Nebiat shifted backward a few kilometers, her stance becoming more defensive. Nefarius was willing to bet that

Krox was feeding her information, and explaining how monumentally screwed she was.

No matter how she faced this situation, she lost. If she stayed, then Nefarius would win, and Krox would die. Krox had to know enough to tell her that. If she fled, her followers would see another god rout her from the field of battle, and would know that she'd fled without even fighting. Her worship would be forfeit, and they'd instead follow Nefarius.

"Where is that confidence of a moment ago? Because I assure you, little godling, that I do intend to pry Worldender from your corpse. What will you do?"

Nefarius enjoyed the torment she knew she was inflicting. Krox deserved every bit of it, and so did anyone even peripherally associated with him.

6

TRAPPED

Nebiat studied the god who'd invaded her system. There was no terror or wonder. There was cold, battle-hardened observation.

You feel no fear, Krox pulsed. *Amazing. Nefarius will end us in moments.*

She didn't reply, instead spinning out possibilities as she planned various attacks. They all highlighted one inescapable fact. Nefarius was faster, stronger, and her body had been created specifically to kill gods.

Now you see, Krox rumbled. *You have doomed us.*

We still have Worldender, Nebiat countered as she readied every defensive magic she knew.

Nefarius still hadn't advanced, though she'd unfurled her wings, and was no doubt preparing an assault.

Nebiat extended her free hand in the Wyrm-goddess's direction, and flung a cloud of *spirit* tendrils that swirled toward Nefarius in a writhing mass. They clung to the dragon's body, her limbs, and her wings, quickly engulfing Nebiat's opponent.

Elation surged, but it died as swiftly as it was born,

turning to ashes as Nefarius began to absorb the tendrils. Every place they caressed the dark goddess, her glittering scales glowed grey, and then the magic was gone.

We are merely feeding her, Krox pointed out, unhelpfully.

"I may not know how gods fight," Nebiat called to her opponent, a bit of confidence returning as she decided her course, "but I know war. I know combat. Come. Show me this legendary warrior goddess I have heard so much of."

Nebiat guided Krox's colossal body toward her opponent, and used two of the arms to swing Worldender in a wide slash. Nefarius danced back out of reach, clearly wary of the ancient weapon.

"You have no idea," Nefarius crooned as she glided further from Nebiat, "how happy I am to hear you say that. I *love* war, little niece. I love death, and most of all? I love hand-to-hand combat. Come. Struggle, before your dismemberment. If you impress me, then I may allow something of you to survive."

Nebiat pushed all emotion away and gave herself to combat. She treated Krox as she would a suit of spellarmor, a tool that could be manipulated. Krox possessed tremendous quantities of *fire*, and *fire* could be transmuted into strength.

She did exactly that, fueling her swings with the immense reserves. The added power made her swings quicker, and forced Nefarius to work harder to evade.

"If you'd had a century and a mentor, then I believe you might have had a chance here." There was wonder in Nefarius's voice, but also amusement, and a touch of exasperation. She twisted around a wild spear swing, banking just out of reach as Nebiat charged again. "What a student you'd have made. Virkonna and I would have both vied for your attention, I think, as we did with Drakkon."

Then Nefarius was gone. The idea that something that large could simply vanish seemed...wrong somehow. In the split second it took her to realize it was no invisibility, but rather a teleportation, she allowed her opponent to get behind her.

Nefarius's barbed tail shot through Krox's abdomen, bursting out in a spray of *spirit* magic. Then that tail retracted, ripping though Krox again in another spray, the hideous damage filling the system around them with globules of grey magic.

There was no pain, but panic flooded both Nebiat and Krox. She instinctively pivoted, then swung Worldender in a tight arc in the area she expected Nefarius to be. It hit!

The spear impacted with Nefarius's right wing, and a wide area around the impact simply...dissolved. The gaping wound in the leathery hide reminded her of a disintegration, but she sensed that this was different somehow. The spear had removed the magic from creation. The universe was less than it had been a moment before.

Nefarius's tail whipped around and curled tightly around one of Krox's wrists, then a clawed hand came down to seize another. The larger dragon forced the spear away from Krox, and the Wyrm-goddess pressed in close.

"You've damaged my body," Nefarius growled, her hellish purple eyes close to Krox's face, "and this is no longer a game. My patience is worn, little niece. Now I will show your followers what I think of their 'elder god'."

Nebiat frantically called upon Krox's reserves of *fire*, desperately channeling strength as she sought to keep control of Worldender.

Nefarius's tail tightened, as did her claws. Both siphoned magic wherever they touched, weakening the affected limb. Krox's cosmic arms tore free at the wrists, spraying still more *spirit* into the system over her world as the limbs spun away.

She managed to seize the spear with a third hand, but Nefarius's black teeth seized Krox's neck and bit deep. The drain was both immediate and unbelievably strong. A torrent of *spirit*, and a lesser flow of *fire*, flowed into Nefarius's gullet.

Krox grew weaker, even as Nefarius feasted on that strength. Nebiat knew a single instant of stark terror. They'd lost, and so quickly. She had badly miscalculated the strength of her enemy.

Nebiat thrashed in Nefarius's grip, but the Wyrm moved with her, and continued to drain magic.

She brought Worldender around in a weak swing, but Nefarius batted it aside. Finally, the dragon raised her maw from the wound she'd left in Krox's throat, *spirit* covering her jaws. "Cease your struggles, child. The battle is done. I will kill your tormentor, but you need not fear."

The Wyrm-god thrust her forearm deep into Krox's midsection, and Nebiat felt something...strange. It was as if someone had walked over her grave, a faint brush, like a breath on the back of your neck when you think someone is behind you.

A flash of pain blinded her, eclipsing all thought, for a moment at least, and then she was tumbling end over end, a mass of *spirit* energy falling like a star, into the orbit of her world.

She watched the battle continue to play out in the sky above her—if it could be called a battle. Nefarius calmly dismembered Krox with the efficiency of a spider wrapping newly caught prey.

You have doomed me. You, a child, with little more than a century's experience, Krox raged, though their connection was different now. Weaker. Muted. *Nefarius will devour my mind. She will overpower me, and the essence that has comprised this entity for millions of years will cease to exist. All thanks to your meddling.*

Satisfaction swelled in Nebiat as she tumbled through the upper atmosphere. She didn't answer. She wasn't even sure she could. All that mattered was that Krox was dead, and that smug bastard would never victimize another race the way it had hers.

Her flight seemed predetermined, and Nebiat quickly realized that Nefarius had chosen deliberately. Her course angled directly toward the mountain-sized dragon effigy she'd created, and relief tingled through her as she realized that Nefarius must intend for her to occupy the body she'd built. Perhaps Nefarius would accept her as a vassal after all. She would gladly and loyally serve.

Her essence slammed into the titanic dragon effigy, the bones of the Earthmother eagerly drinking the *spirit* magic. She could feel herself fusing with the rock, exactly as her ritual had intended. Did this mean that Nefarius had somehow completed the ritual?

Elation soared in her, for a moment at least. Then she realized that she couldn't move. Her energy had inhabited the rock, but the rock hadn't animated as planned. It hadn't become a true body, not as she'd intended. The ritual remained incomplete.

She was trapped. And her enemies were coming.

7

ALL THE WORDS AT ONCE

Voria liked most of the trappings of godhood, but the lack of physical responses tied to your emotions was not one of them. She hated that she couldn't sigh, or even roll her eyes. It made her feel alien. Inhuman. Which, she supposed, she was.

She followed Kazon up the corridor, and out of deference to her brother didn't pepper him with the many questions she wanted answered. How was this ritual to be performed? Could they really resurrect Ikadra? What would the cost be? And were they really going to abandon this place, knowing what it could do?

The others trailed along after them, with Aran bringing up the rear. He strode into the room with a lethal gait, and his hand never left Narlifex's hilt. He was ready for killing, and thought there might be cause. She couldn't blame him. Quite the opposite. She found his vigilance comforting.

"This is my workshop." Kazon beamed at her from the far side of an advanced workstation. A cluster of bundled golden tubes, like fibers of rope, disappeared into the floor, and pulses of white-blue flowed up them, expelled into the air.

That magic generated a field where Ikadra hung, bobbing slowly up and down. Nara stood near a panel, and was tapping away at sigils as she adjusted the field.

"What are we looking at?" Voria asked, folding her arms as she studied the workshop. It was all vaguely familiar from her childhood years with the Inurans, but she'd never been comfortable with magitech engineering, and understood almost none of it.

"The field is a sort of conduit," Nara explained, without looking up from her work. "It moderates the flow of magic into the subject, which enables fine manipulation. This could be used to construct complex enchantments, and you could take years to do it if you really needed the time to puzzle out your spell. It's ingenious, and there are six other workshops just like this one. This place could fuel a magical revolution the likes of which the sector has never seen."

Voria moved to inspect Ikadra. She extended a ghostly hand, and caressed the golden haft. Life still flickered within, an ember at least.

"Ikadra was likely born in one of these rooms," she murmured. "It seems fitting he be repaired here. What must I do?"

"We will be using this device," Kazon said, indicating an odd contraption that very much resembled a spell matrix. "It will collect magical energy, and channel them into the tubes, you see. We'll have Aran stand in one, and supply primal *air*. Then you will provide primal *life*. A sufficient quantity of both will repair the cracks, and theoretically awaken Ikadra."

"You don't sound entirely confident," Voria pointed out

as she removed her hand from the staff. She focused her attention on her brother. "How well researched is this ritual?"

"Well enough," Nara interjected. "Obviously this is all theoretical, but we understand the principles involved. *Life* and *water* form creation. Creation in this case will repair the damaged areas. *Air* and *life* form enchantment, which will stabilize the spell. If I'm understanding this correctly this has an automatic limiter, and will not allow an unsafe dose of magic to be used. Ikadra is at no risk."

Voria eased slightly, and realized that her anger and her criticism were both born out of fear for a friend. She wanted him back. She needed him back.

"Thank you for easing my mind." Voria inclined her head respectfully to Nara, then moved to stand in the closer matrix.

Aran moved wordlessly to the other matrix and slid inside. His cold demeanor was certainly different, and she could sense the intensity lurking behind those eyes. What terrible miracles had he borne witness to? She was glad she didn't know, and thankful that he bore the burden so the rest of them didn't have to.

"Well," Kazon said, exhaling a long breath, "I guess we find out if this works as I believe it does. Aran, Voria, place your hands on the stabilizing ring, and relax. This will feel different from a standard matrix. You are not giving the magic...it is being drawn from you."

Voria nodded, and did as she was bid. Her hands were not flesh and blood, but the ring provided resistance somehow. She gripped it, and held on. More and more she wondered about constructing a physical body.

That seemed not only possible, but prudent.

Yes and no, Shaya said, appearing in her field of vision. It was the first she'd spoken in some time. *Remember that a physical body can be killed. It makes you vulnerable. It offers power, but at the price of vulnerability. You've seen what that cost Xal, and Marid, and Inura. I never constructed a body, and I don't regret that. It made me more adaptable.*

Voria cocked her head thoughtfully. That made a great deal of sense. Krox had never constructed a body either, and Nebiat's attempt to do so were awkward at best. A body could be immensely useful, especially a body like the one the Inurans had built for Nefarius.

For now, though, adaptability was their only advantage, and she intended to use it fully.

The stabilizing ring warmed in her hands, and she felt a smile bloom. She hadn't felt temperature since her ascension. A warm, golden energy was drawn out of her into the ring, like blood flowing into a vial.

She did not resist as the energy slowly bled into the matrix, though she could have, she sensed. Pulse after pulse flowed out of her, but at a measured rate. The energy it gathered was powerful, but hardly what she would have considered a divine level.

Water and *life* were drawn out of her in equal measure, dark blue twined with white pulses, wave after wave.

Across the workshop a similar process was occurring with Aran, who generated icy-blue pulses of *air* every few moments, which the ring eagerly drank from him.

The magic flowed up the tubes at the base of the matrices, then was expelled into the field containing Ikadra. Gold and blue motes of magic swam up around the staff, swirling their way into the crack on the sapphire. More and more magic poured into the staff, and millimeter by millimeter the cracks began to glow with a blazing luminance.

The magic spread until every crack was covered, then a

high pitched whine beyond human hearing began to build. The whole staff vibrated, and the flow of motes intensified. Voria could feel the drain now, powerful and steady, as the staccato of pulses increased.

A deafening pop crashed through the room, accompanied by a flare of intense golden light. When the light faded the cracks were gone, and Ikadra's sapphire was lit with its own inner light.

"Finally. Finally!" Ikadra pulsed, the sapphire flashing in time with the words. "Do you have any idea how long I've been wanting to talk? I've been here the whole time. Does your ship stop flying because you've got a damaged comm? Of course not. I've been here listening. I just couldn't talk. But now? Now I can say all the words. Allthewordsatonce."

Nara was the first to rush forward, and awkwardly hugged the staff. "I'm so glad you're okay. We've been worried."

"I know...here listening, remember?" Ikadra pulsed, though his tone was light. "I could see how you were mourning. Touching. Like, seriously. At first. Then it got annoying. Like, get over it and get back to work. We have a god to resurrect. I've been trying to tell you for weeks."

"A god to resurrect?" Voria blinked at the staff. "You're not back more than a few seconds and you already want to go haring off on some quest? Ikadra, we brought you back to help us retrieve the *Spellship*. We must get that ship back. That's our first priority. If you're up to speed, so to speak, then you know that, yes?"

"Uh, well, yeah," Ikadra admitted, with clear reluctance. "I mean, we need to go deal with Nebiat, like once and for all. But we also need to resurrect Xal. Fortunately, we've got enough badasses to do both at the same time."

"He's right," Kazon broke in, to Voria's mild surprise. "Inura made his wishes known before he left. He built this mech for a purpose, and that purpose involves Xal. He always intended for us to go to the husk, and to resurrect Xal, I think."

"It stands to reason," Aran broke in with a strong, clear voice, "that Nara and I need to be the ones to resurrect Xal. Like it or not, Xal has marked us, more than once, and I'm betting the skull will be a good starting point. Nara, are you game?"

Nara looked torn, and Voria pounced on that. "Nara, I need you to wield Ikadra and take back the *Spellship* while Frit and I delay Krox. Distracting an elder god will not be easy. Please, Nara."

Voria hated the desperation in her voice.

"Umm," Ikadra pulsed, "I get the sense you're really not understanding what I'm trying to get across. The only god that might have a prayer of killing Nefarius is Xal. It won't matter if we somehow beat Krox and get the *Spellship* back, because Nefarius will kill us all eventually. She's already hard at work, systematically building her power base and infiltrating the Ternus government. Do not underestimate her, or we'll all pay the price. We get Xal back in fighting shape, or we lose this war."

Voria hesitated. She wanted to lobby that her mission was more important, but from the sound of it both needed to succeed or it all came apart. "Very well. Ikadra, Frit, and I will attempt to get the *Spellship* back."

"What about us?" Crewes asked, with a nod to the company. "Who we tagging along with?"

Aran's face finally expressed an emotion...indecision. "I'd prefer you with me, but you and the *Talon* are too valuable to risk on a long shot. I'd argue that we need to get Ternus back on our side. Davidson is the way we do that, and someone needs to get him home to New Texas so he can assess the situation. Can you give him a lift, Crewes?"

Crewes shook his head slowly. "I don't like it. Sir, if you aren't going with us, and we're dropping Davidson on New Texas, then who you got in mind for command?"

"You." Aran fixed Crewes with that heavy stare. "It's time. You're ready for it. You trained Bord, Nara, and I from the ground up. Rhea trusts you. Take the *Talon* with my blessing. Get it into the fight where it will do the most good. We need to get people working against Nefarius. We need them to understand who she is. This war is going to be won, partially at least, by the number of souls we can convince to support us against Nefarius."

"Still don't like it." Crewes gave a dark scowl. "I hate being in charge. But, we ain't got a better choice. I'll take command."

"Very well, Captain." Aran nodded at Crewes. "She's your ship now. Treat her right."

"Uh, sir?" Bord spoke up, the first time he'd done so in what felt like days to Voria. Kezia's loss had hit the young mage hard. "How are we gonna move about? We ain't got a void mage, and we ain't got a god that can just like...be there."

"I'll take care of that," Aran said confidently. He turned to Voria. "I guess this is goodbye, for now at least."

Voria nodded sadly. "Take care, Aran, Nara. I understand why you can't go with me. I wish it were otherwise. Know that your sacrifices are witnessed, and appreciated. I'll do what I can to keep them all safe."

"And I'll do the same," Kazon said. "Nara and Aran will

be under my protection, and that of Inura's legacy. Be well, sister. We'll meet again, at the end."

"Huh, huh," Inura pulsed. "Inura's legacy. Sounds dirty."

"Be well, brother." Voria turned from him with a feeling of finality, unmoved by Ikadra's humor, welcome as it was. She sensed, somehow, that she'd never see Kazon again.

8

TRUST

Nefarius appeared in the sky over Colony 3, flush with newly acquired magic. She flung her wings out and basked in the light of the star, partly for comfort, but mostly to display her impressive body to the world below.

It had taken a great deal of effort to stave off torpor after digesting so much of Krox's mind, and she could do it no longer. She needed sleep. Before she could allow that to happen, however, she needed to pave the way for the endgame.

Xal would return; of that she had no doubt. He was too crafty to allow her to arise unopposed, especially given that he'd deliberately chosen his death. She needed to be ready when he did, and that meant creating an army of converts devoted to her.

Time to secure that.

She focused her consciousness down into the tiny mortal avatar, and tapped into the communications array as she'd done before. Nefarius chose uplifting music, something humanity had created endless variations of, and set some of the more impressive scenes to a majestic score.

Nefarius broadcast that footage, and began to speak as it played. Quietly. Humbly. "Citizens of Ternus, I asked you for a great favor. I asked you to place your trust in me, perhaps the greatest favor one can ask during war. Trust comes easy under the auspices of peace. Words like 'honor' and 'duty' are trotted out and paraded about."

She paused for a moment as the battle between her and Krox reached its crescendo. Only when she began her final assault did she speak again.

"War is different," she whispered, so that the audience would strain to hear it. "We trade words like honor for vengeance. We trade duty for extermination. Because let's be clear. Extermination is exactly what we are talking about. So long as one world remains where demons or Wyrms are allowed to flourish, they will always be a threat to humanity. How many billions more have to die under the name of tolerance?"

She paused again, and this time watched and listened. Traffic flooded their social media, and she basked in it all. They might not understand what they were doing, but that didn't matter. They were generating worship. They were turning her into a symbol, the cornerstone of every deity's religion.

"I am weary," she finally continued, and allowed that weariness to leak into her drawl. "I killed Krox. I took vengeance. But his world is still out there. There are millions of Wyrms on it, and millions more Ifrit, all who served Krox and are likely to be a touch angry that I just murdered their god. Now I left those people alive. I did it because Governor Austin didn't order me to wipe them out.

But I wanted to. Because I don't want to see our sons and daughters die fighting them, again, when they inevitably come for us."

The footage showed her devouring Krox's body, feasting on his magic. It was a gruesome, shocking sight. Exactly as intended. "War isn't pretty. But I asked you for your faith and your trust, and you allowed me to prosecute that war. I downed one of our worst enemies. Others remain. I must rest after my assault on Krox, but I will be ready when you call upon me again. Pray to me, people of Ternus. Put your faith in me, and one by one I will deliver your enemies to you. Rest easy tonight. The entire sector knows what transpired and for the first time they fear us, not the other way around."

She killed the transmission, and settled back with a smile to watch the social media. There would be endless arguing and discussion. Battles would be fought. Factions would form. But love her or hate her, all would acknowledge her existence so completely that they would begin to worship her, even if only out of fear.

When Xal returned she would be ready. Humanity was powerful and numerous, and if her ultimate plan came to fruition she would have far more followers than anyone thought possible.

These new gods underestimated the power of worship, but Xal would not. For that reason, and that reason alone, not even Talifax knew the final miracle she planned to perform.

It would devastate her enemies, and in the same stroke deliver her enough worship to overcome every surviving god in the sector. Soon, in weeks at most, this war would be over and she'd finally be able to focus on more important matters, like Talifax's endless treachery.

For now, though, she basked in the notifications as they flooded in from every social media platform in use by humanity, across the sector. Her little speech was having exactly the desired effect.

9

VOID MAGE

Crewes shivered as he reappeared on the *Talon*'s bridge. It terrified him how casually the captain teleported them all from deep within the bowels of the planet onto a ship hundreds of kilometers away.

He tightened his grip around his spellcannon, which he'd carried down there despite the captain saying it would be perfectly safe. That's what everyone said right up until you needed the uptight dude with the spellcannon to save your collective asses.

A low feline whine came from his armor, and Crewes sensed it was directed at Aran. He'd heard enough alley cats back in the alleys of Yanthara that he knew the sound. The cat was scared. Scared of a much larger predator.

Crewes forced himself to exhale, and ran through his mental checklist. Everyone in the company was present. Rhea was already in the central matrix, and Bord had moved instinctively to the support matrix.

The kid had become the model soldier ever since...well, ever since Nefarius had made it personal. He had something to prove now, which deeply saddened Crewes. People with something to prove died badly, most times.

But you couldn't just tell someone that.

Crewes moved on to Davidson, who'd climbed into the offensive matrix. The blond officer had allowed his beard to get more scruffy than the confederate military would have been comfortable with, but then Crewes doubted too many people were checking regs these days.

Nara, Aran, and the bristly-bearded guy Crewes knew as Major Voria's brother, stood in a little cluster away from everyone else.

Nara stood silently, of course, unassuming in her sculpted armor, with a simple ponytail and a staff. They trusted her now, but wasn't too long back they'd had reason not to.

Aran stood a pace away, his right hand resting comfortably on the hilt of his magic sword, which had a name, Crewes was pretty sure. Just like Neeko.

His armor began to purr.

"That's damned unsettling," he muttered under his breath.

"We were about to solve the problem of a void mage," the captain began. His clear eyes swept the lot of them, and Crewes was once again impressed with his casual charisma. The kid had grown so much since he'd been a raw wipe. "You're not going to like the answer, which is why I waited 'til we were back aboard to offer my solution. I can make one of you a void mage. You'll be able to open Fissures and to master gravity magic, eventually."

Rhea's gaze dropped instantly to the deck, making her answer clear. Crewes looked to Davidson, but the Ternus officer gave a slight shake of his head.

"Well," Crewes began, squaring his shoulders, "I gotta be

honest. I was raised to believe demons are evil. Every *void* Catalyst we've seen involves demons. My ma would say that makes *void* magic evil."

"It's a tool." Aran's eyes narrowed slightly, as they often did when he was impatient. "I'm not going to force anyone to accept it, but you guys need to get to New Texas, right? And Yanthara? That was the plan, wasn't it?"

"I'll do it," Bord broke in. He ducked out of the matrix's spinning rings, and approached Aran. He looked so different with the buzz cut. "That's the magic you use to disintegrate stuff, right? And throw void bolts?"

Aran nodded.

"And you can just give me a piece?" Bord asked. He cocked his head to the side. "I thought you could only do that at a Catalyst, because it was the body of a dead god."

"Aran is a living god," Nara whispered. She raised her voice a bit for the next part. "And not just a lesser god. He's nearly as strong as Voria. Stronger, from a purely combative perspective. As scary as we all find it...making a mage is trivial now."

In that instant an emotion flitted across the captain's features. It was there and gone so fast that if Crewes hadn't been looking him right in the eye he'd have missed it.

Aran was terrified. Terrified of the power, and of what it was turning him into. Crewes was certain of it. All the agony, all the terror, it was captured in that instant. Somehow that made it okay. He was still human enough to care.

"Sounds like we got a fix," Crewes said. He knew that, theoretically at least, he was now in charge of this ship, but with Aran and Davidson, and even Rhea, standing right there he certainly didn't feel like it. "Captain will work his mojo on Bord, and Bord will open us a Fissure, then pilot us through. Rhea, help Bord with the navigation in the depths."

"Permission to depart the ship, Captain Crewes?" Aran asked, snapping a tight salute.

Nara echoed it a moment later, as did everyone else on the bridge. Crewes froze, like a deer meeting the hunter. "Uh. Sure thing, sir. Listen, I ain't good at this pep talk stuff, but...don't let this stuff change you too much, sir. I can see you and I are worried about the same thing."

Aran approached and seized Crewes in a fierce hug. At first Crewes resisted, but then he leaned into the hug and embraced his friend. His best friend maybe.

"I won't let it change my principles." Aran took a step back, and offered a grim smile. "I'll become what I have to be to stop Nefarius, and to make sure this sector can make its own choices. I know you'll do the same."

Aran raised a hand and aimed the palm at Bord. "Are you ready, Specialist?"

"Do it." Bord's mouth firmed to a tight line, and his clear blue eyes fixed on the captain. "I'm going to use this magic to make them pay for what they did to her."

Aran hesitated at that, but then nodded. "She'd have wanted that, I think."

A pulse of something that lived beyond black flowed from Aran's hand, a tendril of dense, smoky magic that swirled around Bord. It flowed into his eyes, ears, and nose, and the specialist gave a gasp of surprise.

His eyes closed, but a moment later they fluttered open. He stared down at himself in wonder. "That's it? That was so...easy."

Crewes darted a glance Aran's way, and saw the fatigue etched on the captain's face. It had cost him, whatever he pretended.

"That's it." Aran smiled down at Bord. "I know you never really liked me, but I've always considered you a friend. I'm going to miss you."

A smile ghosted across Bord's face, though it was gone quickly. "I always liked you, sir. You were just too much competition is all."

Aran laughed at that, and shook his head. "We'll see you guys at the final battle."

"Take care, sir." Crewes offered a final salute, and managed to hold the tears in when Aran, Nara, and Kazon simply vanished.

The *Talon* was his ship now, and he had a job to do.

10

UNLIKELY ALLIES

Voria turned to Frit, rather awkwardly, which was to be expected, given the nature of their relationship. The flaming girl—no, the flaming goddess—stared a challenge, ready for Voria to pick a fight.

"We're the last two, Frit. I suppose that means it's time we formulated a plan." Voria folded her arms. "For starters, it makes sense to have you carry Ikadra."

Much of the hostility bled from Frit's expression. "But—why? I don't understand why you'd risk that."

"It's not like I'm going to melt," Ikadra protested, tone indignant.

Voria gave a patient nod. She was happy to explain. "We're going to the stronghold of my enemy. A land of dragons and fire, yes?"

"Yes," Frit allowed.

"And Ikadra is a conduit for worship," Voria explained. "Presumably many of these dragons and Ifrit worship *you*. If you use the staff, you can channel that worship. Channeling *life* has its uses, but channeling *fire* will roast Nebiat. Therefore, you should wield the staff."

"Well, technically—" Ikadra began.

"Please shut up, Ikadra," Voria said, affectionately. "There's also the secondary matter of me lacking physical hands. How would I even carry him? I'd intended for it to be Nara, but we don't have that option. You're the best option remaining."

Frit nodded and wrapped her hand around Ikadra's golden haft. The sapphire pulsed excitedly. "This is so exciting! We're finally going to kill Nebiat. I mean, theoretically. Isn't Krox going to kick our collective asses as soon as we arrive?"

"He's terrifying," Frit whispered, her eyes taking on the unfocused look of memory, "and I don't want to face him. If we attack, it would need to be quick. We'd need to find out where Nebiat is holding the *Spellship*, get it, and retreat."

"And if Ikadra is right? If the opportunity to kill Nebiat arises? What will you do, Frit?" Voria was surprised by the sudden tide of anger welling up within her. "Can you strike a killing blow?"

Frit's smoldering eyebrows knit together. "I can, and I will. Nebiat has duped me time and again. She's made me look like a fool, and she's made my friends mistrust me. I bear responsibility for my choices, but that doesn't mean I can't blame Nebiat for her role in things. She needs to die, Voria. No mercy. No bargaining."

Voria relaxed slightly, the first time she'd done so since her ship had been taken. If Frit was being honest, and Voria believed she was, then she shared Voria's desire to kill Nebiat. She was a true ally, driven by similar motivations.

"I'm still angry about the mirror," Voria snapped, though she had no idea where the comment had come from, "but I'm glad to have you with me. I couldn't agree more. She needs to die. No more chances. We'll find a way to overcome Krox, and failing that, we'll get the *Spellship* and get out."

"I—thank you, Voria." Frit folded her arms, mirroring Voria. "I know things will always be...awkward, but at least we want the same thing. For what it's worth, I'm sorry about the mirror."

Ikadra's sapphire pulsed, but softly, and his voice came out a whisper. "Still can't believe you broke a celestial artifact that predated the universe."

"Let's not talk about it." Voria closed her eyes and once again missed physical reactions. "Can you scry Nebiat's world and give us some idea of what we're facing? Where is Krox? And can you locate the *Spellship*? That will largely determine the efficacy of our plans."

"I will need a few moments." Frit produced a shard from a void pocket, a bit of a...shattered mirror.

Voria's fists balled, but she said nothing as Frit held up the fragment and breathed upon the surface. Fire welled up within it, then cleared to show the Nebiat system. Voria hated calling it that, but it was apt.

Frit opened her eyes, and the image in the fragment spun to reveal the system. "I don't see...wait a minute. Krox isn't there. There's no sign of him. The system...is unprotected right now. We'll never have a better chance."

Voria shook her head slowly, and studied the image in the fragment. "We must be missing something. We know Nebiat went back there after stealing the *Spellship*. Why leave again so soon?"

"I don't know," Frit admitted, "but you can see the same thing I can. It looks like Krox isn't there."

"And the *Spellship*?" Voria hated admitting ignorance, but Frit was far superior with divination. If it could be found, she could find it.

"I can't see any sign of it. There's any number of reasons for that." Frit gave Voria an apologetic look. "I have a vested interest in this too. Kaho is on that ship."

"Yes," Voria agreed, "I have to keep reminding myself that you have as vested an interest as I do. Are you willing to take a chance, Frit? Because if so…let's go to this planet, and see what we can learn."

Frit nodded and even offered a tentative smile. "I'm ready."

11

JUSTICE

Frit materialized in the Nebiat system, the system she'd come to think of as home. She quickly scanned her surroundings with godsight, and began piecing together the situation.

She clutched Ikadra in her right hand, the staff comparatively cool in her hand. She'd never really gotten to know Ikadra, and found his humor juvenile, but his knowledge was vast and his power immense. Certainly worth a few bad jokes.

A moment later Voria appeared, just a few dozen meters away. She was roughly the same size as Frit, and seemed able to change that at will. Frit was tempted to ask her how she did that, as she badly wanted to learn what being a goddess entailed.

But Voria was the very last person who'd help her. Voria had every cause to hate her, and the best outcome from today would be a truce.

"By the goddess," Voria breathed. She pointed. "Is that what I think it is?"

Frit nodded. It had taken a few moments to identify, but

the planet Nebiat had a second moon now. That moon was a shriveled misshapen mass, indicating that it wasn't old enough to have formed into a smooth sphere.

Traces of magic came from that moon. *Spirit* magic and a bit of *fire*. It was the former that interested Frit, not because she sought to claim the tiny ember of power that remained. No, she was interested because it was the same *fire* magic she had been given.

That made this shriveled moon Krox. Or what remained of the god. He'd been siphoned dry of magic. Killed, as fully as a god could be.

"I'm not even sure I thought Krox could be killed," Ikadra pulsed, his tone thick with awe. "Elder gods don't go down often, or easy, and Krox was the canniest of them all. More than anything else he was a survivor."

"Does this mean that Nebiat is already dead?" Voria wondered aloud.

"There's no way we're that lucky." Frit turned her attention from the burned out star and focused on the planet. "There's a lot of magic down there, but if you give me a little time I'll find a way to locate her, if she's here. I expect she won't be. Krox is destroyed and I don't see any trace of Worldender."

"We both know who has it now." Voria frowned, and drifted over to Frit to gaze down at the planet. "I'm curious as to why Nefarius didn't destroy the world below."

"It's not like her," Ikadra pulsed. "She's thorough. Leaving this place intact makes no sense."

"I don't know her reason, but I expect it will ultimately benefit her and Talifax." Frit zoomed a little closer to the world. "There. I see a massive concentration of *spirit* down there, enough to be a god. Shall we investigate?"

Voria merely nodded, so Frit zoomed lower. She enjoyed

atmospheric reentry, as it warmed her all over, like bathing in a star. That kind of warmth was rare, and she reveled in it whenever she could.

Below she could somehow feel millions of pairs of eyes staring up at her. What must she and Voria look like? Twin falling stars, but moving under their own control. They must be terrified after having witnessed the battle between Krox and Nefarius, particularly since Krox had lost.

Their god had been slain.

As she descended she realized that a new settlement had sprung up, and it seemed to be where they were going. The *spirit* magic she'd sensed had come from a mountain-sized statue that had been carved. Of Nebiat, of course. That woman's vanity knew no bounds.

The settlement had, apparently, been built to support the construction of the draconic effigy. The fact that it had been carved from the bones of the Earthmother was no coincidence. Nebiat had constructed herself a physical body from a potent magical material.

"Is she in there?" Voria called as she pulled up short midair not far from Frit. Several dozen priests, most hatchlings, stared up at them in wonder.

"I don't know." Frit stared hard at the effigy. She could feel the tremendous power within, but was that Nebiat? Or was this some sort of unfinished ritual?

Power seethed within the stone, and wisps began to coalesce above it. They rose, wisp after wisp, slowly forming a spectral Wyrm, with dark scales and angry eyes. A form Frit would recognize anywhere, and that she wagered Voria would too.

"Hello, old enemy," Voria called, loud and clear like a clarion call. "It would seem the time for running is over."

"If only you knew how true that was," Nebiat said,

bitterly. "I am anchored to this thing. Tethered, like a leashed dog. Yet I am not powerless. If you have come to do battle you will find me more than prepared. Come, Frit, let us show Voria the price of invading our world."

Frit began to laugh. It was a freeing, all-encompassing laugh. It was the best laugh of her life, and she gave herself over fully to its enjoyment. Even more so when Voria began to giggle. She giggled!

"Nebiat," Voria managed, around a smirk. "When you consistently and systematically betray every relative, every ally, and every enemy, you eventually reach a point where you must be called to account for your actions. Did you really expect Frit to side with you? To save you?"

"Frit, we are kindred. We've built a world together," Nebiat pleaded, her spectral form somehow less menacing than the real thing. "You've seen what I've built, not for myself, but for our people. And we have a greater enemy. Have you not considered how I came to be like this? What of Nefarius? She is a dark and terrible goddess that will consume us all, unless we band together."

"I seem to remember," Voria broke in, "you sending Frit to offer a very similar message, just before stabbing us in the back and stealing a tool you can use to create gods."

Nebiat's wings flapped, although since she had no body Frit doubted it was strictly necessary. She stared at Voria as if searching for the right mixture of words to free herself from this situation. "You're saying you don't trust me, and that's understandable. But surely you understand what I was trying to accomplish. I was merely borrowing the *Spell-ship* so that I could escape Krox. Frit, you may not like me, but you know that's the truth."

"It is." Frit nodded. She seemed unmoved. "It is also the truth that you could have asked your allies for help to accomplish the same thing. Instead, you betrayed them and ensured there will never be peace between us, not so long as you live. You have become a direct threat to your people, Nebiat, and your many enemies will now come to exact vengeance. It will be our people that are harmed by your actions."

Nebiat adopted a contrite expression, which may or may not have been feigned. "You're right. I am a terrible, awful person. I have done unforgivable things, and would again. I have labored to create a home for my children, and I have succeeded. Because of my ferocity in combat Nefarius chose to spare me, even as she devoured Krox. Now I know why. Because she wanted us to fight here, to weaken each other. Is that really what you want? Us, playing into her hands."

"Nebiat, daughter of Teodros," Voria called, a nimbus of golden light, "on behalf of our sector I name you anathema. You are an enemy of all sentient races, and shall be treated as such." She turned to Frit, and there was sympathy in her expression. "It is your world, and she has wronged you as much as anyone. I leave it to you to pass judgement."

"Well, that's easy," Frit gave back without a shred of hesitation. "Nebiat, I sentence you to die."

12

INSTRUCTIONS

Nefarius had finished digesting Krox's magic, a huge quantity of *fire*, which she kept, and *spirit*, which she transmuted into *void*. Would that she could have created *dream* with it, but one could not transmute an aspect into its opposite, even if one was a god.

That meant part of her plan remained out of reach, for now at least. There were several *dream* Catalysts in the sector, and one in particular she had her eye on. First there were other matters to attend to.

An annoying buzzing flittered at the edge of her consciousness, an email marked priority one, something she wanted to review personally. She accepted it, and watched the attached video.

A well-groomed human with dark, slicked-back hair sat behind an impressively wide desk. It had an age to it, and the kind of well worn luster reserved for artifacts of the state. She'd used them long enough to recognize them, and imagined this was one of the symbols of the office of the governor. She approved.

"Madam Nefarius." The human fixed her with, what she assumed was, his sternest gaze. He ruined the moment by adjusting his tie, a nervous habit she'd wager. "We both understand something that most of humanity, most of the sector, does not. We both know you are a good deal older than the fiction that the Inurans created. I didn't know that at first, but I do now, and I'm starting to understand what that means."

The young man leaned back in his chair. He wore his years well, but they were already taking a toll. It showed in the lines on his youthful face, and the patches of grey in otherwise black hair. It showed in the tremble in his hands as he straightened the tie.

"You are a goddess, and you've picked my race for, well, for lack of a better word, assimilation, I guess." He licked his lips, then leaned forward again. "I won't have it. We will not follow you blindly. Sure, we want you to destroy the enemies of mankind, but we will never be your slaves. I already see what you're trying to pull here, and I will fight you. There aren't many of us left. We're banding together. Now I'm smart enough to realize you can kill me whenever you like, but if you do that I've left enough footage behind to ensure I'll be a martyr, and that my name will be the rallying cry to bring you down. Working with the Inurans was a mistake, no matter how bad off we were. Well, I'm rectifying that mistake, before it's too late."

The missive ended, and the Quantum logo flashed.

"Oh, Governor," Nefarius purred, feeling delightfully wicked as she observed the effect of her stratagem. "It's already far, far too late."

She considered sending a response, but none was warranted. Let him wonder at her reaction, and build up plots in his own mind. Let him jump at shadows while she won the hearts of his people.

Instead, Nefarius focused her consciousness fully in her mortal form, settling into the avatar's android body. "Attend me, Talifax."

"Of course, terrible one." The dark sorcerer appeared before her, even as her words died away. He sank to one knee, his bulky black armor making no sound as he moved. "How may I serve your dark will?"

"You can stop using language like that, for starters. Adapt to the vernacular, sorcerer." Nefarius snapped, disguising neither her anger nor her distaste. Her hand twitched, but she resisted the urge to draw her blades. "The humans have been prepared, as best I can until I give them the miracle that will secure my place as their god. It is time to deal with my sister."

"And you wish me to perform a flame reading?" Talifax prompted. His tone bore mild curiosity, but nothing more.

"Do not anticipate me, sorcerer. Ever." Her eyes whirred as she narrowed them. "All your contingencies and all your schemes will not save you if you earn my full attention. Surely you have seen *those* possibilities."

"I have." The words were...contrite. An emotion one did not often hear from the sorcerer. "And I would not enjoy any of them, mistress. You are one of the few who could stalk me across realities. But I also see how unlikely they are, because you know that I exist to further your aims. We both know why. They are watching. Always. And you are our best hope of flushing them into the light, where they can be killed."

Nefarius kept her doubts to herself. Once, she'd considered Talifax her closest ally, and believed him the only other being uncorrupted by those who lurked beneath. Now? She believed he was the most insidious of their agents. Such a shame that he needed to be one of the last to die.

"There is much to be prepared before my confrontation with Xal." She took a step closer to Talifax, and loomed over the kneeling sorcerer. "Which puppet have you placed in charge of Inura's children?"

"Matron Jolene, a fine agent." Talifax's voice was perfectly subservient, his posture doubly so, and yet there was something there. An unspoken challenge. "She is the biological mother of the new lady of light, but that is not why I selected her. She is utterly ruthless, and absolutely addicted to your blood, mistress."

Nefarius nodded. It pleased her to have the consortium in their pocket, but the trouble was that it was in Talifax's pocket, not hers. She needed a direct connection to this Jolene, and to her people, so she could cut out the middleman. Eroding Talifax's power base would be vital after she disposed of Xal.

"Very well. Instruct this Jolene to increase production on the black ships." Nefarius longed for the time to deal with the matter personally, to connect with Jolene, but there were simply too many other important tasks only she could deal with.

"Mistress." Talifax glanced up with that unreadable mask, dark and plain, and utterly unassuming. "Who will crew these vessels? We've stripped nearly all mages from Ternus, and you're systematically removing them from our allies, as well."

"You are a master seer, so I hear," she taunted. "I will allow you to discern my motives on your own. Get it done, sorcerer. If your usefulness is ever exceeded by my urge to crush your throat, well, be certain you are far from this sector on that day."

“Of course, mistress. Pardon my impertinence.” Talifax genuflected, though she doubted he meant any of it. “May I ask where you will go next?”

“To Virkon.” She turned from the sorcerer, and extended her senses into her divine body. “It is past time my sister and I had a chat.”

13

OBLIVION

Virkonna waved a finger in a minute gesture, and a scale drifted from her arm onto the Kem'Hedj board. It joined a group clustered in the southern quadrant, which was currently her strongest area.

Her opponent was a crafty young Wyrm who'd been cagey about his past. Kheross had been present for the disastrous battle, and had even played a pivotal role, or so she'd heard tell. Given his performance in the game she didn't doubt their veracity. He was a true master.

"May I ask a question, mother?" The white-haired Wyrm asked, nodding his head deferentially as he placed a scale of his own.

"Of course. You've proven a tremendous boon, both on the field of battle, and to morale in the days since." Virkonna avoided flattery, but if not for Kheross constantly circulating among her children, many would have already fled her world. They were abandoning her, and who could blame them? She'd been struck down before them, and their enemy was coming. They all knew it.

They all knew it would be today.

"Why stay?" Kheross asked. He brushed a lock of hair from his face, and peered curiously in her direction with those frosty eyes. "You could flee to another sector. You could take your children and depart. The war is lost here. You know this. You know she will be here soon, and we do not need to be flame readers to know the outcome."

"Have you so little faith in me?" Virkonna regretted the heat in her words as soon as she'd uttered them. Not because she feared offending Kheross, but rather because it showed how close to the edge she lurked. Her nerves were frayed, and that wasn't a good position to be in before the kind of fight she was about to engage in.

"That's not it, mistress." Kheross inclined his head respectfully, then added another scale to the board. "I have absolute faith in you. But I have lived in a universe where you stood in defiance and died. Your children were cast adrift. We had nothing to live for. We held on as long as we could, but in the end Nefarius devoured us all."

"And you assume the same thing will happen in our universe?" Virkonna asked mildly, then added a scale of her own. She was slowly but certainly encircling his pieces. Victory was all but assured. Would that real battles could be won so easily.

Kheross nodded, then added another scale. He leaned back in his hovercouch, and eyed her directly. "Your children will scatter. Some will stay. They will be unequal to the task, and their Outriders will watch them fail. In our reality a small group of us persevered because we had a mission. You asked us to guard the *Spellship*. Here, though? There is no mission. Your supporters will fragment, and this world will be deserted or overrun."

Virkonna found that immensely troubling, because he delivered the news with absolute certainty. He was convinced these events would occur, exactly as he'd outlined them.

"Are you a flame reader now? Have you been studying with my sister?" She raised an eyebrow and made no attempt to disguise her growing ire.

"I do not need divination to predict the future." Kheross met her gaze without flinching. "Nor do you. So why stay? I notice you avoided answering."

Virkonna's ire rose, but then broke just as suddenly. Why *had* she stayed? She'd been avoiding the answer, and she couldn't any longer.

"Because I am tired of running," she answered simply. "My mother is dead. My eldest sisters are dead. My little brother is dead. If I run I might live for a while, but the day will come when Nefarius arrives and tears it all down. So I will make my stand here."

A high-pitched ring began beyond the edge of hearing. She knew it immediately, and what it heralded. "If you wish to depart this is your final opportunity."

Kheross nodded, then placed another scale. He made no motion to rise from his hovercouch, and his staunch confidence meant more to her than she could possibly express.

She placed another scale, the keening wind the only break in the silence.

Another celestial body appeared in the sky, the dragon's dark body gleaming in the light of the sun, its hellish eyes menacing as they settled upon her world. Virkonna glanced up and met her sister's gaze. It didn't matter that she was a tiny avatar, thousands of kilometers away.

They saw each other in that moment.

Nefarius loomed in the sky, the largest Wyrm in the sector by a good margin. Her claws could rend continents, and a single swipe from her tail would end all life on this world. Virkonna knew that would never happen, though.

This was too personal, for both of them.

Nefarius's avatar materialized a few meters away, both unfamiliar and terrifyingly familiar at the same time. The voice was perfect, but the body was entirely new. An android, of Inuran design. "Hello, sister." Her accent...the slow drawl sounded like the humans.

"Hello, sister." Virkonna rose from her hovercouch and approached Nefarius's strange incarnation. The dark metal gave off no aura, though after their last confrontation she understood how dangerous that made it. "You're a human now? Interesting. I wonder what mother would have thought."

The android showed no reaction. Nefarius had always valued their mother's opinion, and Virkonna was gambling that it was button she could still press.

"I suspect," Nefarius murmured as her metal heels clicked across the tiles, "that she would have been proud." Nefarius raised her arms in a slow circle, and displayed her new body. The bright sunlight glittered off that sleek metal skin. She moved as she always had, as Virkonna had trained her to move. "This body is the union of her children, after all. The magics in its construction required both *life* and *void*, which are nearly impossible to combine."

"Don't lecture me on basic spell craft, sister." Virkonna narrowed her eyes. "We both know that while mother might have admired the craftsmanship, she'd have detested what you've become. And why? You've never adequately explained why you started acting so erratically. Why you started killing your siblings, and devouring their magic."

For just a moment Nefarius's android face, so alien and

unreadable, adopted an expression of pity and...loneliness. Then it was gone, subsumed by rage and paranoia.

"Nor will I. My actions do not require that you understand their motivations." Nefarius extended both hands, and a void pocket opened on either palm. Twin blades flew out of their own accord, snapping into place in Nefarius's metal hands. "I respect you, sister. I love you. And I will miss you."

Virkonna knew in that instant there was no reaching her. There'd never been much chance, of course, but she had to try. And perhaps this was as close as Nefarius could come to asking for help.

Perhaps that was why she chose to face Virkonna, avatar to avatar. Their contest would be largely decided by their respective skill with a blade, instead of through raw magical might. Had the latter been the case, then Virkon and everything on it would likely have been disintegrated.

"You have always been accounted the finest swordsman in sector history," Nefarius said, circling now, waiting for Virkonna to arm herself. "Do you still believe that to be the case?"

"No," Virkonna admitted simply. Instead of summoning her artifact blades, which would then belong to Nefarius when she lost, she created a pair of perfect blades from hardened *life* and *air*. The weapons were impossibly sharp, and conductive to spells. It would be enough. "Though I don't believe the title falls to you either. When you strike me down today, as we both know you will, it cannot prove what you want it to. You are not besting me through strength of arms. What did mother call it? You brute forced it. And you will learn, I think, that that approach comes with certain limitations. When you meet him you will know him, and none of your tricks, or your technology will avail you."

"Is that a prophecy?" Nefarius taunted. Then she charged.

Her avatar blurred toward Virkonna, but Virkonna simply shifted to *air*, and exploded into electricity. She sought the gaps in Nefarius's armor, but could find no purchase.

Virkonna's cloud of electricity continued on past Nefarius, and coalesced back into her hybrid form. She flared her wings behind her, and conjured a new pair of swords, then she kicked off the ground, and used her tail to add more momentum.

She launched a flurry of blows at Nefarius, who expertly parried, blades ringing like a staccato of ever faster bells. Virkonna quickened her pace, and Nefarius allowed herself to be driven back across the balcony.

Behind her she was dimly aware of Kheross, who still hadn't risen from his hovercouch. He was watching their duel with a quiet intensity, his eyes showing knowledge only a master could display. He knew what he was seeing, the rarity of it.

Martial gods fighting, gods who valued their skill with a blade above all else. Such a duel had never been fought, not in this sector at least, and it salved her to know that a master stood in witness. She knew in that instant that Nefarius would let him live for that reason alone. She would want him to spread the tale of this fight.

Nefarius's foot flashed out suddenly, slamming into Virkonna's gut and flinging her back a pace. Nefarius twisted and used her wings to add power to the motion. She came around and her first blade flashed down at Virkonna's face.

Virkonna interposed one of her blades, but the move was hasty, and the sheer power of Nefarius's blow knocked her parry aside. Virkonna desperately brought her other blade around, and narrowly deflected Nefarius's attack, then rolled away.

She came to her feet panting, and began to circle at range, which Nefarius mirrored. The preamble was over now. They'd both opened strong, enough to take the other's measure. Now they'd try to bait each other until someone made a mistake.

Virkonna knew that was unlikely to be her. Nefarius had always been impulsive. She'd always charged in. The brute force approach suited her personality perfectly.

That meant all Virkonna had to do was outlast her, until an opening presented itself. Then she'd capitalize, or fall back to a defensive position until she could punish another mistake.

Nefarius charged again, this time with a wordless snarl. She hacked at Virkonna with both blades, and there was no subtlety to the attacks. There didn't need to be. The raw strength was irresistible, and now it was Virkonna falling back.

She knocked her opponent's blade aside, then ducked another slash. Nefarius followed up with a vicious head butt, and Virkonna's snout split in a spray of black blood. The wound was superficial, but painful.

Pain wasn't something Virkonna was used to feeling, and she didn't much like it. She rolled away from Nefarius, and came to her feet. "You're enjoying that body. Inura would be horrified that his best work is being used to murder the sector. Did you enjoy devouring his essence? Cannibalizing another one of your siblings in your mad quest for endless power? Oh, that's right. You weren't able to."

"Your Outrider denied me that." Nefarius raised a metallic hand and wiped Virkonna's blood from her face.

"But I would have relished it, devouring little brother's magic."

Virkonna cocked her head, and lowered her blades, a hair at least. "You really mean that, don't you?"

"Of course." Nefarius charged again, faster than before. Virkonna smoothly parried, and drank deeply of *air* to increase her speed to match.

She launched a pair of quick strikes, which Nefarius easily parried. Virkonna followed up with a kick that mirrored Nefarius's. It caught her sister in the midsection, and threw her back a pace.

"I have no need to breathe." Nefarius laughed and began to circle. "You cannot harm me, not in the same way I can harm you. I know what you're thinking. Technology is vulnerable to electricity. Fortunately, little brother circumvented that particular drawback. I am immune to your magic, little sister. And I am your equal with a sword. Eventually...I will win."

Virkonna fell back. She altered her body language, and allowed some hallmarks of panic to leak in. She couldn't tell if Nefarius bought it, but her sister continued her relentless assault in silence.

Finally, Nefarius's blade punched through Virkonna's defenses. It would have carved a furrow in her side, but Virkonna phased that part of herself into pure *air*, and the blade passed through without further harm.

The move left her sister off guard, and Virkonna capitalized on that. She glided forward, and her blades darted forward like serpents. They slammed into Nefarius's midsection, in what would have been fatal blows had she been flesh and blood.

But Nefarius was not flesh and blood.

The hardened magic touched that hellish alloy, and the

metal simply absorbed them. The blades sank into her abdomen, but did not emerge. That part of their magic was simply…gone. And her sister was the stronger for it.

"Your weapons cannot harm me, little sister." Nefarius delivered a cruel smile, and rammed her blades into Virkonna's chest. "I haven't been the student for a long time, but never before have I commanded this kind of advantage."

Virkonna did not resist the blow, though she could have easily. She did not flee, or quibble. Nefarius had beaten her. She had no weapon to pierce her sister's magic-resistant hide, so she allowed the blades to strike home, and end it.

She coughed up a mouthful of acidic blood, which flowed freely down her face. "You…will live to regret this path, sister. You've destroyed…the last dragonflight. The last of our people…"

Nefarius's blades flashed down, and finally ended Virkonna's suffering. She embraced oblivion gladly.

14

REGRETS

Nefarius stared down at her sister's corpse, wisps of magic drifting up and curling around her ebony legs. The magic seeped into her metal, a trickle compared to that which awaited her in orbit, but this bit far more important than the rest.

This was her sister's mind. Her intellect and her memories, extending back a hundred millennia or more. Nefarius devoured them with reverence, and whispered a prayer to their mother to watch over Virkonna's spirit. Though, if such a spirit still existed, Nefarius would have devoured that too.

She closed her eyes, though that didn't stem the flow of information, either from the humans' Quantum network, or from her sister's memories. It was overwhelming, even for a goddess. She stood, and endured.

In that instant, had she an enemy lurking nearby, she'd have been vulnerable. But her enemies were afraid and far from here, and thus missed their opportunity.

Nefarius finally opened her eyes, and looked around the terrace where Virkonna had been hosting her final decadent party. The place was deserted, save for a single Wyrm, his body a near perfect imitation of a human form, except for the eyes, which were slitted as Virkonna's had been.

She strode over to him, noting the ivory hair and haunted eyes. There was no fear there, only resignation. "Why didn't you flee?"

He laughed and extended a hand. Nefarius almost lopped it off, instinctively, but realized he was merely gesturing for a goblet of lifewine, which floated into his hand.

"Because," the man explained, swirling his glass without drinking, "I have seen what running gets me. I have seen what defiance gets me. I have even seen what collusion can do. All I have left now is apathy. Kill me. Drink my power, minuscule as it is. My daughter is safe, and protected by those capable of thwarting you. I am tired, mighty Nefarius, and ready for it to end. I have seen all I built torn down. There will be more tearing down, I think, but then our children will rebuild, and the cycle will continue. Without you."

Nefarius opened her void pockets and deposited her blades, then turned back to the melodramatic Wyrm. She wasn't sure what to make of him. He was old, and carried a not inconsiderable quantity of *air* magic. Yet she felt no urge to slay him.

"You are the perfect messenger," she decided aloud. "I won't slay you, or any other Wyrm, provided you abandon this world. Flee. Flee the sector, and live. I will no longer slaughter my own kind. I grant amnesty, but only to those willing to accept exile. Tell them, Wyrm. Save a remnant so they can rebuild in some distant sector. So that this was not the last dragonflight."

The compassion wasn't characteristic, and she wasn't certain why she was doing it. No, that wasn't true. Nefarius knew exactly why she was doing it. Guilt. Guilt over murdering her sister, as necessary as it had been.

She was easing that guilt by ensuring that some of her sister's children survived her wrath. Nor was she wrong to do so. She had other threats to tend to, after all. Let them run, for now. It was a small mercy, but a mercy nevertheless. The same mercy she'd granted the children of the Earthmother. More guilt.

"No." The impertinent Wyrm brushed a snowy lock from his face, then drank deeply from the goblet. He placed a booted foot upon the Kem'Hedj board, and flung the other over the arm of his hovercouch. "I'm quite comfortable, and since you've frightened the rest of the Wyrms away, there's no one to drink the wine. I plan to stay here and get good and drunk, but even were I a better Wyrm I'd never be your harbinger." He gave a bitter laugh. "You're overconfident, Nefarius. You think you've won, but you've never tangled with my daughter or the people she keeps company with. I have a feeling you're not going to enjoy your first meeting with them."

"You're referring to this Outrider I've heard so much about." Nefarius had reviewed countless hours of Ternus interview footage, commentary, and commentary on that commentary, all about this Aran, a seemingly humble hero defending the sector against impossible threats. Well, she'd dealt with heroes before.

"Yeah, that guy." Kheross gave a half chuckle. "He's the leader of their motley crew, and pretty scary in his own right. I don't think I could take him when I met him, and he's a lot stronger now. But that isn't what makes him so powerful, and it isn't the reason he'll win."

"And what," she asked, sarcasm evident, "is the reason for this supposed triumph?"

"His team," Kheross answered simply. He gave a fanged smile, one of the flaws in his human appearance. "Aran surrounds himself with the best. With gods, and demigods, and heroes. He'll rally them together, and they'll defeat you. The whole sector will cheer him on. All your attempts at cowing people with fear? Or getting them to worship you because they saw you kill Krox, or Virkonna? These people love Aran. They've seen him save world after world. They love Voria. And when you meet them, they will be backed by the entire sector."

Nefarius began to laugh. It pleased her that the creators of her body had thought to allow that mechanism, and she reveled in it. "I like you, little Wyrm. I will allow you to live, for now. I do so because I want you to observe your heroes as they assault me. Watch as one by one, they fail and die. And when the day comes, the sector will be united behind their god, little Wyrm. But it won't be this Aran, or Voria. It will be me they worship."

Nefarius teleported her avatar back into her greater body, and lent the greater form her full consciousness. When Virkonna had died her true body had become visible. It floated in orbit, a massive, snow-blue dragon of unparalleled size.

Nefarius glided closer, and began to feast. Let Virkonna's children watch as their mother was devoured before their very eyes. They would never follow another god after she showed them what happened to those who did.

15

A FITTING END

Nebiat pulled more *spirit* from her prison, the anchor where Nefarius had tethered her essence, and used it to increase her size. She flew up into orbit, and projected herself in a way that all the children on this continent would see.

"War has come, my children," she began, knowing that her only hope lay in persuading them to support her, "First Nefarius came and destroyed Krox, our guardian. Now the traitor, Frit, has led our greatest enemy, the goddess of *life*, to our home. She has brought Voria to slaughter us all, in retribution for the war with the Confederacy she once served. I call upon you to rise up, and fight these invaders. Rise up and drive these gods from our system. Together we will triumph."

She was particularly proud of that speech, and could feel worship swelling from the planet below. But only a trickle. Only a shred of what she'd have expected. Nothing near what would be required to do battle with her greatest enemy and one-time ally.

Frit streaked up into orbit, a meteor in reverse, flame and

brimstone filling the air around her as she came to a halt no more than a kilometer away. She held a staff in her right hand, and not just any staff. Ikadra, the key both to the *Spellship*, and to Nebiat's ultimate freedom.

She looked majestic and powerful, and confident. It terrified Nebiat. She'd never felt so out of control, and not having the ability to run meant this was a fight or die situation.

Voria appeared in orbit not far from Frit, arms crossed as she observed. "How do you want to handle this?"

"She's mine," Frit snarled, the flames in her eyes and mouth flaring into an inferno. "I know she wronged you first, but I need my people to see me slay her."

And there it was. If Nebiat lost this fight she was dead.

Wisps of power rose from the planet, invisible to the naked eye, but very much visible to hers thanks to the bit of *fire* she'd retained when Nefarius had cast her from Krox.

The vast, vast majority of that worship flowed to Frit. These people had lost faith in Nebiat, but still very much believed in their warrior-goddess. Their seer. The very god that Nebiat had taught them to love and respect. The god who'd always triumphed, and had not been present for Nebiat's great defeat. She was unstained by it.

"Frit," Nebiat pleaded, one last time. "Don't do this. Is this really the type of god you want to be? A vengeful one? Is that what you want to teach our people?"

"Yes." Frit's eyes narrowed, and she raised Ikadra. A kilometer-thick wave of blue flame leapt out, blanketing the sky. It moved with incredible swiftness, but Nebiat had been expecting such a move.

She translocated behind Frit, as Nefarius had done to Krox. Nebiat possessed some *earth*. She had some *void*. She even had a bit of *fire*. But her only real power was *spirit*, the heart of binding. If Frit wouldn't serve, and wouldn't form an alliance, then Nebiat would bind her, like she should have done in the first place. In the end Krox had been right.

She concentrated on her reserves of *spirit*, and flung a tendril toward Frit. The fire-goddess had already begun to turn, but it was far too late. The tendril slammed into her back, and immediately began assaulting her will.

Elation, hope, and righteous anger welled.

For an instant, anyway. Then a spear of brilliant golden light severed Nebiat's *spirit* tendril. She looked up to see Voria hovering there.

"If you think I will ever allow you to control another being, you are sadly mistaken, Nebiat. You took Aurelia. You took Eros. You took my world, and my friends, and my dignity, and the Confederacy itself. You took all that from me." Voria's voice grew louder with every word, and the nimbus of brilliant light around her increased in potency and radius.

"Never again, Nebiat," Frit said, reminding Nebiat that she had another enemy to deal with. She shifted to battle both, just as both cast their respective spells.

A lance of pure *fire*, hotter than the heart of a star, punched through Nebiat's chest. Far more damaging...a spear of golden *life* punched through her abdomen. That light dissolved every part of Nebiat it touched.

As she began to plummet to the world below, mortally wounded, Nebiat fled from the pain, into memory.

She remembered being taught about the aspects. About the realms, and how they stood in opposition.

About how *life* cleansed the cardinal aspects, known as realms. How it could eradicate *void*, or *dream*, or *spirit*. Entities like her—pure *spirit*.

She'd labored so hard to create a body tailored to kill

Voria, but in the process had become an entity that Voria was tailored to kill.

The irony wasn't lost on her.

Her fragmented essence fell into the atmosphere, unaffected by reentry. She could feel herself unraveling, as the grim work began by Voria's spell continued.

Nebiat's mind began to fragment. She lost herself, one bit at a time. What was her father's name? She'd been enslaved by a god, hadn't she? She needed to get to Shaya, before Eros discovered that she'd converted Erika. That was a dangerous gambit, but could pay off in the long run.

She glanced down and realized she was falling toward a stone statue of a dragon. A magnificent statue. She hoped she grew up to be a Wyrm like that someday.

Nebiat slammed into the statue, and her consciousness shattered, leaving nothing but fragmented dreams and twisted ambitions.

16

RIDE IN STYLE

Aran suppressed the wave of sadness as they materialized back in the Crucible. He knew Crewes would do fine, but giving up his ship, his life, and his friends...it was a lot, even if he knew how necessary it all was.

Not far away, Nara wore a similar expression, though for different reasons, he realized. She was giving up a lot too. They all were.

"You didn't get a chance to say goodbye to Frit," he pointed out, though he wasn't sure why he vocalized the thought.

"Yeah." Nara nodded sadly. "I was just thinking about that. Maybe we'll get a chance before the end, but if it's anything like...well, like it always is, then I have a feeling we'll be fighting the whole time, right up until most of us are dead."

"And all of them are." Kazon gave a broad smile. "You two are far too glum. Look around, and marvel." Kazon gestured at the workshop where they'd appeared, and at the mecha still standing in its stall. "Only a handful of beings, gods and mortals both, have ever set foot in this place. Inura has gifted me with a piece of his power, and left me his legacy. I know what I need to do. There will be a cost, certainly, but that doesn't mean we can't enjoy the journey. Don't focus on the ending. If we are to sacrifice our lives, let us not also sacrifice our happiness."

Aran found himself grinning. "Always look on the bright side, right? Why don't you show us what you and Inura have built. That thing can get us to the Skull of Xal, right?"

"A good deal more quickly than a standard spellship," Kazon said. He hurried over to the mech and planted a hand against the golden metal. "We will translocate as soon as you are aboard. Touch the mech, and think about being in the cockpit."

Golden brilliance flared where Kazon's hand touched the mecha, and then he just sort of flowed into the metal.

"I wish I had more time to study this," Nara said, crouching next to the mech. "That technology could be used in so many ways. Imagine a ring of metal encircling a planet. You touch the ring and appear anywhere else along it."

Aran loved that all the horrors hadn't beaten the curiosity out of her. "A global transport network. It took his clothing too, so theoretically you might even be able to use it to ferry goods."

Nara laughed, and it pulled a laugh from Aran. She shook her head, but she was still smiling. "If we survive this maybe we'll go into business together."

Then she touched the mecha and disappeared inside. Aran approached as well, and extended a hand. He hesitated.

What do you fear? Narlifex pulsed. *Is there a foe?*

Aran shook his head, but didn't answer. Sweat beaded

his brow, and he forced his hands to his sides, at least until he overcame this.

"It isn't a foe," he managed through gritted teeth. "*Life* magic is the antithesis of *void*, and everything in me is screaming that I should drink the power from this mech."

Narlifex pulsed thoughtfully, but said nothing.

Aran forced a series of deep breaths, and when he was positive he was in control he finally touched the metal. Something light and bright rippled through him, and then he was sitting in a comfortable leather command couch in a climate controlled cockpit.

He glanced around and saw two other couches. All three faced the center of the cockpit, and a shimmering golden ball of magic hovered between them. Countless sigils flashed across the surface, too fast to track.

The walls were utterly blank, suggesting the orb was the interface he should be concerned with.

"What am I looking at?" Aran asked, blinking up at the interface. If that's what it was.

Kazon gave a sheepish smile. "This ship works, ah, a little differently than vessels you might be used to. It is a bit more...invasive. But it is not painful, I assure you."

Aran was about to ask him what he meant when a tendril of golden energy shot out from the golden orb. It latched onto Kazon's forehead, and sent several pulses of light into him. Kazon's eyes began to glow, until the white was consumed with golden brilliance.

"I am linked with the ship now." Kazon's voice came through speakers in the walls, as well as his mouth. "I can feel his subsystems, and can control movement. The two of you can do the same, but you need to will the process to occur."

Aran remained unconvinced. That golden energy was... wrong somehow. At war with everything he was.

Nara closed her eyes, and a golden tendril drifted from the orb and touched her forehead. She gasped, and the gasp came through the mech's speakers.

"It's...amazing. This thing is so much more than a vehicle." Her voice was filled with wonder, not fear.

Aran steeled himself and willed the ship to connect. It took everything in him not to shift to *air* when the tendril moved for his forehead, and the metal beneath his hands bent as he instinctively tightened his grip when it finally touched.

A splash of warmth washed over his entire body, then was gone. He was standing in a stall, in a workshop. He *was* the mech. In the back of his mind he could sense streams of sensor data, magical scrying, and countless other things waiting to be explored.

"This *is* amazing," he murmured. "The interface isn't at all like a spell matrix."

"This is far more advanced," Kazon proudly replied. "This is Inura's finest work, but the link is only one of many reasons. Watch."

The mech stepped from the stall, narrowly avoiding crushing a workbench with its left foot. Then golden energy rippled out around them, and the mecha began to change.

Its legs retracted into the body, and its arms flattened and extended behind the back. The transformation was swift, and when it was over a corvette class vessel floated where the mech had been.

"We can assume many forms," Kazon explained, "but this one is the most suitable for travel. I will show you more as time allows. Are you ready?"

"As we'll ever be." Aran relaxed into the mecha, and

began to enjoy the piloting experience. "What's say we hit up the Skull of Xal? Malila is our best starting point."

"Hold on a moment," Kazon offered. "Now where is that...ah, here we go."

There was a brief moment of vertigo, and then the entire ship translocated. They appeared in orbit, around a very familiar world.

The Skull of Xal floated in orbit, staring at them with those hellish, unseeing eyes. Perhaps what terrified Aran the most about seeing it was the instant realization that he had come home.

17

TIME IS SHORT

Nara rested her hand on the staff Eros had presented to her all the way back on Shaya, back when she'd begun her brief tenure as his apprentice. A trio of rubies rotated around the silver tip, the magic hot and urgent, and ready to augment her *fire*.

It was a tremendous gift, but it wasn't truly sentient. Not in the way Ikadra had been. She'd grown used to him as a companion, and while she was thrilled that he was alive again, it pained her to send him off with Voria and Frit. She should be there too, and it was killing her that she wasn't.

Nara rested the staff against the side of the command couch, which was plenty spacious enough for her lunch, a book she'd brought to read, and her staff. Unfortunately, she'd have neither the time to eat nor read.

The skull floated there...taunting them with its familiarity. She could feel her connection to it, to Xal, she realized. It smoldered coldly within her, a conduit to the vast magical reservoir contained within the skull. Xal's mind. His memories.

"Are you two ready?" Aran asked, his voice made strange by the golden tendril connecting him to the ship.

"As I will ever be, brother." Kazon gave a gruff nod.

"This is the easy part," Nara pointed out. She observed the ship through its senses, and saw a riot of magical signatures coming off the skull. "How many millions of demons are in there do you think?"

She could feel them all, with the ship, and it rocked her to the core. Confederate estimates had put the demons in the tens of thousands. No more than a hundred thousand, tops.

"They've been here right under our noses," Aran murmured. The ship began moving closer to the skull, flying slowly to the same ocular cavity they'd docked in one year ago, moments after Aran had woken up with no memory, and she his captor, or one of them anyway.

This would be her third, and hopefully final, visit to the skull. She didn't hold any particular hatred for demons, but they made their dislike of humans pretty clear, and Nara didn't imagine they were all that thrilled by their little party arriving in a literal ship of light, crafted from their opposite aspect.

The ship sailed gracefully toward the decapitated behemoth, and eventually entered through the eye. They flew straight and slow, a clearly broadcasted approach.

Nara had been wondering what kind of reception they'd get. Nothing could have prepared her for this.

Hundreds of thousands of demons stood arrayed in countless orderly squares, each legion armed with state of the art spellrifles and spellarmor. Each with their own standard. She was shocked by the level of organization. These were no savages.

"If this army attacked Ternus before the war with the

Krox," Aran whispered in awe, "they'd have swept the planet. There's nothing the Confederacy could do to stop it, either. Shaya wouldn't be able to stop them, even back when they were at full strength."

The ship glided over countless ranks, until they spotted a conspicuously empty area on a field of bleached bone. A precise one hundred meters had been left empty, and the precise center of the army.

"I get the sense they are trying to intimidate us," Kazon said. He gave a weak smile. "It is working. I do not know what I have gotten us into. Apologies for whatever is about to happen. I truly believed Shinura, ah, I mean Inura, when he told me this was the best course. Would that he'd stayed to counsel us, but in his words, 'I'm out.'"

Nara noted the slip with the name, and the body language surrounding it. There was definitely something he was hiding, but she didn't press. It couldn't be that important in the grand scheme of things. She needed to trust this man, as hard as that was.

She trusted Aran, and Aran trusted Kazon, but she was finding that trust was not a transferrable property. Kazon seemed to mean well, but he didn't exactly exude competence, and good intentions only went so far.

"That assembly isn't meant to intimidate," Aran corrected as the ship glided to a halt in the landing. "This is an honor guard. They're welcoming us."

Nara disengaged the tendril, which slithered back into the orb, and felt the immediate loss of the ship's countless senses. After this nameless vessel, and the *Spellship*, she understood now why gods created such complex artifacts to aid them.

Gods weren't gods. Not the storybook version of gods

anyway. They were basically just immortal mages with a lot of time on their hands.

"How do we exit the craft?" Nara asked. There wasn't really enough room to rise from the couch.

"As we entered. Touch the wall and think about it." Kazon touched the side of his couch, and disappeared in a flash of golden light.

Aran did the same a moment later. Nara took three deep breaths to steady herself. She didn't fear what they were about to face in any sort of combat sense, but they were attempting to resurrect a dark god to fight a living one, and that was going to demand some steep sacrifices.

She savored her last few hours of ignorance regarding the cost.

Nara touched the side of the couch and thought about exiting. After a warm, pleasant flash she was deposited next to the corvette's base, not far from Aran and Kazon. The ship was a sleek wedge without much definition, and the golden surface was completely smooth.

"Who comes before the host of Xal?" a feminine voice bellowed from the center of the army.

"The Hound of Xal!" the crowd chanted in unison.

A single figure rose into the air, drifting high above her army, resplendent in archaic plate armor at home on some medieval world. Bat-like wings extended behind her, and a slender tail also curled behind her, its barbed tip glittering in the thin light of Xal's glowing mind.

"Be welcome, Aran. Be welcome, Nara. Be welcome, Kazon," the demon queen called. Malila smiled, and opened her arms wide. "You have come home. You are of Xal, and Xal is of you. We recognize your service, champions of the void."

Nara was absolutely positive she didn't enjoy being

named a champion of the void. The same void that Talifax seemed to worship.

Aran kicked off the ground, and floated into the air. His Mark XI spellarmor was a marked contrast to Malila's more primitive set, but Nara suspected that Malila's was far more powerful.

"Thank you, your majesty." Aran executed a perfect bow, then straightened. "I recognize you as a fellow hound and ally. You know why we have come."

"I do." She gave a slight nod, and her smile slipped a hair. "I also know time is short. Come. Accompany me to the throne and we will discuss this further."

18

BACK TO THE SKULL

Aran followed Malila as she zoomed up and away from the army, high into the cavern overlooking the pulsing purple orb of Xal's mind. The ranks of demons gazed up at them in awe as they spiraled into the brain cavity. Xal's mind shone below them, a blazing star that pulsed in time with Aran's heartbeat. If he wasn't imagining that.

Nara zoomed along in his wake, silent and introspective. He honored that, and left her to her thoughts as they glided up to the throne where Malila had first judged them.

By the time he set down near her throne Malila was already seated, her posture ramrod straight, and each arm resting just so on the arms of the bleached white throne.

He set down gently a half dozen meters from the throne, and approached at a slow walk. Nara landed next to him, and they arrived at the base of the steps leading up to the throne as a pair.

Malila leaned forward, and fixed Aran with the most intense stare he'd ever had to battle. She stroked a lock of thick hair over one dark-skinned shoulder, the curve of her neck not so different from Nara's. "There are many things I do not wish to discuss in front of my army. What will follow in the coming days are chief among them. If they knew what we were about to attempt, and what it could mean, there would be no containing them."

"And just what is it," Nara broke in quietly, "that we're attempting to do?"

"Resurrect our father," the demon queen answered smoothly, without an ounce of hesitation. "There is no stopping Nefarius without Xal. You know that, or you wouldn't be here."

Aran inclined his head. Sort of a nod, but a frosty one. "Maybe, but our goals are definitely different. You said 'our' father. And *your* primary goal is bringing him back. Our primary goal is stopping Nefarius, and we realize that means we need Xal. Resurrecting him is a means to an end."

Malila gave an impatient nod, and leaned back on her throne. "Yes, yes, I understand. Your motives are irrelevant so long as you restore our father. I say our father, because that is the accurate term. You have begun to come to terms with what you are, but Nara and Kazon labor in ignorance. They still believe that the void is simply another type of magic they were blessed with."

Kazon gave a snort of amusement. "Blessed. More like cursed."

"Take your pick," Malila allowed. She leaned forward again, and fixed Aran with her stare. "All three of you are vital in what is to come. You are tools forged by Xal, specifically to facilitate his resurrection. We can accomplish that, but only if you give yourself fully to the task."

"And what's involved exactly?" Aran demanded. He didn't make the words an accusation, but he was already hating where this was going.

"Ah, and now we come to the heart of it." Malila gave an amused laugh, then settled back on her throne. Her wings fluttered behind her, as if she couldn't get comfortable. "I must find a way to teach you things that every demon knows before they've first learned to cast a spell. Xal's body is, as you know, divided into two parts. The skull, and the husk. The short version? We must reunite the husk and the skull, and convince the demons on the husk that we aren't invading, and are in fact returning their dark father to them. Without their belief, the ritual will fail. We need to win the hearts of demons, Aran."

Aran didn't respond immediately, choosing instead to process everything she'd just said. "I understand conceptually what you're asking us to do, at a high level anyway, but what does that mean specifically? Which demons do I win and how do I win them? And why should it even be me? You're a hound too, and you know a lot more about demons. Aren't they a lot more likely to trust one of their own?"

"Oh, without a doubt." Malila gave a truly wicked smile, and there wasn't a shred of kindness there. "They will not follow you unless you are also a demon, or demonically touched at the very least."

Nara cleared her throat, and spoke when she had Malila's attention. "How does that work exactly? We've been to several Catalysts now, and the magic has altered us a little, but certainly not enough to change our physical forms."

"Ahh, I must remind myself of your relative youth, and your ignorance. I can remedy you of the latter, at least." Malila rose from her throne, and walked down the steps to stand near Nara. "A god has a choice to make, and most make it early in life. One group focuses on their magic, their soul for lack of a better term. Krox was a good example of this mindset. He accumulated magic, but was careful never to build a physical body. Xal came from a different generation of gods, one where every god was expected to be capable on the field of battle. He built a physical body, a task that took countless human generations. Over the eons he has grown and improved that body, always making it stronger."

"I'm tracking everything you're saying," Aran broke in, "but I don't see the connection. Are you saying we need to build demon bodies somehow?"

Malila gave a delighted laugh. "Nothing so grandiose, I assure you. The point of my explanation was this—if you ingest the body of a god, then you become that god, in part. You've touched Xal's mind. That changed you mentally. If you eat of his body it will change you physically. You will grow stronger, and more resilient, but you will also look a good deal more like me. Or another species of demon. That is for our father to decide."

"You never answered my question," Aran pointed out. "Why don't you take the skull to the husk and unite them? You've been a hound longer than I've been alive. Won't they trust you more?"

"Sadly, quite the opposite." Malila looked suddenly troubled, and didn't speak until she returned to her throne. She turned and faced them as she sat, and all humor was gone. "They will see me as an enemy, because I have kept the skull from them for so long. They have long sought our father's resurrection, and see me as a traitor to our father for not returning home sooner. If I come now, they will assault me and we will see a civil war. No, Aran, you, Nara, and Kazon must convince them to work together. Only then will I translocate the skull home for the ritual."

Aran nodded, suddenly understanding the play. "You

need a third party. I'll bet money that's why Xal prepped a trio of unknowns. So what else can you tell us about the demons we're going to have to win over? What's the best starting point?"

"All in good time." Malila pointed down at the light below. "First, you must eat of my father's flesh, and be changed by it. Whichever of you survives can take your ugly ship to the husk, where you can try to convince the demon princes to follow you."

19

DRINK

Nara shivered as Malila walked to the rear of her throne. That shiver had nothing to do with the cold, and everything to do with what lay behind it. An enormous stone, or bone, cistern had been set into the floor, and it was filled to the brim with a viscous black fluid. Dark and goopy, and familiar.

"That's the blood of Nefarius," she said, walking to the water's edge. "I'd recognize it anywhere." She knelt, and inhaled deeply of the aroma of power wafting from it, while also being horrified at the very idea of it.

Aran didn't approach the cistern, nor did Kazon. Both kept their distance, and both broadcast their discomfort in the way they angled their feet away from the pool.

"No," Malila corrected, as she knelt next to Nara, "this is the blood of Xal. They are similar, in some ways. Xal and Nefarius were close once. The only two void gods in a pantheon that mistrusted the void. They bonded in many ways, and shared many secrets. The creation of the blood was one such, and both have employed it, though Nefarius to much greater effect, obviously. To Xal his blood was simply a means of animating his magical body, and infusing it with power, and a storage device for genetic memory."

Nara stared down at the blood. The pool was utterly still. Placid, unknowable depths. She looked up at Malila. "And you're saying that all three of us need to drink this?"

Malila nodded.

"Why?" Aran asked. He folded his arms, and moved to stand before Malila. He'd adopted his confrontational stance, and that usually meant he was about to dig in his heels.

"Because," Malila explained coldly, "the blood will strengthen your physical body. It will make you tougher, and stronger, and better able to withstand magical attacks. Because if you are to fight for and lead our people then all three of you need to made equal to the task, and this is the only way I can think to accomplish such an impossibility."

"Fine." Nara reached down and scooped a double handful. She nearly retched as the brackish fluid filled her gloved hands, and she was thankful it wasn't touching skin. She raised it to her lips and drank.

The thick, syrupy liquid was icy, numbing her mouth and throat as it slid down. She cupped her head in her hands instinctively as pain flooded her brain, and some distant part of her realized she'd smeared god-blood all over her hair.

The ice flowed through her belly, and out into her limbs. It crawled up her spine, and finally into her head. The world spun, and she toppled to the bleached bone, its coarse surface scraping against her suit.

"My people," Malila explained, her voice distant, but distinct, "didn't begin as we are. We were much more similar to humans, or Shayans, in our natural forms. We lacked wings and a tail."

Nara groaned, but that was the best she could manage from her throat, numb as it was. Her entire body was wracked with spasms, and she twitched and struggled.

The demon queen moved to the pool, and scooped another handful. She held Nara's head, and gently poured the liquid down Nara's throat. Malila was beautiful up close, less monstrous.

"Drink, and relax," she explained in the distance, as more ice flowed through Nara. "The change is swift. In a few moments you will be stronger than you were."

Nara forced herself to focus on her breathing, the sort of thing she'd learned in yoga, which had been a great way to center herself when she'd been imprisoned.

Each breath was labored, but after the first few she realized they were getting stronger. Easier. She relaxed, and the cold began to abate. The shivering stopped.

"There." Malila gently released her, and stepped away. "Aran, and Kazon, you must do the same."

"It isn't that bad," Nara rasped, her voice barely rising above a whisper. "I feel...stronger. Like she said I would." Nara extended a hand and flexed it.

"Nara?" Aran asked. Something in his voice snapped her attention back to him. "Your face."

Nara conjured an illusory mirror, and gaped at herself in shock. The changes were minor, but very pronounced. Her skin was now the same shade as Malila's, and her eyes smoldered with the same *void* magic.

"At least I don't feel any different," Nara pointed out as she dismissed the mirror. She gave Aran her full attention. "This seems a small price to pay, and if it proves to be a bigger price in the long run, well, we've already decided we'll do what we have to do to stop Talifax...and Nefarius."

Nara stood tall and approached Aran. She was shocked

to realize that he no longer loomed over her in the same way. She'd gained several centimeters in height, and her suit had apparently grown to fit her new body.

"You have ingested immeasurable power," Malila said. "Maybe enough to accomplish what you will need to do. Your task, in particular, is the most difficult I think."

"And what about my task?" Kazon asked, wearing his agony like ill-fitting clothing.

Malila's eyes narrowed. "Drink, and I will tell you."

Kazon approached the pool with a resigned sigh. "If there is no other choice."

"And you, Aran?" Malila asked.

Aran licked his lips, and took a few tentative steps closer to the pool. "I don't trust that stuff, but the alternative seems worse. Before I drink, though, I'd like to hear Nara's task."

"Very well." Malila shrugged, and her tail flicked behind her like a cat deciding whether or not it wanted to grant someone a favor. "Nara must become Xal's Vengeance. When you arrive at the husk you find will several nations of demons. Each nation followed one of the demon princes in life. Nara's previous incarnation was known as Kali Ken Xal, Xal's Vengeance, just as you and I are hounds. She must claim that legacy."

"And how am I supposed to do that?" Nara asked, struggling to suppress her irritation. "I don't know anything about my predecessor."

"Don't you?" Malila raised an eyebrow mischievously.

Nara realized...she dimly remembered something about vengeance. But she couldn't quite recall.

"It will come to you in time," Malila explained. Then she turned to Aran. "Come. Drink. I suspect your answers will come much more swiftly, Hound. Your body has already been prepared, and Xal has stored much within you that this blood will unlock."

Nara put a hand on Aran's shoulder. "I'm here. Whatever this entails...we'll get through it."

He gave her a grateful nod. She turned to Kazon and gave him her full attention. "That goes for you, too. We're in this together."

"Thank you, Nara." Kazon nodded stiffly. "I know we are not...friends, but the woman who originally enslaved me bears no resemblance to you. You are someone I respect, and trust."

"Less talk," Aran said, kneeling next to the pool. "More action. Let's get this over with."

20

DOWN THE RABBIT HOLE

Aran forced himself to kneel at the pool's edge. He stared down at the liquid magic, understanding that the changes it would wreak within him were a necessary step to victory. In short, drink or lose.

He didn't care about skin color. He didn't even care if this stuff gave him wings, or a tail, or horns, or gods knew what else. He needed this magic. The knowledge.

Yes. Drink. Take this power, and rule in father's name, Narlifex pulsed in his mind.

He wished things were as simple for him as they were for the blade. That things could be boiled down to power and the ability to mete out death.

"I'm doing this," Aran decided aloud, but I am doing it my way." He turned to Kazon. "Brother, I'm going to need you to drink first."

Kazon paled under his big, bushy beard. "Of course. If you ask it." He knelt next to the pool, and scooped up a large double handful in his gauntleted hands. He drank deeply, until the liquid was gone.

"What is it we're ingesting, exactly?" Aran asked. "I have

my suspicions, and what I do here will be determined by the answers."

"The blood is the genetic memory of Xal. In a way it is Xal," Malila explained with a shrug. "What you are ingesting is the blood of our god. His life force, if you will."

Aran nodded. That settled it. He knew what he needed to do. "And we're going to resurrect him, which will take all of this, right?"

Malila nodded.

"And they'll only accept us if we look like them?" Aran unsheathed Narlifex, which earned him looks from everyone.

"In part." Malila nodded again. "Demons respond to demonic princes. When Xal lived he had a voice, a memory, a vengeance, and several hounds. He created gods to serve him. Demon lords, like of old, he would say."

"Then if I want to lead these demons," Aran said, wrapping both hands around Narlifex's hilt, "then I am going to have be the strongest demon." He plunged Narlifex deep into the pool, until he felt the blade meet stone.

Aran pulled at the magic in the pool with his hound ability.

"What are you doing?" Malila demanded, aghast.

Aran poured his power through Narlifex, into the pool. He drew the blood into the sword, pulling it inside the metal. The blade drank it eagerly, the metal going darker, until the color became a hole in reality, beyond black.

That blood thickened the metal, millimeter by millimeter, then began moving up Aran's gauntlet as well. It seeped through the metal, into his flesh. The very instant the chill blood touched skin he dropped to one knee, all strength stolen.

Aran gritted his teeth, and leaned against Narlifex. He

positioned the blade to prevent them from toppling into what remained of the pool, and held on as the blade absorbed more magic.

Now that metal was saturated, flesh was the only place for it to go. It seeped up his arm and into his chest. His heart thundered as he wondered what might happen when that terrible cold reached his heart, but it came and went without any problem.

The cold spread through his limbs, and eventually up his neck. It continued up his spine, and finally into his brain. Vertigo rocked him, and then Aran tumbled into a memory of the being who'd borne the blood originally.

Xal, as he'd been in his youth.

21

THROUGH MY EYES

Some distant part of Xal's mind understood that this was a memory being played out in another time, witnessed by another being, born countless eons after his mortal body had become cosmic dust.

The rest of Xal, however, was focused on an event of singular importance. Today would dictate the future of not only their reality, but possibly all realities.

If they failed, then the universe itself could fracture, and those who lurked beneath would be free at last to devour everything.

"Attend me, Xal," his master called, the stately demon prince standing near the prow of his airship.

The magitech vessel was one of the most powerful ever crafted, its feathersteel hull enchanted to mimic the sky around it, allowing them to ambush their opponents.

Today that enchantment lay dormant, and the hull had instead faded to a flat metallic black. Mighty Xakava stood boldly near the prow, his face exposed to the wind, and visible to their enemies, who were many.

They were not the only airship to approach, or even the

only demonic host. Others had come, the stately jin and mighty oni. The Wyrms had come, their largest with a seat at the bargaining table, while the rest wheeled and dove above like a flock of errant birds.

Even the titan Trakalon had sent a representative, a craggy behemoth the size, and roughly the shape, of a mountain.

"I do not see the elemental lords," Xal pointed out, hoping his mentor might have an explanation. They were some of the most powerful of the elder gods, and their primal armies were highly courted by all sides. "I could see air not attending, perhaps, or water, but all four? That seems...odd."

Xakava's face fell, his dark skin suddenly a shade lighter under the midday sun. "They do not define time or consciousness as we do. But even they understand our mutual destruction. This is no calculated move, I think. It is far more likely that the rumors we've heard are true. They are dead, killed during the final battle that fractured Om himself."

Xal sagged against the railing running along the prow. The elements were primal forces. They couldn't be defined as living, or dead. For them to have been slain...what did that even mean?

"Their deaths," Xakava continued forlornly, "have probably created more fractures in the Great Cycle. Already we see the damage this has wrought. By linking the Cycle as we have, it is tied to all realities. A master stroke, or so we thought. But it also means that destroying the Cycle will effectively break reality."

Xal merely nodded. He already knew all this, of course. They all did. But if it helped his master to vocalize it, then he welcomed the chance to provide a bit of solace.

"Observe; the council begins." Xakava straightened, and his gaze fixed on a tiny figure who'd stepped into the Arena. How odd that they were using it as a means of communication, rather than the endless games it had been created to facilitate. "Reevanthara takes the stage."

"His avatar isn't much to look at." Xal did not bother to hide his skepticism. "I thought the architect of the Great Cycle would be...taller."

The tiny bearded figure raised both hands, and the entire Arena began to thrum with power. The sky changed, and a colossal version of the architect appeared in the sky. He had an ugly, bulbous nose, large flat teeth, and a thick, bushy beard. He was unkempt, to put it nicely.

"My fellow gods," Reevanthara began, stroking that brown beard, "I've called you all here today for the most important of reasons. Today, we save creation. We save it by giving it up."

He paused, a wise move as conversation exploded on every ship, and between every Wyrm. Xakava said nothing, so Xal said nothing either.

"For us to save creation, to save everything, to keep those who lurk beneath imprisoned in the depths, well, that requires the Great Cycle to keep going." Reevanthara's face fell, and a mouth made for smiles conveyed nothing but sadness. "I linked the Cycle to all realities. If it is destroyed, then they will be destabilized as well. All wards, all blocks, all seals...all of it would break. Every binding in creation would be undone all at once. If that happens we'll have bigger problems than squabbling over our children and their kingdoms."

He paused again, though now conversation had ceased. All eyes were on the dwarf. He licked his lips, and spoke the words that damned them all. "We must agree to leave the

Cycle. All of us. Every deity. No god can be allowed to dwell within the Great Cycle, for doing so risks its destruction. We must preserve it, away from all of us, with mortal stewards to keep it safe."

Reevanthara's eyes narrowed, and took on a flinty look. "Those who do not agree to this accord will be hunted down and destroyed by all those who understand the necessity of what we do. Good. Evil. It doesn't matter. When all is said and done, I will sacrifice my own godhood to preserve the cycle, and to prevent any gods from invading it for their own benefit."

"What of the rest of us?" the Wyrm-mother called, her eight heads rearing over the arena and her children. The sunlight was bright on her multicolored scales, and Xal admitted, privately at least, that he wasn't positive his master could best her.

"Exile," Reevanthara called back without pause. "Every god goes out into the void, and carves out their own little kingdom. Build a world, or a galaxy even. Do whatever you wish, war upon whomever you wish, so long as it is not allowed to take place in the Cycle."

Reevanthara extended his hand, and his great hammer appeared. He raised it skyward. "Look. Look to the sky."

Reevanthara's magic exposed a purplish crack, which extended down a quarter of the sky.

"That is a Fissure in reality. A crack. There will be more, and worse. I can heal them. Slowly. But our war has created hundreds, and it will be countless millennia before I can repair them all."

Reevanthara lowered his hammer, and turned in a slow circle. "What say you?"

"I am Xakava and I speak for the eru demons. Aye, I say, we will depart, in peace," Xakava called, his clear, deep voice ringing over the battlefield. "I urge all others to do the same, for if you do not, then we will also join the host hunting down those who refuse to respect today's edict."

Xal experienced immense pride that his master had been the first to speak. Every history that recorded this day would remember that, and remember the greatness of Xal's people.

Dimly, he sensed that whoever or whatever was watching through his eyes had seen whatever they needed to see. He wished the silent observer well, and wondered what their time must be like.

22

GAMEPLAN

Aran rose shakily to his feet at the pool's edge, and if not for leaning on Narlifex he'd have collapsed entirely. Thankfully, the weakness passed quickly, and within a few moments he was able to stand under his own power.

He awkwardly sheathed his now much heavier blade as he waited for the side effects to fade. He didn't fully understand what he'd just done, but he knew it was the right thing to do. What Xal had wanted him to do.

They were all still staring at him, Nara and Kazon in curiosity, and Malila in an alloy of anger and disbelief, her beautiful features more easily betraying her inhuman nature.

Aran glanced down in the pool, and the rock was a pristine white. There wasn't even a residue left behind. He had take it all, for good or ill. What did that mean exactly? Did Xal somehow live inside Narlifex, and within him? It was unclear to him exactly what the blood was or could do.

"What have you done?" Malila choked out. "I have

husbanded that pool for a thousand generations. And just like that...gone."

"No, what Aran did was right," Kazon broke in, surprising them all. His eyes were veined through with black, and his hands were trembling. "I do not think the void is agreeing with the life within me...but it will settle down." Sweat beaded his brow, and there was a quaver in his voice. "We will need the blood to waken Xal. I don't know how I know that, but something in the blood...I remember how to conduct a ritual like this. Somehow."

Malila's ire shifted to Kazon, but morphed into consternation. "That would only be possible if..."

"If what?" Nara demanded. "You can't just trail off like that."

"If Kazon were the reincarnated guardian of Xal," she explained, blinking at Kazon in awe. "Not yet, but it would appear he possesses some of Gorr's helixes. I believe I am beginning to grasp father's full plan."

"I think I am too." Aran folded his arms, and stared at the lot of them. "Xal wanted to raise a new demonic host, right when it would be needed most. To do that he had to ensure that the sector had no idea the host existed. Thus, they couldn't ever attack their neighbors, which is probably why the husk is so remote. He chose the site of his death to keep his children isolated. Now he's groomed the three of us, well, four with Malila involved, to become the new demonic princes."

"I can't tell if you're enjoying that or terrified by it." Nara eyed him with an emotionless expression.

"Both?" Aran shrugged, though he realized he was intrigued by the concept of being a reborn demon prince. He'd had no place, not anywhere, not on Virkon, or Shaya, or even on the *Hunter*. Maybe this would be his place.

"Mostly excited, because if we're right it means we have a clear path forward. Actionable steps. We show up, prove we're badasses, get nominated as mayors of demon-town, and then we use their worship to resurrect Xal."

"I suspect," Kazon said with a snort, "that it will not be that easy."

"Maybe not," Aran allowed. "But as I said...we have actionable steps. We know what we need to do. It's time to go to the husk, and to show these demons who we are, and why they should follow us. Xal has given us all the tools. He foresaw this moment. All we have to do is figure out how to use them. Malila, what can you tell us about the existing demonic leaders and who we should approach first?"

Malila sauntered from the pool, and returned to her throne without a word. Aran followed, feeling a damned sight better than he had a minute ago, though still shaky. He paused to let the queen get her bearings, which thankfully didn't take long.

"I must," Malila allowed with a grimace, "accept what has transpired here, however much it horrifies me. Perhaps it is father's plan. I pray that it is. I will act as if it is. You asked about the demons on the husk. There are many nations, but three in particular will be necessary if you are to unify them. The largest of these tribes is the jin. They are also the most proud, and are unlikely to deal with you unless you find a way to win their respect. They love blades, and respect blade masters immensely. The jin control Xal's heart, and consider other demons to be...uncivilized. "

Malila rolled her eyes at that last part. "The second group, the oni, are violent. They define themselves by their strength, both physical and martial, and they see a difference. The last guardian was an oni.

"The final group is my people," she continued, "the eru.

We pride ourselves on gathering knowledge and mastering magic. We have few great warriors, but many of the best spellsnipers come from my tribe. This last will be the most hostile to me, but all three will hate me. It is best you don't mention my name until after you've found a way to unify them."

"And what about their leaders?" Aran asked. "What can you tell us?"

"Little," she admitted with a frustrated shake of her head. "Their leadership has likely changed entirely since I dwelt among them, so you'll have to learn about their situations on your own."

Aran nodded, satisfied. "I only have one more question. If we pull this off, if we unify these tribes, then you'll bring the skull and help us raise Xal?"

Malila nodded gravely. "You have my word on it, brother. We will succeed. Father will return. And our kind will once again dominate the sector."

Aran ignored the vicious smile as best he could. Terrifying allies were better than no allies at all.

23

DREAMING

Nara understood on some level that she was dreaming. Colors were too rich. Everything was vibrant. But there were gaps, too. Time was strange in dreams, and skipped about from scene to scene.

Nara looked around and tried to get her bearings. At first she believed she was on some strange world in a forgotten corner of the universe. A sea of stars spilled across the night sky, except for the southern horizon which was completely dark. No light shone there.

To the west stood what she thought at first must be the universe's largest mountain. When her brain began to contextualize she understood that it was no mountain. It was a wing, as titanic as a planet in its own right.

She was living on Xal.

Her perspective zoomed in, and suddenly she was a person, as sometimes happened in dreams. She stood there confused while two people talked, neither familiar.

"I hate it," a woman from Malila's species was saying, her wings flared behind her. "If we do as you ask, then not only does father die, but most of our people will die as well. We have many enemies, and there has never been a better time for them to act on their grievances."

"I understand," a male demon from a different species rumbled. He was taller than her, easily four meters, and his limbs were corded with a preposterous amount of muscle. He shared her dark skin though. "It must be done. We will die, but our tombs will remain, so that when father's vision comes to pass, they will be available. We will return, reborn to lead our people anew."

The demon woman spun, and snatched up a spellrifle that had been propped against a rock. The demon woman fired and the rifle discharged a...micro singularity?

A black hole punched through the wall, and stopped in the next room. Then it imploded, and the walls, ceiling, and floor in that room were simply gone.

Half of a dead hatchling remained. The lower half. Everything above the waist had been destroyed by the spell, and Nara was thankful that the dream insulated her from smells. She really was a bit squeamish, although she'd never admit it.

"Do you see, Gorr?" The woman demanded. At least she had a name for the larger demon. "Their spies are already here. They are dividing up our father's body, getting ready to claim the choicest bits. It's heinous. It cannot be borne."

"In that way father has granted us a final mercy, Kali." There now, the woman had a name too. Somehow, when she heard the name, Nara realized that she *was* the woman, somehow. "We will die in battle. We will kill as many enemies as we can, heaping their bodies up. They will bring us down, eventually, and then they will leave saying they killed the demon princes. Nothing less will satisfy them. If we hide they will keep hunting until every prince is dead. They will account for us all, even your sister."

"Malila?" The woman shot a concerned glance up at a shadow on the horizon. Xal's head, Nara realized. "Xal's breath, no."

Gods of all shapes and sizes translocated into the sector. Some Nara recognized, like Shivan and Marid. Others she did not. They began to attack Xal, tearing into different parts of his body.

The god did nothing to resist, though a tremendous groan of pain reverberated through the world as Shivan seized Xal's head. He jabbed the spear Worldender into Xal's neck, and with a tremendous grinding sawed the head from the demon-god's body.

Xal's skull spun away in a shower of black droplets, his scream fading, but not stopping as the head shrank into the darkness.

"Malila—" Kali raised a hand. Then she lowered it. "Malila will fight. She is strong enough to battle even Shivan. She will—"

The skull disappeared. It translocated from the system, leaving Xal's headless corpse naked before the fury of his enemies. All around her battle erupted. Screams echoed from every corner of their world.

She turned back to Gorr. "It's all coming apart. Just like you said it would."

"Father did prepare us." He shrugged those too-muscular oni shoulders of his. "We knew this day would come, even if we didn't know why or what would be asked of us. Come. Let us kill some dragons. We will make the water flight pay for their insolence."

Gorr extended his hand and his mighty silver gauntlet shimmered into existence. The runes covering the surface were actually inscribed atop another layer of runes, which was inscribed on still another layer. The gauntlet was the most heavily enchanted artifact still possessed by the demons, and had been used to forge most of their wonders.

"For countless centuries the Gauntlet of Reevanthara has been used to craft our arms and armor. Today it will bathe in the blood of our enemies."

Gorr leapt through the hole the woman's spell had created, and landed on the field outside. A dragon screamed by overhead, but Gorr leapt into the air at precisely the right instant, and shattered the Wyrm's skull with his gauntleted fist.

The headless Wyrm crashed to the ground, tearing a scar on the land for a full three hundred meters. Ragged cheers came from the surrounding demons, who began to rally.

"I hate this," the woman murmured. She picked up her spellrifle, and wrapped the shadows around her like armor.

She began running from perch to perch and each time she paused she fired a single spell. Each void bolt killed an adult Wyrm, expertly coring it through the heart.

The dream blurred forward, leaving Nara with the impression that Kali had been killing for some time. Her position was different now. They were...on the wing maybe?

"Mother, please," an agonized young demon was asking Kali, "do not leave us. We need you."

"I must go, little one." She stroked the child's cheek. "You must live, and you must lead. Keep our people safe. Go."

The woman turned and gazed out the window. When had they gone indoors? Now it was a balcony, and she was gazing out at an approaching army.

Hundreds of water Wyrms filled the sky, and they were descending on the demons. Those who stayed and fought, most of them, would die. They'd die nobly, but they would still be dead.

What a waste.

And the worst part? She would need to join them. She'd have to let them catch her. They'd never manage it on their own.

Kali leapt into the sky and used her *void* magic to keep herself aloft. She raised her rifle to her shoulder, and cored the closest Wyrm. Rather than returning to cover she cored the next one, and the next one.

She'd killed fifteen adult Wyrms before they finally became aware of her, but she kept firing at those who seemed to have noticed. Wyrm after Wyrm after Wyrm died.

Dozens fell, but when you were dealing with hundreds those dozens weren't enough. Smart demons fled when facing greater odds, but since her father had forbidden her to do that, Kali kept firing.

She cored another dragon, and another. Every spell drew deeply from her reserves, but thanks to her rifle, Shakti, she could fire very nearly endlessly. She'd be dead long before she ran out of magic.

A Wyrm finally got close enough that she was forced to blink away, and then execute it. That let two more get close, and she was only able to kill one before the other breathed on her.

Ice covered her body, and while it did nothing to harm her it did slow her...which allowed other Wyrms to close.

Something hot and brittle punched through her chest, and she couldn't tell what it was. A barbed tail maybe? It ripped loose, and she tumbled end over end away from it.

As she lay there waiting for the Wyrms to close she forced herself onto her side, enough that she could see Xal's headless neck. "Why, father? And why would Malila abandon us? I don't understand."

Wyrms landed all around her, like vultura, a species of two-headed birds on her world.

Magic pulsed from deep within her father's body, the kind of spell only an elder god could manage. Energy boiled up around Kali, and then her body was gone.

Where she'd been now stood a labyrinth of impossibly sharp platforms, all rotating around each other to conceal something at the center. Then the whole thing sank beneath the surface of Xal's skin, burrowing from sight.

Dragons greedily charged the new structure as it disappeared, but one by one they were butchered as they approached. The platforms moved without warning, severing wings, and tails, and necks.

The tomb, with its lethal traps, disappeared from the surface. Nara's perspective changed and she saw that it had moved to a cavern, though not a particularly well hidden one.

The location burned into her brain, she awoke with a gasp.

24

RIBS

Lieutenant Davidson walked onto the bridge of the *Talon* for what he hoped might be the last time. It wasn't that he didn't love the ship, or the crew. He did. Both had been good to him, and both had saved his life.

He was just damnably tired of war, and ready to muster out. He'd signed up for a war against the Krox, fighting for the Confederacy. Now the Krox were maybe allies, or at least neutral, and only Nebiat was the enemy? He couldn't keep it all straight any more.

"Davidson." Crewes nodded in his direction as Davidson strode onto the bridge. "Good timing, man. Bord's about to get us out of the black."

Bord stood in the matrix they'd designated for defense, sweat beading his brow. He tapped *void* on all three rings, and a Fissure veined across the black, suddenly illuminating them.

Something slithered away from the light, smaller than their ship but still large enough to be menacing. Depths, but he hated the...depths.

Crewes guided the ship through, and they returned to

normal space. The Fissure snapped shut in their wake, giving Davidson his first look at New Texas since he'd left with Aran.

"My god that planet is beautiful." Davidson grinned up at the scry-screen, which showed the dirty-orange world. Not a lot of people love desert country, but Davidson had grown up there. Besides, he could bring his own water.

"Will you look at that." Bord gave a low whistle. "They've already repaired the factories, and looks like they've almost completed a brand new fleet of ships. Don't these people ever take a day off?"

It pleased Davidson to hear Bord making jokes. He hadn't known the specialist, or his lady friend, that well. But they'd both been nice to him, and no one wanted to see a friend lose the love of their life.

"Never, especially not after someone punches us in the face like the Krox did." Davidson smiled at the closest station with pride. "Looks like they're operating near peak capacity. My people bounced back, just like they always do."

"Sir, we're receiving a missive," Rhea said, business as always. "It's from that station. We've been given clearance to land. They have a delegation waiting to receive us, or Lieutenant Davidson specifically. They have you listed as a Major Davidson, though."

"Davidson, you know I love you," Crewes began from the central command couch. He spun it to face Davidson. "But I ain't gonna sit through some big dinner. I ain't the captain. How about we drop you at the airlock with your stuff, and call it a day?"

"Suits me fine." Davidson shrugged. "I wouldn't wish bureaucracy on anyone, and you're needed at Yanthara. You've got an uphill fight there convincing them that NEF-1 is anything but a savior."

"All the more reason to get on the road." Crewes struggled out of his matrix, and walked Davidson down to the airlock. He cleared his throat a couple times, then finally spoke. "Listen. I ain't good with words, man. But I want you to know that you always have a home here. You're a good soldier. You fight hard. And I'm proud to know you."

Crewes extended a hand and Davidson shook it.

"You too, man." He offered a smile. "Never expected this journey to lead where it has. Gods and magic and all that crap. I wish it were simpler."

"You and me both. Take care, brother." Crewes turned on his heels and walked away, leaving Davidson facing the translucent blue membrane separating him from the station.

Davidson stepped through the membrane, and into a new life. Knowing his tank would be joining him helped, but only a little. So much change, so rapidly. So many new faces, and so many old ones gone.

He was damned tired of war.

Davidson scrubbed his fingers through his beard, hefted his bag, and walked up the corridor. He followed the icons toward the restaurant quarter, which wasn't that difficult to find as they were all near the center of the station.

The first thing he noticed was the foot traffic. There was a lot of it. People were wearing Ternus uniforms, not Confederate, which he'd sort of expected. They laughed and joked, and acted just like servicemen everywhere. It was a damned sight for sore eyes.

People stopped in front of stores and bought ice cream, the fake stuff anyway, or sat and talked with friends over soy-noodles. It was normal. It was people. Living life. It was a desperately needed sight, always surrounded as he was by aliens in strange parts of the sector.

Davidson caught sight of a *Louis's Cattle Rustler's*, the most popular chain on New Texas, and apparently a favorite of Governor Bhatia as she'd asked to meet there. He strode up to the place, which had a glowing cowboy on the sign, and ducked through a pair of swinging doors into something that was supposed to look western themed.

It fell a bit short, but only a bit. Good enough for him, anyway. He strode deeper inside, and stopped near the receptionist, a tiny brunette with a brilliant smile. An ancient Terran cowboy sang softly in the background, something about a ring of fire. Must have been a depths of a battle, from the sound of it.

"Mr. Davidson?" The hostess approached and beamed that perfect smile in his direction. If he were ten years younger and less exhausted, maybe. "The governor has arranged for a private dinner. This way, please."

Davidson followed her into a private dining room with twelve chairs. Only one of those chairs was currently occupied, to his surprise. Governor Bhatia sat by herself, drinking a cola, and eating the biggest dang plate of ribs anyone outside Texas of Old had ever seen.

"Ah, Davidson, have a seat." The handsome woman's dusky skin was made rosy under the dim lights. "I ordered enough ribs to feed at least twelve people. Where are Aran and his crew?"

"Ahh, it's just me, Governor." Davidson sat in the chair next to her, and dropped his pack on the chair next to him. He pulled up a plate and scooped some ribs on it. "I promise not a single rib will go to waste."

"You've earned every one, son." She gave him a smile that was ruined by hot sauce. "Pity Aran can't be here, but with the war over nothing is going to get my mood down. We're finally rebuilding, and things are looking up all over."

"Wait, what do you mean with the war over?" Davidson stuffed his face with a rib as soon as he'd gotten the question out.

"Wow, you must have been isolated. Krox is dead." She beamed him a proud smile. "The NEF-1 unit tore Krox apart. It returned to Ternus for further instructions, but Austin's approval rating has never been so high, and even I'm starting to come around."

Davidson set down the bone, and used a napkin to start wiping sauce from his face. His appetite vanished. "Governor, you are not going to like what I'm about to tell you. About the NEF-1 unit. About Aran, about who our real enemy is. The war is just getting started, and I'm going to need your help to put things right."

25

WARM WELCOME

Aran was fairly certain from the thrashing in their command couches that both Nara and Kazon were dreaming. They'd translocated into the system where the husk was supposed to be, but when they'd arrived he'd been the only one conscious, and now both were in the throes of some deep dream, whimpering.

"Nara?" Aran called. He unbuckled his harness, and leaned over to gently shake her shoulder. Nothing. He tried Kazon next. "Kaz, buddy?" Nothing.

Aran willed the ship to connect, and braced himself as the awful golden tendril attached to his forehead. It was unpleasant, but piloting the ship wasn't unlike guiding a spellfighter, and he focused on that.

Now that he could see through the ship's senses he confirmed their location. They'd arrived in a system with a dead star, the cracked remains floating in darkness.

Xal's titanic form slowly orbited that dead star, a headless god with bat wings and a long curled tail. That god emitted the only light in system, and it came from many places across the corpse. The lights resembled cities, though he was too far out to be certain.

A dense debris field had accumulated around various parts of Xal's body, mostly ancient space hulks, stations or random battle wreckage.

They were currently orbiting one of Xal's feet, well, his only remaining foot, to be precise. The other leg had been severed at the knee, and ended in a ragged stump.

Similar wounds dotted the god's body, where his enemies had feasted, something that had been going on for longer than humanity had plied the stars. In that moment Aran finally gave in to despair, for a minute anyway.

"This is what we're supposed to restore?" he muttered. The god's desiccated, headless body might be larger than Nefarius, slightly, but there was no way it would be able to oppose the monstrosity the Inurans had created and that Ternus had helped fuel with immense magic.

Nara suddenly awakened with a gasp. She clawed at her harness, chest heaving as she sought escape, eyes wild. Her long, dark hair was plastered to her neck by a thick sheen of sweat.

"Nara," Aran murmured, soothingly, "it's okay. It was just a dream."

Nara blinked a few times, and settled back into her harness. Her breathing was still elevated, but she seemed otherwise all right. The new hue of her skin was the only visible clue to the physical changes they'd undergone, but if Malila was right they were also far tougher now. That should mean Nara was safe physically.

"Graal?" Kazon's eyes fluttered open. He looked around in confusion, gaze unfocused. The big man licked his lips, and finally seemed to detect his surroundings. "I am aboard the ship. Oh, thank Inura. What a terrible nightmare."

"What did you dream?" Nara whispered, her eyes haunted.

"I was a champion of the demons," Kazon explained slowly, gaze still far away. "A guardian. I wore a gauntlet."

"Your name was Gorr," Nara supplied, straightening in her command couch. "You were the guardian, and I was father's vengeance."

"That would make you...Kali? You died too, didn't you?"

Nara nodded. She clasped her hands in her lap, and seemed smaller somehow. "We were overrun. Our people were dying. They wouldn't leave unless all the princes were dead, so we sacrificed ourselves."

Aran considered what they were saying, then reached down and rested a hand on Narlifex's hilt. The blade was awkward in the command couch, but he'd never be separated from it again.

Yes. We stay together, Narlifex pulsed. *My knowledge is vast now. I see...so much. I hold the memory of our people.*

"These princes," Kazon was saying, stroking his beard as he spoke, "they left tombs when they died. Xal's magic created them at the precise moment and location of their death. I saw mine form around me as I died."

"I saw the same," Nara agreed. "Mine was a series of interlocking blades, all moving in patterns. Dozens of Wyrms died trying to get in."

"Convenient," Aran allowed, "in that both of you have an easy way to prove yourselves. You know you're going to have to get into those tombs, right?"

"What about you?" Kazon asked, scandalized. "Why do we have to do the work?"

"Oh, I'm sure I'll have my part to play." Aran shook his head. "Odds are good I'll have to fight some unbeatable swordsman, or head butt a wall into submission. I'm sure I won't like whatever it is."

Nara turned her attention on the golden orb, and a tendril extended to her forehead. Her gaze went unfocused. "Looks like there are dozens of settlements. Most are single species, but some are mixed. The most numerous are the oni. Looks like the jin are the largest physically, and are mostly concentrated around Xal's chest cavity. The eru are all over, but the densest concentrations are on the wings."

"So where do we start, brother?" Kazon asked.

"I imagine we pick a tomb, and land near it. I'm sure the locals will introduce themselves." Aran realized it wasn't terribly imaginative, but when dealing with demons who prided themselves on strength, subtlety didn't seem the smartest play. "Let's set down near the oni, on the leg there, unless one of you knows where your tombs are?"

Both shook their heads.

"All right, guess we'll just have to start looking." Aran quested into the ship through his link, trying to understand it better. He was having very little luck though, and most of what he saw was gibberish. "Kazon, how do you transform the ship, and how much control do you have?"

"Like so," Kazon explained. Aran tried to follow what he did, but couldn't. It happened too swiftly. The ship transformed from its corvette form back into a metallic warrior. "I assume this is the form you're after?"

"That'll work." Aran focused on piloting, which he did understand. The mecha became an extension of his body and he expertly guided it toward Xal's desiccated right leg. "I'm going to set down outside that settlement there. I see a lot of markets, and where there's trade there's also information."

As Aran descended he noticed that every last demon in that market turned to gaze up in their direction. All of them.

"Uh, Aran?" Nara whispered. "We're in a giant glowing mech, and we represent the antithesis of void..."

The demons closest to the edge of the market began lumbering toward them. More followed. It quickly became a flood with hundreds of oni charging in an enraged horde, all bent on their destruction.

"Well," Aran said, suppressing a sigh, "guess we're in the right place."

26

THE ONI

Aran gave himself over fully to the link with the mecha, and immediately noticed a difference. Always before when he'd piloted a spellship, or even a suit of spellarmor, it had been a tool. An interface.

Not so, this thing. He *was* the mecha. He could feel the frost accumulating on the metal plating. He felt the rock crunch when two hundred tons of mecha slammed down onto the plain outside the city.

Aran scanned the approaching horde, and considered options. "We're going to have to fight. Does this thing come with a sword?"

"I can make one," Kazon murmured, his voice distracted.

A moment later a bar of pristine golden light appeared in the mecha's right hand. The sword had no definition, really, no edge to speak of. It was more of a club, but since that club was made out of pure *life*, and demons were touched by the *void*, that should do the trick.

"Is a shield out of the question, or can you get me that too?" Aran slid into a combat stance, and hoped for the best. He could use a single blade, or a pair, but the strongest style when outnumbered was blade and shield, in his opinion.

"On it," Kazon barked.

A moment later a translucent golden shield flared to life on the mech's left wrist, several rings of brilliant sigils spinning within it.

"Now we're talking." Aran gave a whoop, and started toward the enemy ranks at a trot.

The oni ranged in size from about two meters to about ten meters, putting the largest nearly as tall as the mecha. Those larger ones were rare, though, and the average was closer to about four meters tall.

Aran glided into battle, and was amazed by how fluidly the mecha moved. Despite its size he lost none of his agility, and could fight as if he were on foot.

His sword was everywhere at once, slashing and parrying the dark weapons wielded by the demons. A demon in the distance raised a spellrifle, and was about to lob something unpleasant in their direction.

"I'm on it," Nara murmured.

Something whirred outside the cockpit, and a shoulder mounted spellcannon emerged over the right shoulder. A grey counterspell zipped from the muzzle, and met the thick void bolt unleashed by the demon's cannon. Both spells exploded into particles.

"Kazon, what else can this thing do?" Aran spun and raised his shield to parry one of the larger demons, then countered with a wicked riposte that disemboweled his opponent.

Smaller demons stopped attacking the mecha, and began eagerly devouring the larger demon's entrails. It went down with a roar, and within moments was completely covered by its brethren.

"Perfect target," Nara's voice carried amusement.

The spellcannon fired again, this time unleashing a high level void bolt. The beam was wide enough to cover the pile, and killed both the smaller demons and the larger demon they were busy devouring.

Kazon gave a groan, then a high-pitched whine began deep within the mecha, and brilliant golden light exploded outward. It arrayed itself into a dome of wards very similar to what Bord would have created, though this one was larger and infinitely more powerful.

Volleys of void bolts peppered the ward, each spell briefly discoloring that area of the wards. None of the bolts penetrated though, which left them free to deal with only the demons charging into melee.

The wards didn't stop their enemies from entering, unfortunately.

Aran didn't really mind. He twisted and dodged, slicing through the demon ranks with ease. The whole fight felt... well, easy after having had to deal directly with Nefarius.

A towering oni burst through the ward, this one even taller than the mecha. It carried a battle-axe large enough to cleave a tank, and the creature's thick, corded, muscled arms wielded it with ease.

Aran sprinted toward his opponent, then dropped into a slide at the last possible moment. The axe whooshed overhead, while Aran's golden sword sliced through both legs at the knee.

The suddenly crippled oni toppled to the ground with a roar, but Aran had already rolled the mecha to its feet. He spun, and buried the golden sword deep in the creature's neck, ending its struggles.

He looked around for his next opponent, but there were none. There were plenty more demons, but they all stood silently now, simply staring blankly with large eyes under thick brows.

"I guess that one was important," Nara pointed out. "Maybe that was the leader?"

"Now what?" Kazon asked.

"My demon etiquette is a little rusty." Aran straightened the mech, and began walking slowly toward the market. The crowd of demons parted before them, and none made a move to attack. "At least they're not assaulting us, but they don't seem in a hurry to communicate either. We need to find someone who speaks galactic common."

The crowd parted further ahead of them, and a clear path opened up. It led toward a large gaping wound in the thigh, which was crusted over with frost, and worse things.

"Nara can you scan inside to give us some idea of what to expect?" Aran didn't much like the look of it, though he'd known that would be the case before coming here.

"There are quite a few wards inside," Nara said after a brief pause. "Powerful wards. This place is a settlement. An ancient one. It looks like a network of tunnels extends several kilometers beneath the surface."

"They ate their way through the god," Kazon said, his voice carrying the horror they all shared. "Like beetles. Terrifying. These are the beings we have come to win to our cause?"

"None of us like it." And Aran didn't like it. Not one bit. "But we need Xal. And that means we might have to do some disgusting things. It does not mean we need to compromise our principles. We won't betray who we are."

"I'm glad to hear that out loud." Nara gave a relieved sigh. "I've finally figured out who I am, and I'm not in a hurry to betray her."

They walked slowly up a rise, and when they reached

the summit they could see inside the wound. Dozens of large structures had been carved out of bone, which had presumably been quarried somewhere else. The muscle had been eaten away, and a high ceiling vaulted into the air.

A few oni walked between structures, but almost all of them were focused on the mecha's march into the cavern.

"There," Nara said. "At the far end of the cavern there's a large structure I'm guessing is designed for a chieftain."

"Let's go introduce ourselves. Either they'll work with us, or we'll replace them."

Aran guided the mech into a faster walk, and continued up a broad road for several kilometers as they approached the largest structure. The demons were utterly silent as they passed, not even conversing amongst themselves.

The whole thing filled Aran with unease, and his tension grew as they approached a manor. If 'manor' was the right word. It was more of a crude longhouse, and used long planks of bone with stretched leather hides between them.

The crowd of demons continued all the way to the wide opening in the side of the longhouse. It was not quite tall enough for the mecha to enter, which presented a dilemma.

"Do you think we should get out?" Nara asked. "Not sure I'm loving that idea."

"Guess that's the fastest way to get some answers." Aran unbuckled his harness. "Nara, if things go south, be ready to get us out of here."

"Always am," she promised.

27

GRAAL

Kazon rested his hand on the buckle to the harness. He didn't even really need to unclip it. He could merely touch the wall of the mecha, and be instantly transported outside. The buckle, and the harness it was attached to, were symbolic.

The problem was that Kazon was a coward.

It was one thing to venture into the unknown while armed with a god-forged mecha. But leaving that mecha? All he had was a simple suit of spellarmor, and he would likely be easy prey for any of the demons he'd face here.

Sure, he'd gained some magic. He had *void* and *life*. Quite a lot of both. Not enough to be a god, like Aran, but a large amount.

But he didn't know how to use that magic. He wasn't a war mage, and he wasn't a true mage. He could be called a tech mage, if one was being generous, but a tech mage without tech was just a mundane.

If he left this sanctuary, odds were very high that he was going to die.

Kazon closed his eyes, and exhaled. He'd survived so

many things that should have killed him. He'd survived his initial catalyzation. He'd somehow gotten away from Skare and Jolene, snatched from his fate by Inura himself.

Was this the end?

Maybe. Maybe not. But he'd only find out if he faced this. And he wouldn't be able to face Aran if he didn't. Aran would understand, of course, but Kazon had no interest in being a liability to his friends.

He unbuckled the harness and touched the wall. One brilliant flash later Kazon was standing outside next to Nara and Aran. Both wore their suits of Mark XI spellarmor, something he knew well.

Kazon's own armor was a prototype he'd found in Inura's workshop. It was a scout class, but provided quite a bit of additional strength to the user. That made it ideal for engineering tasks, something Kazon found he enjoyed more than any other activity.

He scanned the faceplate's HUD, but all metrics were green. His potion loaders were filled with healing potions, and his armor was undamaged and ready for action. If only the pilot were as ready.

Aran walked into the longhouse, and Nara floated a little behind him. Kazon hurried forward, until he'd caught up to Aran and could walk side by side.

"I'm proud of you," Aran said, his voice coming through the speakers in Kazon's suit. "I know this is more our gig than yours, but I'm grateful you came along. You know things about tech I don't. We need you."

"So long as no one expects me to fight," Kazon groaned. "I'll just stay behind you, brother."

A crude throne cut from planks of curved bone sat at the far side of the longhouse, which was otherwise empty. Thick carpets covered the floor, and areas had obviously been partitioned off to belong to different families. There was no privacy that Kazon could see, which would horrify him. He valued solitude a great deal.

The room was unoccupied, save for a single bulbous-nosed oni, the largest they'd yet seen. He sat atop the throne, an equally massive club propped against one arm. The base of that club had been carved to look like a skull, and the eyes glowed with the telltale deep purple of the void.

"So," boomed the demon seated on the throne, in perfect galactic standard, "tiny humans cut down Brackus. These fools won't shut up 'bout a 'golden knight'. You come to attack us then? Go back and get friends. You? Not worth getting off throne for. Graal should smush tiny humans, just to see what inside."

"But you haven't yet," Aran called, approaching the oni on his throne. He looked comically small, and each step up to the throne was taller than Aran's spellarmor. "Does that mean you're willing to hear us out?"

"Yes." The oni gave a sharp nod. "Tell Graal story. Make story good, or Graal will smoosh."

"Nara?" Aran shifted to face her. "You're probably the best storyteller."

"I hope that's a compliment, and not a way of saying I'm shady." Nara's spellarmor floated closer, until it was at eye level with the oni king. "I'll tell you the tale of Xal's demise. Of his death, and the death of his princes."

"Graal know Xal's death." The oni king gave a frown that exposed a wicked set of tusks. "Graal was here. Graal saw demon father die."

"But you haven't heard the tale from the perspective of Gorr," Nara protested.

Graal's eyes narrowed, and power seethed within the

demon. "What you know of Gorr? Mortal shouldn't say Gorr's name. Graal getting angry."

"Nara," Kazon found himself calling. "This is my tale."

Kazon strode forward, walking toward the demon king's throne. He funneled a bit of *void* magic into his armor, and rose shakily into the air.

The oni king stared suspiciously down at Kazon, but his curiosity seemed to overpower his rage. "Who little man think he is?"

"Once," Kazon began, growing bolder as he reached into the memories the blood had provided, "my name was Gorr. I was a smith. I built things. I enjoyed it. I made tools for killing. Tools my brothers and sisters used to slaughter our enemies, for millennia."

Graal's anger returned as the oni king leaned forward on his throne, jaw exposing a pair of tusk-like teeth with bits of meat still stuck between them and neighboring teeth. "Tiny man better explain how he know who Gorr is. Now."

"I am," Kazon snarled. "Graal shut up. Graal listen." He channeled the memories, becoming the demon that had once mentored Graal. "Gorr powerful. Gorr smart. Gorr make sacrifice, so oni could live. Gorr died. Gorr gave life. Now Gorr reborn as tiny human, but still Gorr. Ask something only Gorr would know."

Kazon prayed that the oni king could produce a fact that he felt only Gorr could answer, and that his memories of Gorr would actually be able to answer it.

Graal adopted a cunning expression that was anything but. "What command word to gauntlet?"

Kazon began to laugh.

Graal's response was immediate. He seized Kazon in a fist, and began to squeeze. Armor plates began to buckle, and protested as the metal fought to hold its shape.

Memory stirred in Kazon, something he barely understood, and he knew that his next words were not his own. "You think me a fool, Graal. You believe that, if this really is me, and I tell you the word, you can claim my gauntlet. I never told you the word. I never will. The gauntlet is mine, Graal. Now release me, or face the consequences."

Graal eyed him, his hideous breath coating the outside of Kazon's faceplate in truly disgusting things that had been lingering between his teeth.

"Graal wondered." He set Kazon gently down on the arm of his throne. "You sound like Gorr. Smart. Oni not smart now. Muscle make us large, but stupid."

"You lack balance." Kazon nodded. He folded his arms and stared haughtily up at Graal. "Focusing on martial prowess is good, but creating is much harder than destroying. That is what separates us from the Shayatin."

"Shayatin?" Aran asked quietly over the com.

"It's their word for true demon," Kazon whispered back, "and I'll explain more later."

"Hmm," Graal rumbled. He leaned down to peer at Kazon. "Graal think there easy way to test. If tiny human really is Gorr, then he can enter Gorr's tomb, and come back with gauntlet."

28

THE GAUNTLET OF REEVANTHARA

Kazon was at a loss, which happened rather more often than he'd like to admit. How he'd come to be standing outside of the unassailable tomb of a demon prince, and told to enter, he'd never know.

Countless would-be tomb robbers had attempted the place, apparently, an endless tide of adventurers knowing that priceless artifacts and untold power lay within. Kazon wanted neither, but needed both.

That tomb was innocuous enough. A patch of absolute darkness covered the base of the neighboring valley, where Gorr had made his final stand. No demons came here, so their little party was left in peace, at least.

"What is it?" Aran asked from his position a few meters away where he hovered in his spellarmor.

Nara hovered in relative silence a few dozen meters away. She wore her full spellarmor over that wonderful suit of personal armor. He'd kill to study that, though he doubted she ever took it off.

"I don't know," Kazon admitted. He started walking down the path, a rough trail that meandered down to the valley below. "According to my vision many Wyrms tried to enter the tomb, but none emerged. In the scores of millennia since, countless demons have entered. None have ever emerged. And the truly creepy part? How do I know any of that? This stuff is in my mind, and I do not like it. It can't belong to Gorr, because he was dead. So who do these memories belong to?"

"Now is a terrible time to get cold feet." Nara propped her staff on the shoulder of her spellarmor, and stared quite judgily at Kazon.

"I am not getting cold feet," he snapped, glaring at her. "But I am neither a warrior nor a mage. I am afraid, yes, but I hesitate not out of fear, but out of a desire not to screw up my one chance to help save this sector."

"Oh." Nara said. "I'm sorry then." It sounded as if she meant it. "Taking time to plan is great. We're here if you need a sounding board."

"Thank you, and I mean that." Kazon continued down the path. He kept his attention on the step ahead of him, looking for loose debris or anything that might impede him. The simple activity helped.

"You know you could fly down?" Nara said.

"Yep." Kazon kept walking.

He ignored her, and ignored Aran, instead focusing on what he was about to do. He had no idea what waited for him in that tomb, but he also knew something with absolute certainty. Xal had planned for this moment.

As difficult as it was, as strange as admitting it felt, he needed to trust in his god. And Xal truly was his god. Having memories of the deity trapped inside of him tended to convert one quite effectively.

It took nearly an hour for Kazon to trudge his way down to the valley floor. When he reached it he glanced up and saw that Aran was still sitting on the ridge line in his power armor. There was no sign of Nara, though that meant little. She was almost certainly watching.

Knowing that Aran was still in his corner helped a great deal. Aran was widely regarded as the sector's hero. Having that hero believe in you when you were going to do something you'd never done before gave one the courage to try.

Kazon turned back to the wall of darkness. There was no distinguishable feature, nothing to differentiate any part of it from any other. What lay inside?

There was only one way to find out.

Kazon checked the seals on his spellarmor, then plunged into the darkness, and held his breath. Nothing leaped out at him. Nothing at all happened, though after a few moments a warning alarm began to chime on his HUD.

He moved his thumb to accept the notification, and a cut away of the armor appeared. It showed a little sun, which Kazon assumed must represent the power supply. That sun was dimming. Quickly. And that seemed to be the source of the alarm.

"Time to get moving," he panted as he leaned into a trot.

More warning alarms began to sound until they were an overlapping cacophony, all pointing to his imminent death. Whatever this field was, it was draining the magic from his armor at an unprecedented rate. Once that was gone it would probably start draining magic from him. And once that happened...well, he couldn't afford to be here when it happened.

If he didn't reach whatever the destination in this tomb was before his armor was more than halfway out of magic, he wouldn't have enough left to get out.

"This sucks," he cursed, leaning into an awkward power walk.

Something caught at his feet and he went into a tumbling slide, rolling end over end as he bumped his way down some sort of slope. If not for the spellarmor he'd have broken bones, or worse.

Kazon prayed for the slide to stop, enduring the humiliation with as much dignity as he could muster, then rose wearily to his feet when it finally ended. He'd strained something in his leg, but not badly enough to warrant a healing potion, as those might further prolong the armor's supply of magic.

This was going to be tricky without being able to see.

He started forward again, more slowly this time. He hoped that the gentle downward slope was the right direction, and that it eventually led him to the center of the darkness.

When the alarms finally stopped, Kazon exhaled a silent prayer to Voria, but then immediately realized what it meant. The suit had been fully drained.

He reached back and withdrew a healing potion from the potion loader, and held the canister up for inspection. The glow of the life magic within should have illuminated the area around him, like a glow stick.

Instead, the canister was nearly dark, with only an ember of life within. "Well, that isn't going to help much." He dropped the canister and kept moving.

Kazon fell into a fumbling routine, but the further he hobbled the colder it grew. His teeth began to chatter, and moving became difficult. He pressed on, but yawn after yawn threatened to crack his jaw.

Everything in him screamed that he should lay down.

"No," he snarled. "I will do my part. I am not worthless. They need me."

Kazon reached for the magic Inura had given him. There

had been so much *life*, and he drew upon it now. Kazon fed the magic to his armor, and the HUD lit up faintly.

He prayed it was enough.

Kazon began hobbling forward again, and slowly fed a trickle of *life* magic to the suit as he moved. It was already growing taxing, and he didn't know how long he'd be able to maintain it.

Minutes passed, and his reserves slowly drained. He didn't know how much more he could do, but he was certain there would be no return trip. Even if he reached the center it would only be to die there alongside every other demonic tomb robber. But at least he'd see it before he died.

Kazon scraped across the ground, tripped, and rolled down another slope. It didn't hurt, though it was jarring and embarrassing. At least no one was there to see.

When he finally stopped moving Kazon rose to his feet again, and was shocked to realize he could see a shape in the darkness, not more than a dozen meters ahead. It looked like a disembodied hand floating in darkness.

He hesitated. The armor chimed weakly, his magic having restored just enough for that to work. But he was almost out of strength.

Could it be this easy?

Kazon took a step. Then another. He forced the armor forward, and fed it the last of his available *life* magic.

Kazon staggered drunkenly through the last few paces and finally reached the gauntlet, floating at about eye level.

Memory stirred within him and he realized he was seeing the fabled Gauntlet of Reevanthara, an artifact used in the creation of the Great Cycle itself.

You wouldn't have thought so from looking at it. The base metal was silver, or platinum, or some greater metal that resembled the two. There was a tiny crease over each knuckle, but the gauntlet was otherwise smooth.

The riot of colors that had drawn his attention appeared to come from an iridescent layer of ever-shifting wards that covered the surface. They danced just beyond the edge of his understanding, and he found looking at them too long disquieting.

Kazon removed his spellarmor's right gauntlet and dropped it into a void pocket. The instant he did so a layer of frost covered his hand, and he lost all feeling. Kazon awkwardly muscled it into the Gauntlet of Reevanthara, which sealed over the hand.

Warmth pulsed into him, restoring feeling, but not in a way that brought pain. Kazon flexed the gauntlet, and his hand worked perfectly.

Somewhere, beyond hearing, he could hear the symphony of the universe. He held up the gauntlet in wonder.

29

TOLD YOU SO

Aran sat atop a boulder and watched the darkness in the valley below. Kazon had been gone for over an hour, though who knew what that meant. Graal had been clear. No one had ever emerged, no matter how long you waited.

There could be any number of reasons why. It could be a portal to another universe. It could have some sort of monster, or monsters. It could confuse anyone who entered, or make them fall asleep. Who knew?

"It's not easy, is it?" Nara materialized from the shadows, and sat on the opposite side of the boulder. Her features were hidden behind her Mark XI's mask, but her relaxed posture and tone of voice filled in the gaps.

"Being the one left behind?" he asked, still staring at the darkness. "I got a taste of it when Crewes went after Rhea."

"You don't sound as if you like it." Nara removed her helmet, and shook her shiny black hair loose. "I can't blame you. I never have either. I spent a lot of time sitting in a cell just sort of...waiting."

"Yeah, I hate that part. He'll succeed," Aran said, with

absolute certainty. "I can...feel him through the blood. He's alive. Beyond that though? I have no idea."

That certainly helped. They had a lot of seemingly insurmountable problems looming. Waiting was easy compared to staring up at that mountain you had to climb from the base.

Just like that, the darkness winked out. The valley was still dark, but it was a natural darkness, broken by gradations.

Something glowed in the center of the valley. A soft multicolored glow that Aran couldn't quite make out. Whatever it was seemed to be coming closer. It was picking a path in their direction.

"Kazon?" Nara wondered aloud.

"That would be my guess. Let's go check." Aran leapt into the air and used *void* to propel himself down to the soft glow.

As they approached he quickly realized that Nara was right. Kazon walked up the same trail he'd picked his way down, and the soft glow came from a gauntlet covering his right hand.

He trudged wearily in their direction, but raised the gauntlet in a wave. His armor was battered from the beating Graal had given it, but he appeared otherwise unharmed.

"I have succeeded," he called, his voice hoarse and cracked. His face split into a grin. "I have conquered the darkness, and reclaimed the Gauntlet of Reevanthara, which my forebear used to create the arms and armaments wielded by Xal's demonic host. I remember my past. I am Kazon, but I am also Gorr."

Aran nodded. Somehow he understood what Kazon meant. He wasn't merely himself anymore, if he ever had been, ever since coming out of the light back at the skull when this had all started.

"Can I just translocate us back?" Aran asked. "May as well save time."

Kazon nodded. The way he carried himself was different...with more presence and confidence. It was as if he'd been missing a piece of himself, and that piece had suddenly clicked back into place. Aran approved.

"I understand what Inura created now," Kazon said, his voice filled with wonder. "Come. Take us back and we will set things in motion."

Aran waved a hand and the three of them were suddenly standing a few dozen meters from the oni king's throne. This time there were far more oni in the room.

The over-muscled demons shot hostile glares in their directions, and more than one flexed in open challenge. It was refreshing, in a way, after dealing with Shayan politics. At least the demons were honest.

It took several moments for Graal to notice that they'd appeared, but when he did he rose from his throne, sucked in a deep breath, and gave a bellowing laugh that shook the walls and challenged the sound dampeners in Aran's helmet.

Silence reigned.

"Little human came back." Graal wore his smugness like evening finery. "Did little human come to beg? To plead not to have to face the darkness?"

"Graal Ka Xal," Kazon barked, his voice somehow carrying an authority it never had before. "You will treat me with respect, or I will make an example out of you. I do not brook insolence, if you remember."

Kazon raised his silvery gauntlet, and it flared an angry

red. The demons seemed not to recognize it, and were clearly unimpressed. All except Graal.

Graal dove from his throne, and dropped into a kneeling position. "Graal sorry, father. How supposed to know you really you?"

"I am not angry." Kazon lowered his gauntlet. "In fact, I am proud of you, my son. You kept the faith. You kept our people together, despite the cost to you personally. Your intellect is much reduced, but now that I am home I can find a way to remedy that."

A missive from Nara popped up on Aran's HUD, and he accepted it. Her concerned face filled the lower corner of his screen.

"Are you hearing this?" Nara whispered. "That does not sound like our lovable Kazon. What the depths happened to him in there?"

"I don't know," Aran admitted. "I get the sense that more than one person is living in his head now."

"Well that should be fun." Nara sounded more angry than afraid. He knew the anger wasn't directed at him. Or he hoped so anyway.

"Listen, Nara." Aran tried to be soothing, but didn't want to stray into condescending. "You can go in, or not, as you feel is right. We've always supported each other, and that won't change now. If you don't want to go in, no one would ever try to make you."

Nara gave a sigh, and shook her head. "We both know it needs to be done. I've got this." She killed the feed.

Aran turned his attention back to the conversation between Kazon and Graal.

"Other tribes won't listen to oni." Graal sounded more petulant than angry. "If I tell them you Gorr they laugh."

"You are right, my son, but I will find another way." Kazon turned to Nara. "I believe you are the next part of the puzzle, Kali. You will need to reclaim your legacy, and gain the allegiance of the eru. If we approach the jin with the eru and oni working together they will have no choice but to listen."

A text-only missive appeared on Aran's HUD. *Told you so.*

30

ENOCH

Nara hefted her neoprene pack, a nicety Kazon had provided, then cinched it behind her back. It was lightweight, and contained a void pocket with all the things she considered essential.

It was just large enough to be useful, but small enough not to hamper movement, or stealth.

The way Nara saw it they didn't have time to work their way up the chain of command. She couldn't simply turn herself over to the first guard she found. She needed to talk to the person in charge, whomever that might be.

She understood that the greatest concentration of eru was on the right wing, so she'd translocated to a shadowy portion near one of the tips, then started working her way down.

Nara moved in a low run blinking from shadow to shadow as she sprinted along the frost-covered terrain. It wasn't precisely rock—the ground was too spongy for that, and more leathery than any ground had a right to be.

Nara used that to her advantage, rolling off obstacles to increase her speed. She'd employed a simple camouflage spell rather than elaborate wards because the people she truly feared would be looking for magic-laden attackers.

She circled around the city, gradually spiraling closer as she sought the best approach. There were endless alleys and warrens, and plotting a path from there to the hollow where the wing met the back seemed doable.

It was more time consuming than anything else.

Nara kept moving, never slowing, always approaching her goal. She crept along rooftops, and down narrow streets. It was a better choice than attempting to translocate as close as possible, simply because she got to see how the eru lived.

They were a quiet, introspective people, and even their children had a look about them as if they were ready to dart for the shadows at any moment. That saddened Nara. She hated seeing a people beaten down like that, demon or no.

Nara paused at the base of a towering growth, an errant spur of bone that had splintered when the wing had been damaged. The entire spur was covered in lights, the densest of any area in the city.

If it were her, and she were in charge, she would be at the top of that spur.

Nara gave a grim smile and teleported to the tip of the splintered bone, several kilometers above. The wind nearly pulled her off as she landed, and Nara had to use gravity magic to pull herself back.

Below her sat a coliseum, where perhaps two hundred eru were watching a play that would have been at home on any one of a dozen worlds. Nara sensed that the language wasn't any she'd known last week, but she had no trouble following the words. From the little bit she picked up it seemed a harrowing drama with a bandit on the run trying to reach her lover.

She hesitated. Finding the eru leader was important, but

it was possible he was at this play. Not likely, maybe, but possible. Even if he wasn't she might learn more about their culture, making it a worthwhile use of her time.

Nara slipped carefully down the wall, blinking from shadow to shadow, until she landed in a seat in the back row of the coliseum, in the darkened corner where no one was sitting.

No one seemed to have noticed her arrival, so she settled in to watch the play. The heroine, as it turned out, wasn't a bandit. She was merely a snarky heroine, always on the run.

"It must be odd," a male voice broke in suddenly, next to her, "to see a play based on one's previous incarnation."

Nara tensed, but resisted the urge to take a hostile action. An ancient eru male was seated on the stone a pace away from her. He had a long wispy beard, and his wings were desiccated and no longer capable of flight. How old must he be?

"Older than you can imagine." He gave a snort, and a self-deprecating smile. "Old enough that I can't stop myself from picking up stray thoughts, especially ones as strong as yours. Old enough that approaching a pretty young lady, even one from a species I have never seen, is an awkward affair. I am called Enoch. What are you called now, Vengeance?"

Nara wasn't sure how to react to that. Simple honesty seemed best, as long as she wasn't revealing something dangerous.

"My name is Nara," she admitted, eyeing the demon sidelong. "What do you mean when you call me the vengeance?"

"I mean that was your former title, or a piece of it. The soul you bear within you was once one of our most powerful demon princes." His leathery face split into an affectionate grin. "I trained Kali, before she was raised. I taught her, as I would a true daughter. I taught her to kill, but also to think so she knew when it made sense to do."

Sudden sadness washed out the smile, and Enoch gave a pained sigh. "Her death nearly unhinged me. She was the best of us, you see. But I knew that Xal had planned for everything, and had faith that one day my daughter would be restored to me. I believe that today may be that day, but I am no fool. I would see more before I accept you."

Nara nodded. "I wouldn't expect you to take a stranger at their word. You seem to recognize something in me, but other than some dreams...I don't know anything about your daughter. I drank from a pool on the Skull of Xal and—"

"You've spoken to Malila." All friendliness evaporated, and Enoch's hands balled into fists. "My flesh and blood. My true daughter. My greatest disappointment."

Nara realized she'd need to approach this carefully, or risk alienating her only contact. "She warned us that you would not react well to her name, and I'm sorry for that. I'm hoping we're seeking the same thing though. I want to resurrect Xal. We need to resurrect Xal."

"Nefarius has come again." Enoch's wings drooped. "Always it is so. Another elder god rises, or the same elder god rises anew. We battle endlessly, and with each iteration we are less than we were."

"Maybe, but this is the only iteration I care about." Nara reached out and took Enoch's hand in hers. "If you think I may be this daughter you hold dear...help me. Help me find this tomb and get inside. Help me unify the eru. We already have the oni on board. If you help me we can bring Xal back."

"And the implication," Enoch replied sardonically, "is

that if I do not then Nefarius will come for the husk. She will devour what remains of father. Is that it?"

"More or less," Nara admitted with a shrug.

"I have long expected this day. Come, Vengeance of Xal, I will show you the tomb you must brave. If you are who you say you are, then you might actually succeed. If not...well, I doubt anyone will remember you, and your bones will be left to mingle with the other fools who've tried over the years."

31

THE TOMB OF BLADES

Enoch led Nara away from the coliseum, but only after they'd stayed for the end of the play. The heroine had ended up in the same inn where she'd started, which Enoch claimed was a metaphor for her reincarnation.

They picked their way down a narrow road that wound past storefronts built into whatever nook or cranny would hold them. Unlike in other cities she'd been in, these people had to work with the terrain, rather than shaping it to their will.

Also unlike other settlements the eru occupants didn't use windows, and didn't advertise their presence in any way. There were no visible lights, and nothing to suggest any shop or residence were occupied. These people had clearly learned not to draw attention to themselves.

"That tends to happen," Enoch said in a low voice, "when you are the lowest rung of a social order."

"The eru are the lowest rung?" She wondered why they put up with it if they were the smartest, and she was also annoyed by how easily Enoch seemed able to read her thoughts.

"We put up with it because we must," Enoch admitted. He paused, and leaned heavily on his staff, his chest heaving and tail dragging along the rough ground. "The other demons do not trust us. The eru were the scholars and the assassins. We took care of the unpleasant business, and our brethren will never forget it, despite it being done for their benefit. They see us as ruthless and power hungry, and they don't like that we occasionally elucidate about our progenitor."

Of the tribes this one sounded the most like Nara, which when combined with her dreams suggested maybe there was something to her being this reincarnated demon prince. She hoped so, because if they were wrong she'd already seen what happened to people who tried to breach the tomb and failed.

Enoch led her down a steep ravine, which ended outside of a wide cave mouth. Inside she could see light glinting off something metallic, the lights shifting along the cave wall.

"That's it, isn't it?" she murmured, though she already knew the answer.

"Indeed. You made your final stand within, and lured countless water Wyrms to their death," he said proudly. "They will never forget the price you exacted."

"Well, that sounds lovely," she murmured, stepping into the cave. The idea that she'd been someone before wasn't terrible. Maybe that person had been better than the woman she'd become in this life.

"Enoch, since I'm probably going to die in a few minutes, would you mind answering a few questions?" She moved forward at a slow walk, eyeing the shadows in the cave, just in case.

A faint whisk-whisk sounded in the distance, like a thousand blades being sharpened. As Nara made it further up the tunnel the glinting began to match the whisk-ing, but it wasn't until she reached the entrance to a massive cavern that she put it all together.

As in her dream, platforms moved through the cavern at seemingly random intervals, hundreds of them. Every one was no more than a single layer of atoms thick. Being struck was instant death, spellarmor or no.

The density of platforms increased the closer to the center of the cavern you got, to the point where they completely obscured whatever lay at the center.

"You have got to be kidding me." Nara began rubbing her temples as she studied the ever-shifting pattern.

"You expected something different?" Enoch asked, his amusement clear. "How would you suggest hiding the legacy of a demigod for thousands of years? Leave it out in the open?"

Nara barked an unexpected laugh. "Good point. I still don't think I'm going to enjoy this. I only get one shot."

"So how will you approach it?" Enoch asked. He hobbled over to a flat, well-worn rock and sat heavily. Once seated he fluffed his wings, then turned his attention back to her.

"I'll study it." Nara sat on a similar rock, a few meters away. "There has to be a pattern, and if I can find it, then I can figure out how to get past them. I've been prepared by multiple gods specifically for this moment. My cognitive abilities increased."

"You sound a good deal like her." Enoch gave her a wink, his leathery face splitting into another smile. He seemed to have an endless supply. "She too believed everything could be solved with science and reason. She gave short shrift to intuition, which is a pity. It could have served her well, at the end."

"Trusting intuition is why everyone who has attempted this puzzle is dead. I could rush in, but I like breathing. Watch. And learn, old man." Nara teleported to the top of the cavern, and used a bit of gravity to hold herself aloft. She turned back to Enoch. "Or, you know, watch and wince if it goes awry." Nara gave him a wink, trying to pretend she felt as flippant she made it sound, and then gave herself to the task.

She was careful to stay to the edge of the cavern, well away from the path of the platforms. Now that she'd changed her perspective she saw more of them. They were effectively invisible if viewed from the wrong angle, and that would be true of other platforms as well.

Nara blinked slowly around the room, and began building a mental map of all the platforms she could see. It took some time, but eventually she was confident she'd found them all. Without Neith's gift it would have been impossible to keep it all straight, but with her abilities she had a complete mind map of the room.

"My gods," she whispered. "It's a fractal pattern. I can predict it, the outer layers at least."

"Impressive." Enoch appeared next to her, held aloft through magic since his withered wings were unequal to the task. "That's more than anyone has ever done, I think. Every poor soul I've seen brave this place has simply tried jumping from platform to platform. It ended predictably."

"I can see why." Nara bit her lip, a habit she'd not indulged in some time. "Even knowing the pattern, a single mistake means death." She released her lip, and turned an excited smile on Enoch. "Why not use *air* or *dream* to make myself ethereal? Then the platforms wouldn't hurt me."

"That one I *have* seen others think of," Enoch confided. "It did not end well. The platforms slice through magic, same as flesh. They are comprised of a material similar to the most ancient of artifacts, like Worldender."

"Got it." She teleported again, to the final location near the bottom of the cavern. It afforded a unique view, which filled in the rest of the pieces. "I'm fairly confident I can make it to the part of the pattern I can't track from the outside, but if I run into trouble once I start..."

"Then you'll die." Enoch appeared next to her once more, as she knew he would. "Your only chance will be your instincts. Your intuition. Once you are inside you will have to intuit the pattern. If you are right about this fractal, then that should hold deeper inside, yes?"

"Theoretically, but it's a depths of a thing to be wrong about."

"True." Enoch gave her an infuriating smile. "And you'll have to decide if it's worth it to unify our people."

It was.

Nara took a deep breath, then put her staff in her void pocket. She wanted her hands free. Just her and her spellarmor. "Well, here goes."

She moved to the edge of the cavern at the angle she wanted to approach from, and watched the platforms. Nara visualized the first jump, and the twist she'd have to make at the fourth platform, and the roll after the seventh.

Nara rehearsed it perhaps a dozen times, and then she jumped.

It felt rash, but also freeing. She landed on the first platform, then jumped to the second, and the third, then rolled to the fourth, where she waited for the fifth to move into range.

Over and over she vaulted from one to another, working

her way around the edges of the room. Her path meandered all over, but gradually, ever so gradually, she approached the center.

By the tenth jump she was winded. By the thirtieth she was struggling. By the fiftieth she was using *void* magic to augment her jumps. She paused, panting, as a platform carried her in a small circle. Sweat fell in a pool all around her, slicking that part of the platform.

Nara rolled off and fell fifteen meters, where she landed on a platform just as it passed. She very nearly slipped and fell, but a quick burst of *void* kept her on her feet.

She was so deep in now that platforms obscured her view of the cavern. There was no going back, even if she had the strength and endurance. She needed to finish this, and soon.

Nara gave herself to the jumps. She rolled, and moved, and anticipated, and just...flowed. It was quite unlike her, and she hated it, especially because she was forced to admit that Enoch was right.

Only intuition would save her.

She rolled suddenly, then leapt into the air just in time to dodge a platform that whizzed through the space she'd occupied.

On and on it went, until finally she spied a dark purple glow between passing platforms. That glimpse gave Nara the strength to continue, and she willed herself to move, dodging and rolling her way closer to that glow.

A hundred times she dodged death, a thousand, each time allowing it to pass within millimeters.

There!

A platform passed and she saw the source of the glow. A rifle rotated in a slow circle. Not just any rifle, either. The rifle she'd been holding in her dream. The one that could core an adult Wyrm with a single spell. One that would prove her legacy, and help them bring Xal back. The legendary Shakti.

There was the catch, though. If she jumped at the precise moment she could grab the rifle, but her fall would be uncontrolled. She might be able to arrest her momentum with *void* magic, but the odds of her surviving were slim.

Of course, Xal had known that when he'd placed the tomb. Kazon's tomb had disappeared when he'd taken the artifact. Would the traps stop her as well?

She rolled again, her time for thinking over. Nara committed. She dove for another platform, then flipped over a passing one, onto a third. She windmilled her arms to keep her balance, and the instant she had it Nara leapt into the air, augmenting the leap with *void*. She seized the spell-rifle, and began to fall.

A platform whizzed by beneath her, and she tracked its flight with a sinking feeling. She was about to die.

The platform dissolved. All the platforms dissolved. She was still falling, but the lethal death traps disappeared, and she was able to hover in the middle of the cavern, her spell-rifle held triumphantly in her hands.

She remembered the first time she'd picked up a spell-rifle again after getting her memories back. None had ever felt right...until now. She just wasn't a staff kind of girl.

"I am impressed," Enoch said as he appeared in the air next to her. "Come, I will take you back to my people. I think you will find them quite receptive now. All demons remember the rifle Shakti, and the list of gods it has killed."

32

SABRA

Aran waited inside the mecha, and wished that he had something more productive he could be doing. Nara would be back soon. Kazon was busy instructing his oni 'children', inevitably surrounded by dozens of attentive ogres, begging for more stories.

If Nara succeeded they'd have enough support to approach the jin, though he wasn't certain what would be involved. Probably a duel.

The mecha vibrated and Kazon appeared in his command couch. He reeked of alcohol, strongly enough that it burned Aran's eyes.

"Ugg." Aran pinched his nose. "How much of that stuff did you have to down before you couldn't smell it anymore?"

"I don't want to know what was in it, but it does erode your problems," Kazon replied, a beatific smile plastered on his face. "The oni are ready to help us resurrect a dark god, so we can kill a...darker god." Kazon adopted a quizzical expression.

A moment later Nara appeared in her command couch. At this point Aran couldn't buy the coincidence. Everything they were doing felt scripted by some deity, most likely Xal, down to the millisecond. Both comforting and terrifying.

Nara held a new weapon, a sleek long-barreled sniper rifle of a design he wasn't familiar with. The barrel was long and slender, and the body had been artfully designed with smooth curves, and a simple trigger guard.

Shakti, Narlifex thrummed. *The legendary rifle of the gods. Old. Powerful.*

How do you recognize it? Aran thought to the blade. *This thing has been in the tomb since before you were created.*

Memory comes from blood of Xal. I hold the memory of our people. I know many things. I have lived and died countless times.

That gave Aran something to think about. He'd taken the blood from the pool mostly by instinct, but perhaps it was more important than he'd thought.

"Nara, that weapon," Kazon breathed. "It is exquisite. Amazing. And Ancient. So ancient. I have never seen the like."

"It's also the very thing we needed to get the eru on board." She delivered a proud smile. "They're willing to follow us. Enoch has sent a missive to the jin saying they'll be sending us as emissaries."

"Who now?" Aran asked, fairly certain he'd never met anyone by that name.

"No one special." She gave him an amused smile. "Just a million-year-old eru. Apparently he advised Xal during his time as a mortal, and has served as the Memory of Xal ever since."

"Oh." Aran blinked. A century he could conceive of. A millennia made sense. A million years? "Whole species have evolved and died out while this guy was living on the husk? Let's hope the jin respect their elders."

"Graal has sent a similar missive on behalf of the oni."

Kazon's smile grew a little wider, if possible. At least he wasn't acting like an ancient scholar.

"Guess that means we're out of excuses. Let's go meet the jin." Aran didn't mention how this whole place, the rotting body and every demon on it, made his skin crawl. Their casual savagery wasn't any worse than the Krox, but it was still shocking to adjust to. He just wanted to go home, whatever that meant. "Kazon, you want to change us back to a corvette and I'll pilot us to the chest cavity?"

"Of course, brother." Kazon set down a flask he'd been about to drink from, and a tendril attached to his forehead from the orb. "Oh, that is not doing good things to my stomach."

Aran felt the mecha shift, and as soon as it became a ship he took control and piloted it up and away from oni territory. The demons all stared wordlessly up at them as they went, and Aran had no idea if they wanted to kill them or worship them.

He guided the craft up and away from Xal, circling wide around the torso as he made for the chest cavity. A tremendous wound had torn open the chest, and a hellish purple glow, not unlike the one from the skull, came from within.

"Looks like that's the place." He flew unerringly for the cavity, and gently guided them inside. To his shock nearly every meter of the interior bore some form of construction. Those areas that did not provided illumination, as the interior lining blazed an angry violet, enough to see by, though probably not to read.

Entire modern cities had been built, dozens of them all made from a dark alloy that disappeared into the tissue at the edges of the cavity. The most surprising structure within that city was a thriving spaceport, which contained a half dozen sleek craft that were somehow more modern than he expected.

"That seems like a good place to land. Nara, maybe try sending them a missive, since you're a reincarnated demon prince?"

Nara nodded. "I'll put on my commander face."

Aran guided the craft into a smooth landing at the edge of the spaceport, and winced when he noticed a knot of armored jin walking over. They wore ornate spellarmor with large, steel-grey shoulders, and layer after layer of hastily repaired battle damage. These guys had been through the thick of it. Often.

"Guess we're about to find out how much parking costs." Aran touched the ship's wall and appeared outside.

Nara appeared a heartbeat behind him, and shot him a low whisper. "Kazon passed out. We're on our own."

"Lovely," Aran muttered. It could be worse, he supposed.

A trio of large purple-skinned demons were approaching. All wore armor, traditional body armor, and carried spellrifles. They looked a good deal like the eru, minus the wings and tail, but with much, much more muscle mass. Even Crewes would have had had good things to say about the jin's workout regimen.

"Who are you, interloper?" One of the demons demanded. She stepped in front of Aran, and glared down at him with void-touched eyes. He'd put the jin at three meters, and didn't spot any weak points on her dark armor.

He noted the curved spellblade belted at the demon's side, within easy reach, but not yet drawn. The hilt was wrapped in something like sandpaper, which looked like it had been replaced recently.

"Well that's the reincarnation of Kali," Aran said, jerking a thumb in Nara's direction, "and I'm a Hound of Xal. We've come to speak to whoever your leader is about resurrecting our father."

"Lower your voice," the lead demon snapped, darting a glance at the other two demons. "Such things are not uttered lightly. Not if you wish to keep your head attached to your shoulders. Who are you? And what is your species? I do not recognize you."

"We're humans," Nara supplied, "And he is telling the truth. I am the vengeance reborn." Nara held her rifle aloft, and the lead guard gasped. "I see you recognize Shakti. Within this mecha we also carry the reincarnation of Gorr."

The demon eyed Nara as if uncertain if she were making fun of him. After a few moments she seemed to decide she was on the level.

"Very well," she said, glancing again at the other guards, "I will take you into custody, for your protection. The attempts on your life will begin as fast as the word of your mission spreads, and will not stop until you are dead. We must get you to Malazra before then."

"Malazra?" Aran asked. The name was vaguely familiar.

"She is a Hound of Xal, and the last of the surviving princes." She puffed up a bit at that, as if Malazra's fortunes were tied to his own. "She will know what to do. How to present your claims in a way that will not fracture our people even further."

"What about our ship?" Aran asked, nodding at the vessel.

"It should be safe here. I see no means of gaining entry. And unless you can shrink it and bring it with us...then it must stay." She gave them a tentative smile. "I am called Sabra. Come, I will escort you to my mistress."

33

IMPOSSIBLE SHOT

Aran trailed after Sabra as she crept up pitted stone steps that were a little too large for a human. Nara came next, with the remaining two guards bringing up the rear.

They moved low and quiet, though the jin carried enough gear that the jingle of harnesses and scrape of armor against stone still carried. Aran thought they were far too loud and too obvious, right up until he heard the first exchange of spell fire in the distance.

The void bolts flashed a few blocks over, quickly followed by screams and explosions. What surprised him was that they weren't only using magic.

"Are those projectile weapons?" he called to Sabra, just loud enough to carry.

She shot him a patient look through her faceplate. "Keep quiet, or we'll all find out the hard way. Those are automatic weapons. They use a bit of *void* to propel bits of whatever ammunition the user has handy. Bone, usually. Metal sometimes. Neither is worth being on the receiving end of. The weapons are easy to maintain and power, and making munitions has become an art form."

Aran nodded, and kept silent. He appreciated her willingness to answer his question, but also understood that keeping conversation to a minimum increased their odds of getting through this alive.

He was shocked that the heart of the demonic civilization had fallen to such ruin. Every structure they passed had some battle damage, most old or even ancient. No one had ever taken the time to repair it. This was a civilization in continuous collapse.

They reached the top of the stairs, which opened into a narrow cavern with only one tunnel at the opposite end. Sabra had paused at the top, and made a series of hand gestures to the pair below. Look. Danger. That was Aran's take anyway.

He crept up and scanned the cavern. This was the perfect place for an ambush. Several burned out hovercraft littered the area, providing excellent cover for snipers. An iron gate lay on the far side, blocking their exit through the tunnel. Aran assumed that Sabra had the key.

The jin officer made another gesture to her unit, then turned and sprinted across the cavern, toward the gate. The instant Sabra crossed the midway point their enemies struck.

A trio of darkly armored hovertanks shimmered into existence, their frames battered and corroded from uncounted centuries of use. Each bore a wide spellcannon not unlike the modern confederate version.

At the same time demons in equally battered body armor popped up behind several of the burned out vehicles, each holding either a spellrifle or spellcannon.

All were aimed at Sabra, and while Aran didn't know what her capabilities were, he had a hard time imagining anyone surviving that kind of assault without help.

He had a split second to act. They had no idea what the political structure of the jin was, or what the consequences of allying with Sabra and whoever this Malazra were.

Aran made a choice.

He blurred forward, kicking off the pavement and into the air. Aran snapped his left wrist down to activate his spellshield, then ripped Narlifex from his sheath.

All three hovertanks fired in rapid succession, void bolts converging on Sabra. Void bolts, and not disintegrates.

Aran flew into the path of the spells, and snapped his shield up to block the first spell, then down to block the second. The third caught Sabra in the chest, and flung her into a crumbling wall, which shattered into rubble.

Aran channeled his momentum into a throw, and hurled Narlifex at the tank that had hit Sabra. The sword grew heavier in the air, and by the time it reached the tank it was as dense as a star. The sword punched through the hover-tank, and the tank exploded spectacularly.

He was about to fetch his spellrifle from the void pocket when Nara teleported. She appeared in midair at an angle that provided a perfect shot at the remaining tanks. Nara raised her spellrifle, and fired the thickest, most potent disintegrate any spellrifle had ever fired.

The spell boiled away the first tank, and continued to the second, then dissolved the wall behind them. All of a sudden Aran understood why there was so much battle damage. When you had demons and demigods tussling, it wasn't good for the surrounding terrain.

The surviving demons turned to run, but Sabra exploded from the rubble that had buried her into the air.

She ripped a spellpistol from her holster and gunned down the furthest demon, then landed next to the closest and decapitated it with a quick slash from her spellblade.

Aran raised a palm toward the last surviving demon, and increased the gravity around him a hundred fold. The demon was instantly crushed flat, and Aran winced. "Guess I used a little too much. I was trying to get a prisoner."

"No need," Sabra panted as she cleaned her sword with a rag she'd ripped from one of the demon's cloaks. "Their sigil was emblazoned on the tank. They're Proud Shayatin, one of a dozen local factions vying for this territory. The Proud are trying to control the tunnel leading to Malazra's estate, and if they can secure access, then they control who she gets to see. It would mean the end of her power, effectively."

"Then it's a good thing we broke the ambush." Nara drifted down to a graceful landing next to Aran. Her rifle was nearly as tall as she was, and even more intimidating up close. "Shouldn't we get moving?"

"Yes, but there isn't as much rush now." Sabra pointed across the cavern and up the tunnel. The purplish light of the veins in the walls provided just enough illumination to make out the single demon sprinting away. "Their spotter will report back, and then—"

"No he won't." Nara raised her rifle to her shoulder, and made the impossible shot. A narrow beam of negative space, the essence of the void, pierced the tunnel wall, disintegrating a path to her target.

The beam caught the runner in the back of the skull, even though Nara couldn't see him. He'd been behind a wall, but she'd tracked his flight so well she'd known where he'd be before he arrived.

Aran just blinked at her. "Wow."

Sabra shook her head. “I can scarcely believe it. You are everything that you promised. Only a demon prince could fight as you do. Come, let us get you to Malazra as swiftly as possible.”

34

UNDER FIRE

Kazon woke up with the most terrible headache. He wasn't fond of pain, and generally reacted badly. He'd be terrible at being tortured.

"Where's that flask?" he muttered, patting the leather around him. He found the wrappers from a pair of cookies and cream protein bars, but it took several moments to identify the pain under his right thigh as the flask. "Ah, there you are."

He was about to take a sip when the corvette shook. Something rumbled outside, and it shook again.

"Are we under attack?" He blinked blearily up at the golden orb. It didn't answer, of course. Oh, how he missed having a verbal interface.

Kazon closed his eyes, which proved a mistake. Everything threatened to come up, so he opened them. Thankfully, the ship had apparently sensed his need, and a golden tendril snaked from the orb.

He swatted at it instinctively as it approached, but the tendril dodged him and connected to his forehead. The interior vanished, and he was suddenly perceiving through the ship.

The regret was immediate. Tanks had surrounded them, and a steady staccato of void bolts was slamming into the hull. Those had, thus far, seemed to have no effect, which spoke highly of the built-in warding Inura had created.

The rocking came from more conventional cannons, which were firing hunks of stone the size of a desk. Those were doing slightly more damage, but it amounted to little more than scraping the paint.

Kazon took a deep, steadying breath. "This is bad." His stomach roiled, but he managed to hold in the contents.

He focused on communication, and thankfully found that the ship was still linked to both Aran and Nara. He had no *fire* magic, and so could not send a missive otherwise.

"Aran," he sent through the tendril, "I am under assault. The ship is in no immediate danger, I think, but I don't know what to—"

Kazon was suddenly and violently ill, all over Nara's command couch. *Oh, no.* He'd never clean it up before she got back.

"How long can you hold out?" Aran's voice came back, his tone distracted.

He wiped at his mouth and tried not to look at the mess he'd made. "I will find out."

Kazon focused on the system. Presumably there must be some sort of magic level to the wards so you knew when they were depleted.

He quested around, and eventually a graph popped up. It showed the shield's magic sloping downward. It was still green, but it looked like it would pass into yellow soon. The graph went into red far more quickly than he'd have liked.

"I have about fifteen minutes, I think." Kazon watched the graph continue to tick.

"Take the ship back to the oni," Aran gave back, almost immediately. "If Nara and I need an evac I'll send you a missive. Get yourself to safety."

"As long as you and Nara will be okay. I do not wish to abandon you." The graph ticked into the yellow. At least he'd have enough time to clean the mess.

"You're not abandoning us. We're almost to Malazra's sanctuary. Get clear, brother. We're going to see the oni soon. See that they're ready for war."

"Be well, brother." Kazon killed the connection, and willed the corvette to lift off. He was confident a single strafing run would kill the demons attacking him, but beyond making them pay for his hangover he couldn't think of a compelling reason to kill them. They weren't a threat.

Kazon guided the corvette into the air, and began retracing their steps back to the oni.

35

MALAZRA

Aran and Nara were led up the tunnel past the cavern, which ended at a secure compound built into the thickest part of the ribcage. The bleak white structure was a veritable fortress, and he noted a good half dozen cannon emplacements. This place was ready for war.

Sabra marched up the path toward the front gate, and seemed unconcerned as every spellcannon trained on their group. She walked straight to the front door, and knocked a precise seven times, at even intervals.

Two answering knocks sounded from within.

Sabra knocked again, then three more times.

The door opened, and revealed a trio of jin guards in the same armor as their escort.

"We feared the worst," a man was saying. He pressed his forehead to Sabra's, and the pair closed eyes as they shared a moment.

"As did I." Sabra pointed at Aran, then at Nara. "I would be dead if not for them. That is Aran, a Hound of Xal, and Nara, the reincarnation of Kali. This is my husband, Jerich."

Sabra's husband darted a skeptical glance at their party, but didn't contradict his wife out loud. "Of course they are. And I am the memory. She's expecting you, but she is...not doing well. She is feeling harried, and has lashed out again."

Jerich led them inside a spacious, but practical, entryway. Murder holes lined the second floor high above them, and would allow mages to rain death from complete safety. The room itself was all marble and granite, which insulated it to a degree, and made it difficult for potential attackers to reach the defenders.

They ascended a wide staircase, and Aran relied on *void* to drift above the stairs, rather than make the awkward little jumps. Nara did the same, and drifted into a parallel course with him.

"I'm wondering if we're backing the winning side," she whispered over the comm. "If this is their demon prince, I am not impressed."

Aran reserved judgement, but only for the time being. "Let's hope she has more pull than it appears, or we're going to have to look elsewhere."

Sabra and Jerich turned up a hallway at the top of the stairs, which emptied into a wide sitting chamber lined with plush couches. A fire roared in a marble hearth, and Aran sensed that the flame was enchanted.

Only one couch was occupied. A bespectacled jin sat, ramrod straight, with a book held in her hands, held so as not to crease the pages. The woman delivered a level look to Sabra, but did not speak. The dignified jin could have been Malila's wingless twin, though her features were a touch more angular.

"Forgive the intrusion, Prince Malazra." Sabra executed a practiced bow from the waist. "I thought it prudent to disturb you. This news warrants it."

"Yes, I can see that." Malazra deliberately removed her glasses and set them on a floating oaken stand next to the couch. She gently closed the book, and set it next to the glasses, before finally turning her attention back to them. "I can feel the power coming from these creatures, though I don't recognize their species. Who are they, and why are they worth bringing into my presence?"

Sabra fell to one knee, and bowed her head. "Highness, I present Nara, Vengeance of Xal, and Aran, Hound of Xal. You are no longer alone. And they have arrived with the guardian."

Malazra studied them again, this time seemingly with fresh eyes. She met Aran's gaze, and gave him a nod of respect. "Brother. I see that what she says is true. It has been long since another hound was called. I have been alone for far too long."

Aran didn't point out that Malila was still alive, and that she was most definitely a Hound of Xal. No sense stirring the pot.

Malazra turned to Nara, and gave a deep bow of respect. "I should have recognized your weapon immediately. How did you defeat the tomb?"

"Math and intuition." Nara rested the barrel of her rifle on her shoulder, and moved to sit on one of the couches, which was designed for someone far larger. She somehow managed dignified. "We've risked a lot to be here, but we've brought the oni and the eru. You have to know why we've come."

"Of course. Every demon on the husk knows." She cocked her head. "The trouble is...the resurrection is a myth. Making that myth a reality? That's a good deal more difficult than simply willing it so."

"We're aware of the immensity of the task," Aran said,

moving to another couch. "Respectfully, it looks like you barely control the land outside your front door."

A mixture of embarrassment and anger flitted across Malazra's face, but it was gone quickly. "You are not wrong, and I take no insult, though it stings to hear aloud. It has been too long since someone was willing to voice a contrary opinion."

Aran glanced through the window and noticed a blocky grey spellfighter; unsurprisingly, it was of unknown design. Just large enough for one person. An escape vehicle? That didn't fill him with confidence.

"So what will it take to unify your people?" Aran demanded, as politely as he could manage.

"I don't know." Malazra exhaled slowly, and looked like she'd rather be elsewhere. "It's true. I do not control the jin. I am no leader. I am a hound, like you." She nodded at Aran. "We are tools of destruction. We are not leaders."

"So we need a leader," Nara pointed out. "What about Enoch? He seemed old and wise. Is he respected enough?"

Malazra snorted a laugh. "That would be nearly as bad as inviting Malila back. No, very few would follow Enoch. He is no warrior, nor has he been in my lifetime. From what I gather he was a friend of Xal's when Xal was a mortal, and has advised him ever since. Enoch was the original Memory of Xal, and has never been replaced. Having him speak for a leader would be good, but that leader still needs to be a warrior they can respect."

"And that's not you?" Aran asked. She seemed the obvious candidate. "Not even if we support you, alongside Enoch?"

She laughed. "Perhaps I could seize control, but I couldn't hold it. I am not nearly diplomatic enough. We need someone strong, wise, and with enough of a backbone that the other princes cannot push her around. That isn't me. If it's one of you, then you'll have my allegiance, so long as you can truly bring back Xal."

Aran considered that. None of them were uniquely qualified to lead, and besides, he was already a hound, and Nara the vengeance. They needed someone to step up and become this voice, from the sound of it.

36

FEAST

Kazon set down just outside Graal's longhouse, and wasn't surprised to see that the oni had already begun to gather. He touched the side of the ship, and appeared next to its base. Chants of 'story, story' began immediately.

"In good time, my children," Kazon bellowed. The oni began to fall quiet. "I must meet with Graal. The time for war will come soon, and we must stand ready."

Kazon felt the shift within him. His walk became more stately. More dignified. He was the embodiment of his forebear, Gorr. Gorr had been a master craftsman, a deliberate politician, and an indifferent Kem'Hedj player.

He glanced down at the gauntlet, which he barely noticed most times. It was so innocuous, but there was so much power contained within it. He didn't pretend to understand what it meant, or what it could do, but he knew that it would be important. He knew that what he remembered of Gorr's life would be important.

Kazon didn't enjoy having his personality encroached on, but after having one's memory hollowed out with a mind wipe spell, this was nothing. At least he could remember who he was.

He crossed the interior of the longhouse and stopped before Graal's throne. The towering oni stared down at him, expression all adoration, as it had been ever since he'd accepted that Kazon was his master reborn.

"Graal, the time has come for war," Kazon explained, channeling Gorr's stateliness. "We must prepare."

"Time for flesh!" Graal pumped a fist in the air.

Every last oni mimicked the gesture, and all began chanting the word flesh. It had a ritual feel to it, though neither Gorr nor Kazon recognized it. He looked to Graal and nodded, hoping that was the sign Graal was looking for.

It was, apparently. The chanting stopped as Graal rose. He leapt from his throne, and the ground quaked when he landed a hundred meters away. Graal bounded across the ground in long strides, sprinting deeper into the wound that tunneled into Xal's leg.

A large oni Kazon didn't know picked him up and placed him on her shoulder, then joined the throng following Graal. They flowed inside Xal's leg, deep within a wound that had been burrowed through the calf muscle.

They stopped at what looked like the sight of a fresh feeding. The place reeked like a slaughterhouse, and fat flies buzzed everywhere.

Graal made for a hunk of exposed flesh, and ripped off a fistful. He bit off a hunk, and then tossed it to the crowd. That seemed to be some sort of signal, and the oni swarmed the room.

Kazon's temporary mount set him down, and went off to join the feeding frenzy. Kazon watched in horror and disgust. The oni were literally eating their father's body, which to them seemed to be a sacred act.

"Gorr!" Graal yelled, face smeared with fresh blood. "You feast too."

And there it was. The Gorr part of Kazon understood that these demons would not follow him if he didn't eat. The mage-engineer in him understood that eating the flesh would change him physically. He'd be stronger and tougher, but there was a very real chance that doing so would impact his intellect, and not in a good way.

"Gorr eat too!" Kazon yelled back, and moved to a fresh wound. He removed a laser-knife from his boot sheath, and used it to slice away a morsel. It looked like beef, which he loved.

Kazon popped it in his mouth, and began to chew. He hoped it did lower his intellect. Ignorance was bliss.

37

10,000 ONI

Aran stared down at the table, impressed by the illusory map of Xal's heart, or the space where it should have been anyway. The map perfectly captured the cavity and showed where all the various factions were based, and where their respective areas of influence extended.

"As you can see", Malazra was explaining, "We have plenty of magical power. We have my fortress. We have arms and armor. What we are lacking is competent demons. Other factions have gradually bled away our support, and we simply lack the numbers we used to have."

Aran drummed his fingers along the edge of the table as he studied and tried to find a way out of this, tactically speaking. "It looks like there are four major districts, and a host of minor ones. Which one would you say is your greatest rival?"

Malazra tapped a section of the map with a purple overlay. "This is house Vakkoru. They are without a doubt my greatest rivals, and the ones with a realistic chance of deposing me. They lack the magical firepower, but have the bodies. You can see the conundrum."

"And who is their leader?" Aran asked, focusing his attention on that part of the map. "Looks like they're sandwiched between a rib and a weaker neighbor."

"They're led by a brute of a jin named Kahaka." Malazra frowned. "She's no match for us in a straight fight, but reaching her would be nearly impossible. I don't see how we can accomplish it."

"That's where we come in." Aran studied the manor where this Kahaka lived. "You want to take down Kahaka? You draft the oni. Give them weapons and armor. Create a... police force, if you will. Then, use that police force to assault your enemies. We hit Kahaka's manor and wipe them out. Show the rest of the jin that you are restoring order, which means you're doing something, and at the same time show them what happens if they don't cooperate."

"Bold," Malazra allowed as she leaned over the map, "but you may not understand how this will influence us culturally. If I bring the oni into the cavity, then many will see that as a betrayal."

"Of course," Aran agreed. He gave a grim smile. "That's why you'll be providing them with an even greater enemy to focus on."

"What do you have in mind?" Malazra leaned back, and watched Aran cautiously.

"Once you've dealt with Kahaka I will send a missive to your sister," Aran explained. "She will translocate the Skull of Xal into this system, so the people can see the resurrection is imminent."

Malazra's eyes narrowed to slits, and her entire body tightened. "You want to involve my sister?"

"How badly do you want to win this war?" Nara

demanded, speaking for the first time. "We can hardly bring a headless Xal to fight Nefarius. If you want to win, then we need your sister, like it or not. I've worked with people I hate, and you're going to have to learn to do the same."

"You are right." Malazra gave a very put-upon sigh. "And I knew this day would come, eventually. I do not wish to see Malila again. Not ever. But I suppose it was always inevitable. Very well. I will take your counsel. Send word to your ally, the reincarnated Gorr. Tell him to prepare ten thousand of his best oni. I will have weapons and armor sent, and I will send jin officers to guide them. We will strike at dawn."

"Will you need us there?" Aran asked. "We might make a difference. Sabra can tell you what we can do."

"No." Malazra's eyes narrowed again. "I am a hound, Aran, just as you are. I deal with my problems harshly. I will not have it said I relied on another prince. Make no mistake. My rival will die. You get Malila here. I will tend to the rest."

38

YANTHARA

Crewes had flown the black for long enough that the depths didn't phase him. He'd done it on dozens of vessels, including the *Wyrm Hunter* and the *Talon*. This was the first time he'd been in charge, though.

Not that it meant doing anything differently. Everyone knew their role. They knew what they were supposed to be doing, and did it. The only discipline case they'd ever really had was Bord, but since Kez...well, that poor kid had become the model soldier.

"Bord, open us up a Fissure," Crewes ordered, trying to sound like Major Voria. "Rhea, once we're in I want you to send a missive to arrange docking. I've got business ground side. Anyone else need to leave the ship?"

In the old days Bord would have been first in line for shore leave, but no one spoke up. Rhea kept to herself, mostly, and Bord did now too. Ever since they'd dropped Davidson off the ship had been a damned tomb.

"Aye, sir." Bord's hands flew across the rings, and a Fissure cracked the sky.

Crewes guided the *Talon* back into normal space, and breathed a bit easier when he saw Yanthara. He'd left his home world to outrun expectations, but it had always comforted him to know she was out there, untouched by war.

No matter what shit had gone down, from Starn to Marid, Yanthara had always been fine. His home had always been all right.

That wasn't gonna be the case any more, though. Crewes had puzzled that part out. Nefarius was pretty straightforward, and she thought a lot like your typical warlord. She was taking all the pieces off the board, and eating the pieces to get stronger in the process.

And Yanthara had two of the pieces. Shi, the goddess of dream, and Van, the god of flame. That represented a lot of magic, and sooner, probably, rather than later, Nefarius was gonna come for that magic.

When she did, it was his job to make sure this world was ready. There was only so much he could do, but it would start with making sure these people knew what they were facing, and were ready to resist.

"Captain, we're cleared for landing," Rhea said, her tone crisp as always. "Do you have a destination?"

"Yeah, tell them we'll be landing at the Temple of Shi." Crewes squirmed in the command couch. He hadn't told Serala they were coming. Was that bad? Shit, he didn't know how this stuff worked. "Uh, and I'm going to head to my quarters. Rhea, set us down in the same place where we picked you up. You remember that?"

"Copy that, Captain." Rhea nodded, and tapped all three *fire* sigils to take primary control of the ship. "I'll inform you when we land."

Crewes exited the bridge and headed for his quarters. He could have taken the captain's rooms, but he liked his, and they were plenty big enough. Besides, it would take time and effort to move them.

He sat down at his desk, and knocked a couple beer cans from in front of the scry-screen. Serala was a proper lady and wouldn't appreciate his, uh, gruffer side.

He tapped the *fire* sigil, and waited for the missive to connect. He had no idea if she'd answer. He was fairly sure she remembered the old days, and that she might even like him like he liked her.

"Linus." Serala's smiling face filled the screen, minus the veil she'd been wearing last time. She was a more handsome version of the woman she'd been when they were kids. "You caught me before I leave for the temple. What brings you back to Yanthara?" Her smile slipped. "I know you do not believe this tripe about the war being over, so it is not to see me, is it?"

"I'm sorry, Serala. I mean, I *am* here to see you," he got out, then closed his eyes and started again. "What I mean is I'm still focused on the war right now. You're right. It ain't over. The Fist was a major loss for the good guys, and nobody seems to even realize it."

"I know, better than any." She leaned closer to the scry-screen, and her eyes grew wet with unshed tears. "And I know more of the cost, though I am forbidden to speak of it. Oh, Linus, I am so sorry for what is to come."

"Don't be." How did one even respond to that? "We can only do what we can do. People are gonna die. Bad shit is gonna happen. I don't want to know about it, Serala, so don't tell me. I'll face my death on my feet, but I don't want to see it coming, and then just lay there waiting for it, ya know?"

"Of course." She wiped at an eye. "Come, visit me. I will be ready by the time you arrive and we will discuss how to approach the coming days. Our people need us, Linus. They need us both."

"Course. I'll be there soon." He allowed the missive to die, took a deep breath, and tried to decide what to wear.

39

MIRACLE

Nefarius paused outside the golden doorway leading into the facility her younger brother had built so many millennia before. The Crucible existed in many realities at once, and could forge incredible wonders, because it could reach places where the impossible was possible, and bring the results back to a lab for testing and integration.

She lacked the ability to properly utilize such a facility, of course. Even if she'd taken Inura's *life* magic, it wouldn't have imbued her with the artificing knowledge he'd spent countless millennia acquiring.

Nefarius stifled her anger as she stepped across the threshold, the servos in her legs whirring as she moved up the corridor. She ignored the walls, which were lined with glyphs. She didn't understand the magic, and that irked her.

No traps detonated. No automatons attacked. There wasn't even a shade to greet her. Nefarius walked through the facility, poking her head into workshops and taking a long moment to inspect the hangar where she presumed the *Spellship* had once lain.

When she'd completed her circuit she was forced to admit that the place had been abandoned, which made no sense to her.

"Talifax, attend me." She waited, and not for long.

Talifax appeared and dropped into a kneeling position. "Yes, mistress?"

"I have questions." She turned from the hangar, and gestured at the hallway leading back into the facility. "This place is incredibly advanced. The *Spellship* was created here. And Ikadra, the key. And who knows what other wonders. It even contains a temporal matrix."

"Yes, mistress. All true."

"So why would my brother abandon it? Why leave it for his enemies? Couldn't he have cloaked it or destroyed it?" That part puzzled her, and put her guard up. Was this all somehow a trap she wasn't seeing? Her brother had been crafty on a level no one but her had ever really understood.

Everyone else had underestimated the shrewd Wyrm.

"This place is greater than any conflict, mistress," Talifax explained, humbly of course. He didn't rise, and kept his large form pressed to the tiles. "It can and will birth countless more wonders, and I don't think a craftsman, such as Inura, is capable of destroying such a wonder. Even Virkonna likely wouldn't, though I'm not sure anyone but Inura even could destroy this place."

"Interesting." Nefarius found that line of logic troubling. What did it matter if this place existed after Inura's death? He wasn't around to see what happened, yet still valued a future he would never see. "You're skilled with these matters. Take me to the temporal matrix."

"Of course, mistress." Talifax rose to his feet, and started up a corridor. The sorcerer moved swiftly and silently, despite the bulk. "It is not far."

He led her through several criss-crossing corridors, until they finally reached a spacious chamber with a single device near the center. It strongly resembled a ship's spell matrix, though this one was far more ornate, far more complex, and possessed an additional ring.

"What use do you have planned, mistress?"

Sudden paranoia welled up within her. Nefarius stepped carefully into the matrix. The very instant she'd linked with it she rounded on Talifax, and her arm shot through the bars of the temporal matrix. Nefarius encircled his thick neck so swiftly the sorcerer had no time to react. She waited, expectantly, for him to realize his predicament.

"I cannot translocate. That should be impossible to block." His tone was calmer than she'd have liked. She'd hoped to provoke him into some sort of reaction.

"I'm standing in a temporal matrix," she explained as her grip began to tighten. The enchanted metal around Talifax's throat began to buckle. "Finding the possibility where you lack the ability to translocate was simple. Imagine what else I could do."

"Are—" Talifax choked out, "you going to kill me?"

"No." She released him, and withdrew her arm back into the matrix. "But I want to remind you that I can. If I ever, for even a moment, suspect that you are working for them..."

"Mistress." Talifax raised a hand to inspect the finger marks she'd left in his armor. "I understand that you suspect everyone, and rightfully so. Their agents are everywhere. But why would I align myself with them? They seek to devour creation. Every possibility. Every reality. How does that profit me? It is not required that you respect me for us to work together, but surely you can see I have no motivation."

"I suppose you're right." Robotic eyes whirred as they

narrowed. "But the threat stands. Be certain I don't learn you're betraying me."

"Of course, mistress. Is it impertinent to ask what you intend to use the matrix for?"

"I'm going to ensure my victory," she explained, deciding to keep the rest to herself. "I will use this device to secure the loyalty of Ternus, and every human throughout the sector."

Talifax allowed a long pause before speaking. "And how will you do that, mistress?"

Nefarius ignored the question. "One of my brother's most clever stratagems was hiding the *Spellship* in a distant, highly improbable, possibility. He knew I'd never be able to reach it, not without the help of greater divination."

"I'm not following, mistress." Talifax sounded genuinely confused, which pleased her immensely. "You plan to use this same strategy somehow?"

"In a way," she confirmed. Nefarius walked toward the temporal matrix, which gleamed under the soft enchanted lights along the ceiling. She ducked carefully inside, noting that the matrix had been built to accommodate a human, not a Wyrm. Odd, that. "Almost every possibility exists somewhere. The less likely that possibility, the more difficult it is to find, even with a temporal matrix."

Her fingers flew across the sigils, activating all eight aspects as she began her quest.

"I'm seeking a very specific possibility, one that is actually quite likely." Nefarius continued to activate sigils, and the domed ceiling began to glow more brightly.

Eventually it faded, and they appeared to be in the void, surrounded by countless galaxies. Nefarius concentrated, and the universe flickered around them. Nothing was different to the naked eye, of course, but she'd shifted their point of view to another universe.

"This place is...the same," Talifax mused. "But we are in the past. Several decades." He cocked his head. "Fifty-six standard cycles."

"Too far." Nefarius frowned and activated several more sigils. The ceiling flared to life, and the galaxies returned. Again she guided them into another reality.

The glow died.

"We are still in the past. Roughly two years before the present date." Talifax approached the matrix. "I begin to understand a part of your plan. You are returning to a specific point in the past, presumably in search of a tool."

"Ahh, Talifax." Nefarius continued pressing sigils, and the rings spun more rapidly around her. "You are so clever, but you do not see everything."

No one could predict what she was about to do, or how it would change the future. The ripples this action would send out would have far-reaching consequences for decades. If she pulled it off, she would be the undisputed ruler of the sector, her worship unquestioned.

She focused again, always seeking a specific marker. Somewhere out there existed a possibility where time moved slower than it did here, almost imperceptibly slower, but was the same in every other way.

The possibilities she'd already located were examples, but she needed to return to...there.

Krox loomed over Ternus and billions of citizens peered up in horror as the god prepared the spell that would doom their world. Nefarius admired the cruelty of it, doubling the gravity of an entire world. It had broken the back of humanity in this sector, and they'd never recover their dominance again.

Nefarius closed her eyes, and reached for her body in orbit. It was flush with newly acquired *air* magic, and *fire*, and *spirit*. But most of all it was flush with *void*, the aspect she needed for the feat she was about to achieve.

She reached for Ternus, the entire planet. She didn't take the objects in orbit, only the world itself, the atmosphere, and everything in that atmosphere. Nefarius used *void*, immense quantities, and she tore the world from its reality, depositing it in their own.

Oceans of magic flowed into the temporal matrix, which began to shake, until it emitted a high-pitched ringing sound. Nefarius poured still more magic into the matrix, and willed this bit of another reality to merge with their own.

Forcing such a change was the epitome of a divine act, possibly only with a great artifact, immense magic, and sheer will. Nefarius used all of those things, pouring everything of herself into the idea that this world was now a part of their reality.

Finally, an eternity later, the spell reached its crescendo. The lights flickered above, and then dimmed as the matrix powered down. The rings slowed, and Nefarius dropped to her knees.

An android could not feel exhaustion, not physically, but it impacted her in other ways.

"What have you done?" Talifax whispered, his voice thick with reverence.

"I have rescued the people of Ternus," Nefarius explained as she rose to her feet. "Four billion souls just returned to our reality. To them, Krox was just in the sky about to obliterate their world. No time has passed. I've saved them. Their friends and their families, and all those in orbit? Now they get to be reunited with those who they thought they'd lost. I've given them back their people, and they will love me for it. Soon, when I am ready, they will tear down their heroes and deliver them to me."

40

JOURNEY

Enoch picked up his satchel, and slid it into the void pocket he'd anchored to his inner coat lining, and prepared to depart on his first journey in nearly a million years. That was an inconceivable amount of time to most species, much less to an individual. The vast majority of beings who styled themselves gods couldn't claim to have lived so long.

But he was the Memory of Xal. It was in his nature to remember, and to try to offer counsel based on that memory. Or that had been the plan anyway. In practice his role had been largely ceremonial, and Xal had never relied on his council.

Enoch had lived out on the wing, alone for much of his life. Over time other eru had come to study with him, assuming he had some secret wisdom. They'd become their own tribe, all without his notice or interest.

He'd watched as Xal had raised his first demonic host. He'd known the first crop of demon princes personally. He'd grown up alongside many of them, in a world that had known nothing of the universe at large, or their place in it. To them the stars were just the stars.

He'd watched that first crop of demon lords fall in battle, and seen their replacements rise, and fall, and rise, and fall. It had been endless, and after the first ten millennia or so he'd staked out a little claim on the left wing.

Enoch had dutifully come whenever his master had called, of course. He served as he was able. But he didn't claim to understand Xal in life, much less in godhood. For all his advanced age, Enoch wasn't a god. He was merely immortal, and the difference mattered more than non-immortals realized.

Since Xal's death, no one had cared what he thought. Now, though, what he thought finally mattered. He knew what Xal was trying to do, and how Xal was trying to do it. All the pieces were here, but someone had to arrange them into the right image.

Enoch didn't use magic. Instead, he walked from his quarters and ambled down the sloped wing until he reached the very tip, the highest point. Enoch flared his desiccated wings behind him, straightening and stretching them until he worked feeling back into the appendages. They weren't much to look at, but they were still wings.

He leapt from the highest point, and glided down toward the chest cavity. The trip would take hours, but he'd decided he wanted to try flying one more time before he died. There would never be a better opportunity. If Xal hadn't planned absolutely perfectly there would never be any other opportunities.

Enoch remembered Nefarius. He remembered what it had taken to mobilize the pantheon, and how they'd always suspected that Xal was secretly allied with her and Talifax. Nefarius had poisoned things long after her death.

The wind cooled Enoch, and reminded him of better days. Of days when hundreds of scholars would make the leap he just made, all gliding back to their families near the heart. A time when their society had flourished and valued learning and mutual advancement.

They'd been quite egalitarian, for demons anyway. Their brethren back in the great cycle would have been horrified by the degree to which Xal had civilized them. They would have been elated and covetous to learn that his magineers had fabricated advanced weapons of war that far outstripped anything they'd ever conceived of.

Xal had eclipsed them all. Then, inexplicably, at the height of his power, he'd sacrificed it all. He'd allowed himself to be killed, despite knowing that he could have triumphed in such a contest. Why? What had Xal been planning?

Enoch had no doubt it was devious. Nefarius had been the master schemer, but most gods had underestimated Xal. Xal was as cunning as any, and Enoch had no doubt that the next few weeks would prove it.

Finally, he would be vindicated for his faith.

Enoch embraced the passage of time, and the exertion of flight, and smiled as the chest cavity's glowing lip grew ever larger. The wound no longer bothered him. It would be healed, in time. In short order, he imagined.

He glided lower, passing the lip, and entering the interior of the husk. He marveled at the city the jin had built, a wonder he heard of often over the millennia, but one he'd never been able to summon the interest to warrant a pilgrimage to.

Picking out Malazra's manor was simple enough. He could feel the surge of power from the vengeance, and her newly acquired artifact, and so Enoch glided in that direction. He noted that many demons looked up at his passage.

Some were hostile, to each other at least. They'd killed their brethren, and would again. But every last one knew Enoch for who he was, and not a one would risk firing at the Memory of Xal. What if they killed him? What if they brought a million year existence to an end?

Enoch almost dared them, just to have something that absurdly unexpected occur. None did, of course. He glided lower, and landed on the foyer, outside the room in which Malazra was entertaining her guests.

He particularly liked the new vengeance, this Nara. Her predecessor had been much more aggressive, and much less logical. Vengeance must be cold, or it threatened the host as much as recipient.

What was this new hound like? And a guardian? After so long? That seemed impossible. Gorr would never be able to adapt to what his people had become. They were as much brute as sentient now, and ruling them would require someone in touch with their baser instincts.

Enoch strode inside, and fluffed his wings. He relished the exhaustion, even as he realized a simple journey would never have taxed him so, once.

"Enoch?" Malazra said, rising slowly from her couch. "Memory? I—how have you come to be here?"

She seemed appropriately scandalized, which Enoch enjoyed immensely as he settled into a couch. "I flew. One of the many racial adaptations of my species, you see. We have wings." He fluffed his for emphasis.

"But...you don't leave your home. Ever." She adjusted her spectacles, which made her eyes appear larger, and thus more innocent. It was an interesting look for a demon prince.

"Unless I have cause, and I have cause." He frowned at her. "Time hasn't mattered for—well, longer than you can conceive of. But now it matters a great deal. We are reaching a confluence, and what happens here will determine the future not just of this sector, but of this plane of existence. Melodramatic, but there it is."

"We need to resurrect Xal," a tiny, but fierce, warrior said. The demon-touched human was the same size as Nara, and the two sat close to each other. There was a bond there. Love, and more. "Can you help us do that?"

"I can." He smiled down at the tiny human. "You must be the new hound. Aran, yes? I am Enoch."

The human nodded. "So you can help us?"

"I can, as I said." Enoch settled into his couch, and waved his hand until a goblet of void blood floated over. He sipped before continuing, and made a big production out of it to further inconvenience the human. "We need to raise Xal. Raising Xal requires a full demonic host. A full demonic host requires a prince in every key role. Guardian. Memory. Hounds. Most importantly—"

"Voice," Malazra finished for him. "You're saying we need a leader."

"You really couldn't wait for me to say it?" He frowned at her. He'd been planning this for some time. "We do need a leader. Find a new voice. Get the guardian and his pretty toy mech to Gorr's workshop, you do those things and I can help guide you through the rest. We can resurrect Xal, if the princes unite."

41

SIMPLE

Aran hoped he knew what he was doing. His plan for recruiting the oni had worked better than expected, and he'd been shocked by Malazra's brutality, even viewed from a distance with a scrying spell, as she'd used them to destroy her enemies.

She was ruthlessly efficient. Like him, but minus the moral attachments. And it appeared to have influenced her people. Approaching her complex today was far different than the last time they'd come. There were no ambushes. No one trying to assault them.

Instead, a veritable army of oni in spellarmor lined the tunnel leading up to the manor. Patrols also threaded through the city, showing people that there was order once more. If you'd asked him, Aran would have predicted this having taken weeks, not one day. That raised his estimation of Malazra considerably.

"You're positive she'll come?" Malazra was asking. She stood on her balcony with a goblet of wine in hand, and stared at the sky.

Aran nodded, and moved to join her. Malazra was taller,

but otherwise similar to a human in most ways. And her spellblade gave him something to relate to at least.

"I'm positive. She's been planning this day for a long time." Aran turned his attention to the sky, to the area where Xal's severed neck ended.

Something stirred in the sky above, past sight or hearing, or any conventional sense. It heralded the coming of a divine being, and called out to that same thing in Aran. A moment later the Skull of Xal winked into existence, in all its terrifying savagery. It drifted a few dozen kilometers from the severed neck, close enough to touch when dealing with objects that size.

The glow from the mouth and eyes filled the system with sudden illumination, brightening corners that had been long hidden. Everywhere that violet light touched, demons scurried, which was probably a good thing. The only demons they didn't want scurrying were princes at this point.

"This should be quite the homecoming," Enoch mused. "I have seen familial betrayal in every conceivable form, and it is rare for both parties to genuinely forgive each other."

"This will not be one of those cases." Malazra's demeanor became brittle. "I will work with her for the good of us all, but I will never forget, nor forgive her betrayal of our people."

"And what was that betrayal, exactly?" Enoch asked, tone innocent.

Malazra's face broke into a snarl. "She took the Skull and the Mind of Xal, when we were under assault by our enemies. When we needed them most."

"What would have happened if she'd stayed?" Enoch asked mildly.

Malazra appeared ready to hurl a retort, but then

thought better of it. She seemed to genuinely consider the question, and chewed on it for several moments. "Our enemies would have devoured Xal's mind. They would have killed Malila in the process. They could not risk Xal rising again."

"And if she'd brought the skull back at any time after they'd left?"

Malazra's eyes flashed. "The sector would have come together against us, most likely, but that doesn't mean we wouldn't have been triumphant. There were many times when we could have at least tried. She left...and never came back."

"She is back now," Aran pointed out. "We can fix things, but not if we let the past get in the way. We need you, Malazra."

The hound nodded. She licked her lips, and then looked up at the skull once more. "I will do what I must. The gain is worth it. She is on her way here now?"

"She is," Nara nodded. "I spoke with her earlier, and explained where we stand. We will never have a better chance to bring the princes together and establish order."

"But we still have the fundamental problem," Aran pointed out, "that we don't have a leader. I still think Voria is our best option."

"Maybe," Nara allowed, "but there's no way the demons will accept her. They see us as outsiders. Voria is a literal goddess of light. Their opposite."

Aran nodded wearily. "Point taken. But we need a leader." Aran turned to Malazra. "I have a question about demon culture."

"Ask, and I will answer if I can." She leaned back into her couch and steepled her fingers beneath her chin.

"How are demon princes replaced?" Aran asked, leaning

back into his own couch, which was too large to be comfortable. "By that I mean, let's say an underling wants to replace a guardian. How do they do that?"

"They murder them." Malazra blinked a few times. "Then they take their place."

"That's what I thought. Might makes right." Aran felt better understanding the underpinnings of their process, and it gave him an idea about how he could force the other princes around to where they needed them to be.

The air rippled and folded, and Malila coalesced not far from Nara. The winged demon queen looked around the room, and stiffened when her gaze met Malazra. The two sisters merely stared at each other, wordlessly, for long moments, like strange cats meeting for the first time.

"Welcome," Aran finally said, drawing the attention of both. "Thank you for coming, Malila. We've paved the way. The oni, jin, and eru stand united and ready to help resurrect Xal. You've brought the skull. All that remains is the ritual."

"As if that were a trivial matter." Malazra gave a snort.

Malila gave an eye roll at the very same moment. "We may not be able to do this at all. The ritual is by far the hardest part."

"What is involved, precisely?" Kazon said, speaking for the first time. He'd been noticeably less talkative since returning with the oni, and Aran wasn't surprised.

Kazon was a half meter taller, and his skin was a shiny ebony. It also looked like he'd spent some serious time worshipping the squat rack.

"No one knows, precisely," Enoch interjected as he swirled a goblet of void wine. "But I can tell you the shape of it at least. Your vessel is the key, I believe."

"So Inura told me." Kazon nodded, and stroked his

beard thoughtfully. "But I do not understand what that means, exactly."

"The secret lies in how you defeated the tomb, I believe." Enoch gave Kazon a knowing smile. "Are you willing to share?"

"I don't see why not." Kazon gave a shrug, and then straightened. "The secret lay in *life* magic. At first, *void* was enough. As I moved deeper into the darkness I reached a point where I could no longer use the *void*. But the *life* warmed me. It powered my armor, and kept me alive long enough to reach the gauntlet."

"So the key, therefore," Enoch mused, "was the blending of *life* and *void*, yes? And we just happen to have all the *void* in the sector, plus a god-forged machine designed to funnel *life*? What's more, we have the gauntlet, one of a handful of objects that can channel both *void* and *life* at the same time. An object capable of restoring a god to life."

"What are you suggesting?" Nara asked, her eyes glittering intensely in what Aran took for intense interest.

Enoch rubbed his dark hands together, giving a mischievous smile. "That we find the central place where Xal's life is tied, and use Inura's creation to jumpstart his body, just as you'd do with a mortal."

"I understand, like a pacemaker." Kazon straightened. "Yes, yes I see it now. If the ship is the key, then this city is the lock. But we will need a tremendous source of magic."

"Worship," Aran and Nara said in unison. Nara fell silent and waved at Aran to speak, so he continued. "We use a spell to get the attention of every demon on this rock. We show them a united council of demon princes, and then we ask them to help us raise Xal."

"Could it really be that simple?" Malila asked, edging a bit further from her sister.

"Probably not," Aran admitted. "There's no way it could be that simple. Nothing is ever that simple."

"I think," Enoch said, darting a mischievous glance at Aran, "that you will find that it is that simple. Not because we are dealing with simple things, but because you are reaching the end of a divine plan set by Xal long before your species became a spacefaring race. Xal accounted for everything. He has placed the pieces together. All we need do is use them."

"If that's the case," Nara broke in, "then why not do it now? What are we waiting for?"

"I can't think of a reason not to try." Aran faced Kazon. "Get your mecha to the start point. Nara will handle the illusion. Nara, can you create one large enough for the whole system to see?"

Nara nodded, but tightened her grip around her new spellrifle. "It will be taxing, and I won't be able to maintain it for every long, but yes I can get you in front of the demons if you want to give them a speech."

"What makes you think you can give the orders?" Malazra asked. Her eyes had narrowed to slits again, which was beginning to irk Aran.

"Because," Aran said, mimicking her expression, "you told me that demons decide things through might. I am declaring myself the voice, right now. I'm claiming my promotion, and I'm giving the orders. Why? Because we don't have a better candidate. If you want to stop me, well, then stop me. Otherwise you have to accept that I am taking charge. Either way we end up with a leader."

Aran watched the war play out in Malazra, and she wore her emotions openly enough that he was fairly certain he knew how the battle was going down. Malazra didn't want to be in charge, but she didn't want to follow any one else, either. She needed to choose one path or the other. Both involved a compromise.

"Very well. I will follow you, but let me be clear that I do not do so out of fear, and that deference only goes so far. And, I have a condition." Malazra turned her glare on Malila. "Malila must be evicted from the skull. The skull is the rightful home of the voice, and as that is now you, she will have to make...other arrangements."

Malila's scandalized expression was so comical that Aran almost laughed. He sensed that it would have been a terrible idea.

"Done." Malila finally said. "If you need my home to make you cooperate? Then I will give it. Anything to have father back."

42

SALES PITCH

Aran translocated into high orbit over Xal, facing the gaping wound in the chest. A lot hinged on the next few minutes, and he was going to need to convince these demons to accept him as a leader. He had no idea if that was even possible, but as all demons seemed to respect strength, and he had plenty of that, he hoped that would be the key.

"Okay, you're on," Nara's voice crackled over the spellarmor's speakers. "Just start talking and I'll amplify it all."

Aran exhaled slowly, then just started talking. "Demons of Xal, I am Aran, thrice marked by our father. Named hound and accepted by my fellow princes. As you can see, I arranged for Malila to come home with the skull, to allow us to resurrect our father, at long last."

As Aran spoke, Nara's magic began. A demonic version of Aran sprang out around his spellarmor, growing until he filled the sky over the husk. Aran rested a hand on Narlifex's hilt, the giant blade a reminder that he was a warrior.

"If our father is to live again," Aran continued, "then we must have your help. The jin, the eru, and the oni...all must work together. All must pray for our father's resurrection. Every last one of you will aid in our father's rebirth."

"Aran?" Kazon's tentative voice crackled over the comm. "The demons in the chest cavity are going nuts. They are cheering. And it is spreading. The orb is beginning to glow. That must be worship."

"I'm seeing the same thing," Nara echoed. "It's working. Keep talking, Aran."

Aran considered his next words carefully. He was, for all intents and purposes, the representative of their god. What he said would shape their culture. He didn't want to inspire the demons to war, but he also needed warriors.

The demons might be stranded for now, but if provided with ships they could invade and conquer the entire galaxy with ease. That prospect terrified him.

"Our god," Aran called, Nara's spell amplifying the words, "orchestrated this day. He foresaw his return, and knew that we would come together. Only with our combined strength can we return Xal. Pray, brothers and sisters. Pray for our father's return."

He'd considered a call to arms, but once a mob was whipped up it wasn't so easy to calm them down again. Right now all they needed was enough worship to get Xal up.

"It's working!" Kazon's excited voice came over the comm. "Aran, you did it. I think we have enough to start the ritual."

Dread filled Aran. They were well and truly committed now. He hoped Xal was everything he believed the god to be, because if he wasn't they were delivering him one depths of a power base.

43

XAL

Kazon stared at the golden orb and wished it had the answers he was seeking. It didn't, of course, and instead he was going to have to operate on feel. That was even harder than usual since eating the flesh of Xal.

He wasn't stupid, exactly. Kazon could still remember everything, and still think, but doing so was...slower. He had to concentrate very deliberately on things in a way he hadn't before. But if he did that...well, he wasn't much different than old Kazon.

He glanced at Aran, and then at Nara. Both wore resolved expressions, but for once Kazon wasn't reassured by it.

For the first time everything hinged on him. They couldn't help or save him. Kazon had to do this alone. He had to initiate the ritual that would resurrect a god, and he had to do it intuitively, drawing on the memories of his previous self.

Everything he'd seen had prepared him for that. His time with Inura had prepared him for that. He had the power and, theoretically at least, he had the knowledge. Everything that he'd endured had prepared him for this.

But what if he screwed up? What if the ritual didn't work? Nefarius would kill Voria, and would kill them eventually. The sector would lose, and that would be on him.

The trouble was that he had his doubts, and knew that would interfere with the ritual. These demons were savage, and so different from either humans or Inurans. If he brought them back and gave them a god, would they slaughter everyone else, or enslave them? Were they more dangerous than the Krox had been?

How could he know what the right decision was? It was maddening.

He placed his faith in Aran, his brother. Aran thought they needed Xal. That was the play, and he would back it.

Kazon raised his the gauntlet toward the orb, operating largely by instinct. A tendril shot from the orb and attached to the palm of the gauntlet.

Connecting in that way was quite different, and a great deal more pleasant. The gauntlet handled the heavy lifting, and all he had to do was think about what he wanted. It was a buffer and a magical intelligence, all wrapped into one.

He closed his eyes, and used the gauntlet to meld fully with the mecha. Only, it wasn't a mecha, not really. That had been its initial form, but this device was formless, and wasn't designed to be a simple transport or even an armored weapon. Those forms merely existed to bring it here, to the place where it had been created to be used.

It was a blueprint. A magical seed containing all the neural circuitry necessary to resurrect a god. Kazon focused on the device's purpose, and on the god they'd come to save. He focused on that entire body, which was cold and desiccated, and weak.

Tendrils shot from the outside of the mecha, identical to those that connected to his forehead. They burrowed into the floor, and into the ceiling, and the distant cavern walls.

Each tendril split into dozens, which split into dozens, which split into dozens, until millions, and then billions of tendrils were worming their way through Xal's husk.

Kazon had spent a great deal of time studying neurophysiology, and understood how the human body worked. These mimicked it perfectly, just on a much, much larger scale.

All the *life* magic that Inura had deposited into the mecha suddenly made sense. If you wanted to heal a dead god, then you needed *life*. Tremendous amounts of the stuff, more than even most gods had ever accumulated.

Kazon had thought that Voria possessed a great deal of the magic, but this ship contained an amount far greater. Voria was a puddle, and this a lake so vast you couldn't see the opposite side.

How much must Inura have possessed?

Life flowed into every part of the dead god, and when it had reached the furthest edge of the extremities the god stretched. Every muscle in every limb went taut at the same time, each filled with immense *life*.

A low groan came from Xal's throat, echoing through space, somehow, the eldritch whispers of an ancient god. All over the husk, from every demonic throat, arose a great collective cheer.

It resounded across the body of Xal, and that belief, that faith, that hope, the ritual captured it all. The worship was drawn to the mecha, which converted it into more *life* magic, which allowed it to further repair parts of the god.

Muscles knit back together. Wounds closed. Bit by bit, Xal healed. The worst of it, at least. There was still a hole in the chest. They were still missing one leg. But the other three limbs, and both wings, were now fully functional.

Kazon didn't even want to think about what had happened to the demons living in the affected areas. How many had just died? The ritual had done nothing to create more demons, or help those that existed. If you lived inside of a wound, as the oni did, and that wound had just healed over, then those demons would be absorbed back into their god.

It was horrifying, and Kazon prayed the grisly cost was worth it. He also prayed that most demons were smart enough to move away from wounds, but knew that the oni wouldn't number among them.

He waited for the god to awaken. For Xal to talk to him, to thank him, or smite him, or do...well, something.

Nothing happened. The god went quiet. The movement stopped.

"Did we fail?" Nara asked, biting her lip.

"I do not think so," Kazon muttered, looking around the cockpit. "There is something I am missing...something obvious."

"Do we need more worship?" Aran asked. Both he and Nara were only trying to help, Kazon reminded himself. What he really needed was space to think.

He closed his eyes and hummed to himself while he considered what had happened. The mecha had established a connection to the god. Even now he could feel that. But the god hadn't reanimated, and the connection was still active.

"I think I see it." Kazon gave a great laugh and grinned at his brother, while simultaneously watching the progress with Xal. "Perhaps we did not fail. This god...it isn't alive again. Not truly. But what if it is a vehicle, just like a spellship or a mecha? Perhaps we are meant to pilot it. This cockpit can serve as the control center for the entire god. From here we can direct Xal's movements. We can, effectively, pilot a god, and no one would be the wiser."

Nara blinked at that, and then she began to laugh. It quickly spread to Aran, so of course Kazon joined in. It felt good to laugh, and to see them laugh.

"It's one hell of a con," Aran pointed out. "I'd rather have Xal back, but if we can't do that, then there's no reason the demons have to know."

"That makes so much sense," Nara was saying, "it explains what Xal was trying to prepare us for. Why we three specifically needed to be here. He knew he wasn't coming back. If this thing functions like a spellship, then we have offense, defense, and piloting, right?"

Kazon nodded. "Exactly, yes. I'm assuming Aran is the most qualified to pilot it. I will try to manage the wards, and Nara I guess you can make the god cast spells?"

"What about the demons?" Aran asked. "They believe we just resurrected a god, right? They heard it groan. I know I thought he was alive again. What do we tell them? Because they won't like the truth."

"He's right." Nara bit her lip. "It's like a house of cards. We need them to believe Xal is back, and ready to lead them. If they stop believing, we're too weak to take on Nefarius."

"Do we bring the princes in on it is the question?" Aran asked, then immediately answered it. "I think we have to. I think they need to know the truth, so they can help us preserve the fiction. They'll get why it's necessary, and understand that it's really them as a council that runs Xal the god. We all have a say."

44

ALLIANCE

Frit stared down at Nebiat's body, or monument or whatever the statue could be called. Three days of rain hadn't changed it, and she hated that it was a life-sized version of the Wyrm. It was more than she deserved.

Most of the spiritual energy had stayed intact, and had crashed back into its anchor point in that stone when Nebiat had died. How much remained she wasn't sure, but she was absolutely positive that what they'd known as Nebiat had died in that explosion.

She wrapped her hand more tightly around Ikadra, who'd been a growing comfort, like a pet who could facilitate divine miracles. Eventually she'd have to give him up to Voria again. Now, most likely.

"I can't believe it's finally over," Frit whispered into the void.

"Is it?" Voria asked. She drifted closer, her expression weary. "I don't know where she hid the *Spellship*, so I'll have to find that. As for Nebiat? Well, I think we just witnessed the creation of a Catalyst. She's dead, but no god can ever really die."

"I find that alarming," Frit murmured, staring down at Nebiat's tomb. "I will have my followers create an order to watch over this place, with instructions that if some shade of Nebiat remains that they stay well clear. She can be dangerous, even now; of that I am positive. We will never be free of her, not really."

"Your followers," Voria snorted.

Frit's eyes narrowed, and the heat within her grew.

"I'm sorry." Voria raised a placating hand. "I wasn't poking fun at you. I was poking fun at us. I have followers too. It sounds so pompous, that's all. Now let's go find my followers. You're the diviner. I would be grateful for your help, Frit. In fact, if you will find the *Spellship* I will forgive you for the mirror, and for being duped by Nebiat. Multiple times. I'd much rather us be allies, long after Nefarius falls. That seems best for the sector, don't you think?"

Frit relaxed, and made a mental note not to be so defensive. She couldn't afford to be rash. That would teach her children to be rash, too. Parenting was already proving difficult.

"I think you're right. It is best for the sector. I think that when all is said and done, we're going to need to talk about forming a pantheon. In the meantime, we need to begin preparing for Nefarius and we can't do that without Kaho and the *Spellship*."

"Aww, you're getting along," Ikadra pulsed happily.

Frit ignored the staff and chewed on the problem. How could she find the ship? It could be hidden anywhere.

"Back when I needed to know if there was a way to free Nebiat," Frit mused, staring down at the draconic statue in a mixture of horror and relief, "I scryed the past to see the coordinates you used to find, ah, the world in the depths. That's what I was looking for when I broke the mirror. Wait, wait...don't get mad. I'm sorry. But I want you to understand why, and how it's useful now. I can scry the past here. I can see where Nebiat placed the ship. Our friend in the depths has amazing wards. Nebiat has nothing. I will find your ship, Voria, and we will part as allies, at the very least."

Voria nodded. "Thank you for that, Frit."

Frit closed her eyes, which helped with most divination related tasks, and focused on Nebiat. She found her easily enough, and traced her timeline backwards. She followed it to the battle with Krox, allowing it to pass in a blur.

Once she reached the combat she went back slowly, and sure enough there was Nebiat arriving with the *Spellship.* There was her going to the nadir of the planet and anchoring a powerful void pocket. Powerful enough to hold the *Spellship.*

Frit opened her eyes. "I know where it is."

45

RESCUED

Kaho sat gently and the hovercouch bobbed to accommodate for his bulk. He was the last to arrive at the council meeting, but it had been worth it to finish the chapter he'd been reading.

"Thank you all for coming," Administrator Pickus said, addressing the hastily assembled council. "As you all know, we are effectively hostages, and we've been presented with an ultimatum. Either we help Nebiat free herself from Krox, and become a goddess in her own right, or she slaughters everyone on this vessel and fills it with her own people."

"That is the same dilemma," groused an older Shayan Kaho did not recognize, "that we have faced since that witch put us here. You do not need to restate it at every meeting."

Pickus adjusted his glasses and addressed the situation with a good deal more tact than Kaho would have. "I'm merely following the protocol we established. Let the record reflect that Sub-administrator Laratha is being a douche about it."

Kaho barked a short laugh at that, which earned him a baleful stare from several councilors. "Apologies. I did not mean to offend, but we have been at this too long. We have no new data. No new answers. We are chasing the same solutions, when we don't have the slightest bit of control. We can't predict when or even if Nebiat will come back. Or if she'll honor her word. We have nothing but ifs."

He had their attention now, whether he wanted it or not. So he kept talking. "These meetings occur to let the people know we're doing something, but we all know that we're not doing anything. Not really. We're biding time until we can be useful, and we have no idea when that is."

He hadn't intended to lay it all out there, but it had needed to be said, and he wouldn't have the words back even if he could.

He started defiantly around the room, but mostly found nods of agreement, even from Laratha.

"I guess we just feel like we need to be doing something." Pickus rose from his chair with a stretch. "Maybe we table these meetings for the time being, or at least reduce their frequency. I only had them set up so often, because I thought there was an actual chance we could come up with a solution."

The room brightened as a luminance appeared at the head of the table. It flared into sudden brilliance, and then resolved into Voria, a literal goddess of light. Kaho had never seen anything so beautiful, except maybe Frit, and he admitted he was slightly biased there.

As if summoned by his thoughts, Frit appeared next to Voria, as smoldering and beautiful as she'd ever been. More so, somehow. Kaho rose from the awkward hover couch. The best he could manage was gawking. All the words were gone, as they often were around Frit.

"Ma'am?" Pickus asked, blinking owlishly up at Voria. "Is that really you?"

"Indeed, Administrator." Voria gave him an affectionate smile. "Thanks to Frit, we were able to locate you. Nebiat has been...dealt with. Permanently. You are safe now, and free to rejoin the war effort."

Tension flowed out of Kaho, and he sat right back down on the hovercouch. They were free. Nebiat was dead. Part of him didn't really believe that. She was unkillable, and if you thought she was dead it meant she had tricked you somehow.

"What happened?" Kaho finally croaked. "How did she die?"

"She's really gone," Frit said, crossing the room to stand near Kaho. "I'm sorry, beloved. It had to be done."

"I know." He nodded. "I'd have helped, if I'd have been able. Thank you for...dealing with it." He looked up at Frit, and found a compassionate woman staring back. Gods how he'd missed her. "I just cannot believe she is dead."

"She became a Catalyst," Voria said, drawing everyone's attention. "The Shade of Nebiat lies below, a brand new *spirit* Catalyst. In that way, she secured her legacy. She was a twisted creature, but at least she loved her people."

"I'm surprised to hear you say anything positive about her," Frit admitted. She shook her head. "I don't think I could manage that. Everything she did. Every word, every gesture, and every manipulation. It was all to get us to do what she wanted. Emotions were just one more weapon in her arsenal."

"You're not wrong." Kaho stood, and placed a hand on Frit's shoulder. It was pleasantly hot, another thing he'd missed. "She's dead now. That's the important thing. We are all better off for it. The question we need to answer, collectively, is where we go from here. What comes next?"

That was the real question, after all.

"We go to war with Nefarius," Voria gave back, voice firm with resolve. "She needs to be stopped, and the longer we take to do that the greater the casualties will be."

"*You* go to war with Nefarius," Kaho corrected. He shook his head. "Not me. I will remain here. This is a war for gods, and I am no god. But there is something I can do. Catalysts need a guardian for a reason. I will become the guardian of the Shade of Nebiat. I will take charge of mother's legacy, and ensure she does no further harm."

Frit's face fell, but she nodded. "I understand. I was just...I always thought you'd be my guardian."

"There's no reason he can't do both," Voria pointed out. "I hate to lose you, Kaho, but I'm glad you made it home. Teach your people well, and teach them that we don't have to be enemies."

Kaho nodded. "I am dreadfully weary of war, and I will see that my people do not embark on it any time soon. I wish you luck against Nefarius. I believe you will triumph. When you do...come home, Mahaya. I will be your guardian, too."

46

R&R

Crewes guided the *Talon* to a smooth landing on a landing platform outside the Temple of Shi, where they'd come to retrieve Rhea not so long ago. The jungle loomed behind it, as unwelcoming as ever.

He hated the humidity the most, which did terrible things to his hair, and was why he'd started shaving his scalp every morning all those years ago. It was worst in the summer, and thankfully it was autumn, so close to bearable.

"All right, kids." Crewes unbuckled his harness and climbed from the matrix. A glance at Rhea and Bord made him rethink his words. Once, that kind of approach made sense. Now the only two people left were grizzled vets. "I'm going to make contact with the Temple. Rhea, you're welcome to pay your respects, but if you'd rather stay here, you're welcome. Bord, you can take some R&R if you like. We're not likely to leave for the next few days, and if an emergency crops up we can swing by and pick you up."

"I'm good," Bord said, unbuckling his harness and crawling from the command couch. He ducked through the rings and paused in the doorway. "Gonna do some studying.

Nara said that if we worship gods, they can give us stuff back. Well if ever there was a god I'd worship, it's the major. I want to learn how to do that proper like."

Crewes felt a smile growing. The kid was recovering. "That's smart, Bord. She'd be proud." He didn't say who he meant, but they both knew.

"I'm gonna make something of myself." Bord squared his shoulders, and for just a minute resembled a proper soldier. "After I finish the research I'm hitting the squat rack."

"Do you even know what that is?" Crewes blinked, shocked. He'd had to twist Bord's arm back in basic to get him anywhere near PT, and the kid had never liked physical exertion.

"Yeah." Bord's voice had gone quiet. "You may not have noticed me, but I poked my head in now and then to see what you and the captain were doing."

In that moment Crewes wondered if he could have done more to foster the kid. No, the man. Had the gruff drill sergeant approach been wrong? He'd been taught to use that, that his role was being the asshole so that the line troops hated him and not command.

But now he was command. He couldn't just be a hammer any more. He needed to be all the tools. That was going to mean a whole lot of learning, and he'd be the first to admit he wasn't the fastest learner.

"Hey, Bord," Crewes called just before the specialist disappeared, "why don't you and I work out together later, when I get back from the temple?"

Bord paused. "Sure. I'd like that, sir."

Rhea said nothing as Crewes left the bridge, and he didn't press. The raven-haired soldier didn't dislike him, exactly, but they were like a dog and a cat who both belonged to the same master. Now that that master was gone, they had no idea how to interact with each other.

Thus far, Rhea had followed his orders to the letter, and seemed to support him unquestioningly. That was really all he could ask for.

Crewes headed down to the cargo hold—well, one of them, now that the ship had grown. He considered suiting up, but then considered better of it. "Hey Neeko, you wanna go see Serala?"

The cat, which had been lounging against the wall, rose with a stretch. Unlike a flesh and blood cat, she hadn't grown since he'd gotten her, though her fur color seemed to change depending on her mood. If she lay against something for too long her fur color would often shift to match, making her almost impossible to find.

Truth be told he'd stepped on her twice, but thankfully she'd forgiven him. After a great deal of petting and apologizing. Neither of which was something he did under ordinary circumstances, but having your armor mad at you seemed like a good way to die.

Crewes hesitated. He didn't like leaving with no weapon, and not wearing armor. Walking around in jeans and a black t-shirt might look good on holo, but it didn't stop spells, or even bullets.

He took a deep breath, and stepped through the *Talon*'s shimmering blue membrane into Yanthara's sweltering autumn heat. A sheen of sweat broke out all over his body at once, which was why he always wore black shirts and thick jeans.

A few robed acolytes walked the grounds, and he nodded politely as he threaded up the garden path toward the temple's double doors. The place had been carved from marble the last time he'd been here. Now it was made from wood, more like what he'd expect on Shaya.

Man he hated magic sometimes. *Dream* especially. Nebulous shifty bullshit.

Neeko gave a low growl.

"I didn't mean you," Crewes allowed, reaching down to scratch the cat behind the ears.

The cat rubbed against his thigh, then darted through the temple doors when an acolyte suddenly opened them and stepped into the afternoon heat. She delivered a slight bow.

"Ahh, Linus Crewes. You are expected. Please, follow me and I will escort you to Serala."

Crewes followed the orange-robed woman into the temple, which was blessedly cool inside. The walls were wood, which shouldn't have kept the heat out, but it was as if they'd stepped into another season somehow.

"Ahh, Linus." Serala's melodic voice came from deeper within the temple, behind four thick wooden pillars filled with elaborate carvings of animals. "Be welcome within the halls of Shi. We welcome our cousin Van, and greet you as family."

"Uh, I missed you too. You look good—from what I can see, I mean." Which wasn't much. Serala wore a purple robe that covered everything but her dusky eyes. But having just seen her on holo he could fill in the details.

"Leave us, please." Serala waved a hand and the other acolytes in the room suddenly found other places to be. After a few moments it was just them in the spacious chamber, which only made it more awkward. "Linus, our time together is short. I know you've come to warn me, but Shi has already done so. My course is determined. If you still wish to warn me I will hear you out, of course, but I'd rather this be a social call."

Crewes wasn't really sure how to react to that. "So, uh, this is a date then?"

The cloth over Serala's mouth whispered in what he took for a smile. "Indeed, Linus. One I think we've both wanted for a long time."

"I can get behind that." Crewes nodded, and felt immediately better. "I've been wound tight a while. It would be nice to take a little R&R, and I feel like I've earned it. Not like we can do much but sit around and wait for Nefarius to take an interest."

Serala winced at that name, and Crewes realized she must know something about a coming attack. He was tempted to pry, but knew there was no way she'd tell him anything she didn't think he absolutely needed to know.

"So I don't know this part of Yanthara. You got a restaurant around here you like?" Crewes was kind of in the mood for fajitas, which he almost never got to have any more. The *Talon* could make them, but it just wasn't the same as having a real chef bring a sizzling platter out to you.

"I can do better than that." Serala gave one of those laughs that, ah, affected Crewes very profoundly.

The room went dark. When the lights came back he was somewhere else. Somewhen else. Someplace familiar.

"Is this—are we back in the library at school?" Crewes spun in a slow circle and looked around, a grin gradually taking over his face.

Every day at lunch they'd sneak into the school library, where it was quiet. Just the five of them. They'd sit around and role play. Crewes hadn't understood most of the rules, but he knew when he needed to roll his d20, which was whenever something needed to be smashed.

Serala had almost always been the game master, and she'd been damned good at coming up with great stories.

"Hey, bro," Marcellus's bored voice came from a neighboring table. Crewes was positive it had been empty a moment ago, but now a fourteen-year-old version of Marcellus sat there, playing a competitive word game on his Dx7, an old portable game system. "We need to get started. Bell's gonna ring in 20 minutes, and we've got time to down that beholder."

Crewes turned to Serala, and was so overwhelmed that he couldn't force words out. Crewes inhaled through his nose, and then out through his mouth, until the odd, wet sensation in his eyes went away.

She'd picked a time when Marcellus and he had still been close. A time when he'd been a star athlete, and no one mocked his lack of brains.

"Thank you." Crewes took two steps forward, scooped up Serala, and kissed her.

He was damned well going to enjoy some R&R.

47

OUTFLANKED

Davidson reached for his gun when he woke up, then relaxed back into the bed. The sheets smelled too clean, and through the windows he could hear the muffled sounds of distant construction.

He liked the quarters the governor had provided, but they didn't feel like home yet.

He rose with a yawn, and retrieved his discarded shirt from the nightstand as he moved to stare out the window. A crane was maneuvering a massive steel girder into place, completing another layer of superstructure in the building.

New Texas was alive, booming, and devoted to full recovery. They'd endured their own personal hell when the Krox had invaded, but that was over a year ago, and now their planet was recovering.

Part of that terrified Davidson, because he felt like any world doing too well for too long was due for a crisis. Gods seemed to have a pretty sick sense of humor so far.

Bleep, bleep, bleep. He jumped when his new comm vibrated on the nightstand, then moved to retrieve the small black rectangle.

Davidson pulled his shirt on, straightened it a bit, then answered the com. "This is Davidson."

"It is so odd to hear you address yourself without rank," Governor Bhatia said, her voice pleasant and friendly, instead of panicked and overwhelmed as it had been the last time they'd spoken. "During our last meeting you mentioned generating a groundswell of support for Voria and Aran, yes?"

"That's the long and short of it, yeah." Davidson tore open a coffee packet and poured it into a mug. It began to steam and bubble and a moment later the wonderful aroma filled the room. "Belief matters, as it turns out. And I'm here to try to get more people on our side, because the time is going to come real soon when we can't pretend that NEF-1 is some benevolent servant."

"You mentioned that before too." Bhatia's expression grew concerned. "I was hoping you'd be more coherent after a night's sleep. Are you seriously saying that Austin's super weapon is a problem? It destroyed Krox, and now Virkonna. I'm not seeing the downside, and the rest of the sector won't either."

"Both self-serving moves, I assure you." Davidson took a sip of his coffee, which was warm, but not precisely hot. "This tool they've made isn't some new technological marvel. It's an ancient goddess, reborn and ready to pick up right where she left off. We're playing right into her hands, Governor."

Bhatia stared silently at him for a long time. He could see the wheels turning behind those brown eyes.

"I know you wouldn't lie about this. If we're really playing into her hands," the governor allowed, "then I'm not sure what you're going to make of this. Because it certainly seems benevolent."

"Make of what?" Davidson gulped down the rest of his coffee and set the mug back on the counter.

"The capital world of Ternus has returned, as if it never blew up." Bhatia raised an eyebrow. "The world, and all its inhabitants, reappeared this morning. Our people are back. Everyone we thought dead? The nightmare we all lived through? It's as if it's been erased. Overnight. Our families, friends, media icons...they're all back, billions of people safe."

"And Nefarius is behind this?" Davidson had gone cold. He sat heavily on the edge of his bed. This was so much worse than he ever could have managed.

"The recording is all over the holo. You're going to want to watch that. Contact me when you're done, because I have a great many questions about the NEF-1 unit. If what you're saying is true, then it paints all this in a sinister light."

Davidson nodded. "Couldn't agree more. Give me a bit to get up to speed, and I'll get back to you with a plan of action. This sounds good...on the surface. But there will be a hidden price tag, and I'm going to find out what it is."

He killed the connection, and browsed Quantum for the video she'd mentioned. It wasn't hard to find. In fact, it was the most viewed link in the sector at present.

Davidson clicked it, and Nefarius's feminine android body filled the screen. Despite being forged from the same dark alloy as the ships, she still managed a compassionate expression. "Citizens of Ternus, many of you are rejoicing right now. You are rejoicing at the return of your brothers and sisters, your sons and daughters. At the return of your home. To those on the world of Ternus, you must be confused."

Nefarius gave a broad, motherly smile. "Your world was about to be destroyed by Krox, the terrifying god of our enemies. Thanks to your worship, your belief in me, I had to the strength to stop Krox. I have slain him, and claimed the vengeance we craved. But I have also undone the most heinous of his crimes. I have given you back your capital, and returned humanity to its rightful place in the sector. Once more we are the dominant species, strong enough to resist the Wyrms and the demons. Soon, a new fleet of black ships will arrive, to be crewed by volunteers from among the saved. Together we will force the monsters back, ladies and gentlemen. We will pave the way for our children's future."

The video died away, and then showed a cut-away of the Ternus system. Sure enough, the planet was back, just as pristine as it always had been. Somehow, Nefarius had performed a miracle.

How were they supposed to compete with that? Every last one of those people was going to worship her. He would, if he'd been saved like that and didn't know Nefarius for the snake she was.

Somehow he needed to find a way to show his people the truth. If they couldn't catch her showing her true colors, then this war was as good as lost.

48

NEBIAT'S FATE

Kaho approached the monolithic statue of his mother, perfect in every scaly detail, but rather than reverence, all he could summon was pity. He'd loved her, as much as someone could love a genocidal planet-dominating tyrant. She'd been a profoundly unhappy woman, and also a product of her upbringing.

Not an excuse, certainly, but a mitigating factor perhaps. It helped to understand her origins, what little he knew, because it contextualized his mother's cruelty. His upbringing hadn't been about him, or even about Nebiat. It had been about the world she'd been born into, and had instinctively perpetuated.

How odd that he empathized with a monster.

Kaho walked to the very foot of his mother's statue, unarmed and wearing nothing but a simple robe. There was no protocol for this sort of thing, but to his mind becoming the guardian of a Catalyst was important business, and should be treated as such.

He'd come alone, as seemed fitting. It was bad enough

he'd have to deal with his mother in some fashion. "Well, brother, I never thought I'd see the day. I outlived you all."

Kaho raised both arms and both wings. He'd spent long years working with *spirit* magic. He understood the nature of Catalysts. To become a guardian all one needed to do was dominate said Catalyst. Enforce your will upon it.

At the moment of bonding, that Catalyst would surrender whatever knowledge it contained to you, and from that moment forward you would control its magical resources. It was an incredibly powerful position, but as the human Eros and his predecessor had demonstrated, it was not without risks.

"Mother," Kaho called, closing his eyes, "I have come to claim stewardship of the Shade of Nebiat. I have come to claim your power."

Mocking laughter sounded, just past hearing. Subtle enough that had it happened at any other time, in any other place, he'd have laughed it off as imagination. At least he'd confirmed something of his mother survived.

Clouds boiled out of a point in the sky directly over the Catalyst. Heavy, dark clouds, filled with rain. Lightning crashed as they blotted out the sky, and a cold rain began to fall.

It drenched Kaho, but he ignored it and stood with his arms raised, basking in the immensity of the magic. Nothing like what Krox commanded, but this place still held tremendous power.

The rain fell thicker and thicker, until the land around Kaho was blotted out. He could no longer see anything, save the looming shape in the rain, the mountain that had nearly become Nebiat's divine body.

She had come so close to victory, but had fallen short, as

her father had before her. Overreaching seemed to be a family trait, one he vowed not to fall prey to.

Lightning fell and thunder crashed, until he could no longer even see the mountain. When it cleared he was locked in some sort of vision.

His point of view hovered over the shoulder of a female hatchling, one of a dozen, all armed with spellblades and wearing spellarmor. They'd landed at a temple that was so ancient nearly every glyph had been worn away by rain.

Kaho couldn't tell contextually where this world was in relation to his own. It could be his own for all he knew. All he could do was watch.

The hatchlings continued in a combat formation, until they eventually stopped in front of the temple, and spoke to each other, though their words were carried away by the rain. Eventually one of them, a larger male, shouldered his way past the others into the temple.

The rest followed, with the female Kaho was following being the last inside.

Once out of the rain he could hear what they were saying, which mostly amounted to grousing about the miserable weather. He studied their equipment, and tried to piece together either when or where this scene was taking place.

Their spellblades were archaic, but that meant little since archaic spellblades were highly prized. Their spellarmor was traditional Krox fare, sculpted to enhance the wielder's draconic nature. Even their speech would have been at home during his childhood.

"Nebiat!" The largest male bellowed.

The hatchling he was following sprang into motion and rushed over to the male, then dropped into a crouch, wings spread submissively. "Yes, elder brother?"

"Go and forage. Bring me food. Meat. Do it now. I hunger." The elder Wyrm flicked his tail menacingly.

"Of course, elder brother." Nebiat pressed her face to the stone, until her brother turned away.

She rose silently, and no one but Kaho saw the venomous look she shot her elder brother. Nebiat left the cave and braved the storm. She hunted until she found something that resembled a gazelle, and quickly downed it.

There was only enough meat for one, in Kaho's estimation. He watched as Nebiat expertly cleaned the animal, then noted that she withdrew a flask of glowing green liquid from her pack. She made three small gashes in the meat, and carefully put one drop of the liquid into each.

She carefully wrapped the meat so as to hide the liquid, then leapt into the air and flew back to the cave. Kaho already knew what was coming next, but he winced anyway.

Nebiat presented the food to her elder brother, who wolfed it down without a second look. Then he shoved Nebiat away, and she slunk into the corner to bed down for the night. Only Kaho saw her smile.

He knew his uncle would never wake up, and that no one would ever trace it back to Nebiat.

The vision flashed and Nebiat was older now. Still a hatchling, but older. There were nine siblings now, and they were led by a female. She was ordering Nebiat and two of her elder brothers to assault a tech demon position, and take it.

Nebiat followed her brothers into battle, one of them in charge, of course. She kept to the shadows, and only struck when certain she could do so from safety. Her brothers led her deep into a compound, and finally spotted their quarry, the enemy leader. They charged in.

Nebiat fell back to the shadows. She watched as her

brothers were overwhelmed. They managed to fatally wound their target, though they were both killed.

Nebiat returned to her elder sister and reported her success and the deaths of her siblings.

The pattern continued, until Nebiat was the last of her siblings standing.

"I don't know what I expected," Kaho muttered to himself as the vision reached its crescendo, and then started over from the beginning. "I thought maybe...maybe I'd see something that would put your life in context. Would give me some reason to understand, or love, or forgive you. There's none of that. You were a terrible person, right from the egg mother. I am glad you are dead. The sector is better off. And I will keep you from ever harming anyone again."

There was one more mocking peal of laughter, then the storm broke, and Kaho found himself standing before the statue. He rose and wiped water from his eyes, then looked up at her stone face.

The sector was better off.

49

RULE THROUGH FORCE

Aran rested his hand on Narlifex's hilt, and strode into a council chamber that had not been used in an age, as evidenced by the thick dust and debris on the floor, and the odor of disuse.

He was the last to arrive, which hadn't been a conscious choice, and more a result of his body...adjusting to the food here. Eight chairs sat around a table cut from dark stone, and the four corresponding to elements were already taken.

Kazon sat in the element corresponding to *life*, so Aran sat opposite, in the element that corresponded to *void*. As he was the voice now, that seemed fitting. He didn't know if they had a leader, but the voice seemed the closest.

"Welcome," Malila called as he seated himself. "Now that the voice is here we can begin."

"Shouldn't the voice conduct the meeting?" Nara interrupted. She sat in the element corresponding to *fire*, at his right hand. Vengeance. Fitting.

"Yes," Malazra added, quite smugly. "Don't try to usurp power, Malila. You are merely a hound."

"As are you," Malila bristled.

"This is getting us nowhere." Kazon rose from his seat and planted his palms against the table. "We need—"

No one save Aran paid him the slightest attention.

"Kazon," Aran boomed, at a volume that would have made Crewes proud, "was speaking. Sit down. Shut up. And let him finish."

Silence reigned. The princes all gave their attention to the bearded half demon.

Kazon sat back down, but continued. "As I was saying—we need an official leader. Someone we all agree to follow without question, in battle at least. Each of us is, well, I guess we are demonic princes, though that term is strange to me. Presumably we each have one vote?"

"Vote?" Malila scoffed. "We fight for dominance. The voice speaks for Xal, but each of us executes his wishes as best we are able. We do not answer to each other, nor are we required to work together, though most of us do."

"Most of us," Malazra snapped, glaring at Malila. Malila didn't meet her stare.

Aran rose slowly to his feet, and planted his hands on the table. "All of you remember Nefarius, I assume? Reborn Wyrm-goddess with a body that we don't even fully understand?"

"I do," Enoch growled, "even if the rest of you do not. Nefarius is the gravest threat Xal ever faced, and she killed him from the grave. We must not underestimate her."

"You are here as a courtesy, old man." Malazra's eyes narrowed. "Do not presume to lecture us."

"If you wish to fight for dominance." Aran instinctively flared his divine aura, though he couldn't explain how. A nimbus of *void* infused his words, and the room darkened around him. "Then let's get that out of the way, shall we? Kazon, Nara, and I will be happy to put down any dissenters, right now. If you're telling me that I just need to dictate terms, fine. Here's what's happening. You're going to tell your followers that Xal has returned."

"They are already aware of that," Malila groused. Her eyes narrowed. "And I would be careful who you threaten. You might—"

No one saw Nara move. One moment she was seated across from Malila. The next she was two meters behind her, the barrel of her artifact rifle pressed against the back of Malila's skill.

"As I was saying," Aran continued, "here's what's going to happen. You are going to tell your followers that Xal has returned. This is a lie. We failed. What we've created is effectively a massive super weapon, but we have not restored Xal. His...mind is elsewhere."

"I knew it," Malazra snapped. She stabbed an accusing finger at Malila. "You did something to his mind. Robbed him of something to increase your own power. What have you done?"

"Do you really think I'd stoop to the kind of tactics you would use?" Malila raised an eyebrow, and eyed her sister coldly. "I wish our father's return more than any of you. Xal can absolve me of any wrongdoing. What I did, I did at his behest. I need him to return to clear my name, so you can see, sister, that I have as vested an interest as you do."

"It isn't her fault," Kazon protested, his tone mollifying. "Please, everyone calm down, and listen to Aran. Time runs short. Very short."

"Do you know something that can shed some light on things, Kazon?" Aran asked, before he realized that particular colloquialism probably didn't work as well in this crowd.

"I do, Voice of Xal." Kazon bowed deferentially. "I believe

that we are missing a piece of Xal. A piece we assumed that was located in the skull. Xal's—well, his soul or consciousness if you will. It is missing."

"Regardless of the reason," Aran said, allowing his gaze to roam the room. Most dropped their gaze when his touched theirs, all save Malila. "We have a job to do. We need to stop Nefarius. I don't care how much or how little you know about Nefarius. She's bad news, and she is devouring magic in our sector. If we don't come for her, then she'll come for us."

"Very well," Malila agreed. She looked like she'd eaten something distasteful. "I will do as you ask. I will tell my children that Xal has returned, and that we will make war on his enemies. I will keep your secret, for to do otherwise is suicide. Likewise, I will defer to you, Voice. I approve of the way you have handled matters, and if the day comes when I disagree then I will simply take the position from you."

"You will try, you mean." Aran met her stare kilo for kilo.

In that moment, Aran learned what staring down a goddess was like. Malila's power boiled within her, and she seethed in silent rage as her glare grew ever more intense.

Aran refused to look away. Demons respected strength and little else.

Finally, after their wordless battle had drawn on, Malila averted her gaze. "I will accept him. How about the rest of you?"

One by one they assented, as Aran had known they would. They didn't really have another option, not a good one anyway. This was the only way they were getting their god, and their unity, back.

"Do we have a chance?" Malazra asked. She leaned back in her chair. "Since we're conspirators I think we should at least be honest amongst each other, whatever mask we wear in public."

"More than a chance," Aran said, and meant it. He smiled grimly at each of them in turn. "Xal prepared us. All of us. For this day. For this moment. He went to his death willingly, because he knew someday the gain would be worth it. Today is that day."

There were no cheers, but they nodded, at least. They were as united as they were going to get. Now, it was time to engage Nefarius. "Nara, can you get in touch with Frit and Voria? If anyone knows where Nefarius will appear next I suspect it will be them. Besides, we still have no idea if they even got the *Spellship* back."

"And what are you going to be doing?" Malila demanded.

"I'm going to learn to pilot a god." Aran turned away without a word, and strode from the room.

50

CREWES VERSUS THE VOLCANO

Crewes was pretty much walking on clouds by the time he arrived back at the *Talon*. Even Neeko was in a good mood, and the cat had been batting at a thick tree branch the entire time they'd been walking back.

Currently the cat was carrying the stick in her jaws, prancing along as if it was deadliest predator to have ever lived. Crewes snorted a laugh, which the cat pointedly ignored.

They strode up the *Talon*'s ramp, and through the shimmering membrane into blessed climate control. Of course, even without the heat the planet had left its mark. Crewes was now cold and clammy, as the sweat became a new kind of problem. He badly needed a shower.

He ducked into his quarters, but before he took care of that he moved over to the scry-screen and placed a call to Serala. It hadn't even finished chiming the first time when it connected, and her smiling face filled the screen.

"I was expecting your call." She delivered a wink that robbed all the words from his head. "You wanted to say goodbye, but part of you also wants to ask what comes next."

"Not in a 'tell me the future' kind of way," he protested. "I just wanna know what I should be doing. If I'm right about that big scaly dragon, then this planet is in a whole lot of trouble. They're going to need to come together, behind Voria and Aran."

It still felt weird calling them by their first names.

"Nefarius comes to devour all magic." Serala's face hardened and he was glad he wasn't the cause of it. "We will do all we can to resist. I will rally my followers, but you must do the same with yours."

Crewes gave a snort. "Uh, I ain't got followers. Unless you count Rhea and Bord."

"You underestimate yourself, beloved. This world adores you. Your captain may get much of the credit, but your people love you. Give them a hero." She gave him the kind of reproving look his mother loved to dole out. "No one speaks for Van. It alone, of all Catalysts we know, has no guardian."

"Well that's because," Crewes countered, "anyone who goes into the flame dies. No one's every been able to seize the place. What makes you think I'd do any better?"

"You possess not only the blessing of Van, but also the blessing of your mysterious fire goddess." Serala licked her lips, which made him think of...other things. "I cannot know where you acquired all the *fire* magic you posses, but you might be the strongest wielder in our time. No one will have a better chance of claiming Van's strength than you, and if you do not...we are naked before the storm. Please, Linus, there is no one else."

He nodded. "Yeah, I get it. I'll jump into the volcano." Curiously, he wasn't even all that scared. "At least it's something I can do. I loved our date, but too much R&R and I start to get itchy."

She gave him a sad smile, and he didn't like the finality to it, not one bit. "The sector is fortunate to have you, Linus. Be well. I love you."

The missive ended before he could reply. Damn, she'd really thrown down the gauntlet. He loved her too, and he hoped she knew that. She must know. She seemed to know everything else.

Crewes rose reluctantly from the bed, "Neeko, I got work to do, and you can't come with me."

The cat gave a low growl.

"Don't give me that shit," he countered, eyeing her balefully. "You ain't made of fire, and I ain't taking you into that place. What if you don't make it out?"

The cat's tail swished, and she pointedly looked away from him and began cleaning herself.

"I'll be back soon." She'd forgive him, as long as he came back.

Crewes left his quarters and headed to the bridge. Rhea was on duty, but there was no sign of Bord. "Rhea, can you take us to the Temple of Van? You can find the coordinates in the planetary network."

"If I can get the blasted thing to work," she growled. "I am still adjusting to that tech. I'll get it taken care of."

The *Talon* lifted off and began heading north.

Crewes watched the scry-screen, grateful that someone else was flying the ship so he could think about how monumentally screwed he was. Basically he'd agreed to jump into a star.

That wasn't entirely crazy. He'd been to Van once, when he'd first gained *fire* magic. Then he'd met Neith, and spider-chick had given him a bunch. And finally, Aran had stolen a bunch from Krox and had been nice enough to share.

Could he survive this? Probably. That seemed likely, or he doubted Serala would have told him to walk into fire. I mean, he wasn't that bad at sex. He hoped. Not like he had a lot of recent practice before today.

The *Talon* sailed north and gradually exchanged the jungles for harsh fields of dark lava rock. The further into those fields they made it, the larger the lakes of lava they passed. Cruiser-sized salamanders basked in those lakes, though the only visible sign was the ridge on the lizards' backs rising above the lava, like a sea of fans.

Beyond them lay a ring of tall volcanoes, each with wide rivers of lava flowing down multiple slopes. This entire continent was an open wound in the planet, and it was still bleeding thousands of years after Van had slammed into it.

"Should I set down over there, by the encampment?" Rhea asked as she guided the *Talon* toward the tallest mountain. "That's what the planetary network recommends."

"Yeah, that will work." Crewes breathed in through his nose, and out through his mouth.

"What are we here for, sir?" Rhea finally asked.

"I'm going to jump into that volcano." Crewes kept his tone matter-of-fact, mostly for his own benefit. Inner Crewes was a very turbulent place at the moment.

"Oh." Rhea flew closer, and set down on the very lip of the volcano. "I made it as short a walk as I could, sir."

"Good. I'm so over symbolic hikes. See this is a Catalyst I can get behind. I jump in. If it works, I live. If it doesn't, I'm just dead." Crewes strode to the doorway and paused. "If I don't come back, you know the ship is yours, right?"

"You're coming back." Rhea didn't look up from the sigils on the rings of her matrix.

He didn't see any sense arguing with her, so Crewes walked down to the cargo hold, crossed the berths for the spellarmor, and walked through the blue membrane, into the blessed heat he'd grown to love as a kid.

This was dry heat.

He stood at the edge of the caldera, and stared down at the dark bubbling magma filling the mountain like soup in a bowl. A normal human couldn't get this close. Even a mage would be uncomfortable.

For him? It was pleasant.

"Well," he muttered, "here goes."

Crewes stepped off the edge, and knifed his feet down at an angle like he would if he were diving into water. Lava was probably not very much like water, but then he wasn't very much like a diver.

His legs punched into the crust, which was more like rock than water, as it turned out. Fortunately, Crewes punched right through it and into the lava underneath. He tensed, but only for a moment. The lava was warm against his skin, like a bath.

Crewes swam downward, and used a bit of *fire* to increase his strength. That was a trick the captain had taught him, one of the first things he'd done that made him a war mage now, instead of a tech mage.

He needed to update his résumé.

The lava was thick and hard to swim through, even with the excess strength. Crewes kept after it, and forced himself deeper and deeper. The heat rose the deeper he swam, but it merely went from pleasant to tolerable.

Up until that moment Crewes had been holding his breath, but pain was building in his lungs, and he was realizing there was a dangerous flaw in his plan. He wasn't a very good swimmer, and couldn't hold his breath for more than a couple minutes.

He pushed deeper, rather than trying to work his way

back to the surface. If he died, he died. Honestly? At this point it would be a bit of a relief. He'd never give up willingly, but if you got taken out fighting your hardest? There was no shame in that.

Of course, having the end of his story be "and then he jumped into a volcano" wasn't his favorite thing ever.

Crewes finally couldn't hold his breath any longer. He was disappointed with himself, but he'd been swimming through lava for hours, it felt like. He let go, and exhaled his final breath.

When he instinctively tried to suck in another breath his lungs filled with lava...and he kept breathing. It didn't even burn. Quite the opposite. It was a little strange, but it didn't feel bad, precisely.

Crewes kept swimming, deeper and deeper. It was easier now. The lava seemed to be sustaining him. Empowering him. Changing him. He grew stronger, tougher, and denser. He realized that not all the lava was being breathed out. Some was being ingested somehow.

And there was more.

Crewes could feel the lava. All of it. Not just the lava in his lungs, or even the lava in this volcano. He could feel all lava, everywhere on the planet. And he could control it, if he wished.

And right now he wished.

Crewes ordered the lava to pick him up and carry him out of the volcano. And it did. He shot up through the warmth, which parted before him with increasing speed. Within a few seconds he'd climbed through hundreds of meters of lava. That's what he told himself anyway.

It was probably more like twenty meters. All the effort had only taken him down twenty meters. Talk about embarrassing. At least no one had seen it.

Crewes shot up into the air, but he wasn't flying. He was standing on a pillar of lava, which extended from the volcano below. He'd done that.

"I guess I'm the guardian now." That had been a whole lot easier than he'd expected, which seemed odd. Shit like this was supposed to be hard, he thought.

Something beyond hearing came from the sky, and Crewes looked up. He went cold when the familiar ebony dragon appeared, wings flexing.

Nefarius had arrived.

"Well, that tracks. So much for R&R."

51

SEIZING POWER

Nefarius appeared in the sky over an unfamiliar world, its citizens numerous, largely secular, and completely unprepared for what was about to happen. Roughly two thirds of Yanthara was covered by dense jungles, which reminded her of the world she'd grown up on in her youth.

The last third was all volcanoes and magma, harsh, blasted lands twisted by fire magic and the world's own natural forces. She had no interest in that latter half, the strength of Shivan, potent though it may be.

That *fire* had been gifted to him by Xal originally, back when the pantheon had some semblance of unity. Shivan had risen in their ranks, and eventually Xal had entrusted him with the great spear Worldender, the very weapon clutched in her talons.

Nefarius concentrated and manifested in her android body. Her good works on Ternus had been proceeding, and many volunteers had come forward to crew the new black ships that the Inurans were producing.

In a matter of weeks she would be prepared to begin invading other sectors, and she'd never have to leave her domain to do it. Converting these people into zealots willing to spread enlightenment would take time and a deft hand, but she'd done it before, and relished the opportunity to improve upon her previous works.

All that remained were a few formalities.

What she did here, today, would precipitate her dominance in the sector. She would assault this world, which would draw Xal out prematurely, because for whatever reason he considered these people valuable.

She'd dispose of him, devour whatever of his magic remained, and then move on to the next phase of her plan. Easy, and blessedly swift if her scrying was accurate.

"People of Ternus." She began her broadcast, her android self superimposed over an image of the world below. "I have destroyed Krox. I have slain the Wyrm that terrified the planet Marid for generations. I have decapitated the last dragonflight, and killed their goddess. And, once the sector was safe, I returned the planet Ternus from obliteration."

She paused to allow them to take it all in, to remember how much they trusted her. Of all the things she'd done for them.

"Now, the time has come to be pro-active." She gestured at the world behind her. "Yanthara contains a cancer. An evil that, if left unchecked, will grow. Once upon a time this evil was known as Shivan, an elder god who terrified the sector. An elder god with a notorious hatred for humanity. This god was killed, but as it turns out you can never really kill a god. So long as the pieces remain they can be put back together.

"So we have a choice, ladies and gentlemen. We can wait

for those pieces to form something we can identify clearly as a threat, or we can rip it out at the source right now." She smiled magnanimously at the drone recording her. "In a moment you will have the opportunity to vote. No representatives between you and power. Cast your votes, and we will tally them. Do you want me to end this threat before it arises? Or should we wait for it to grow in strength?"

Nefarius hijacked their own governmental systems, which underlay their entire Quantum network. The whole thing was a system from their home world, a place called Terra, and their modern engineers had little understanding of how to fully utilize it.

They didn't understand, for example, that she could force all relays to carry her message, or jam communications that New Texas had been trying to send. That was something that needed to be dealt with, and soon. She couldn't abide insubordination, and she'd have to make an example of this war hero, Davidson.

For now, though, she needed to convince her people that they were responsible for what was about to happen.

The poll contained two graphical bars, a green, correct choice, and an angry orange to represent the wrong one. Nefarius monitored the poll, and noted to her surprise that almost 70% of their citizens voted against attacking Yanthara.

Nefarius reversed the numbers, and the polls displayed overwhelming support for ending an evil threat before it was fully unleashed.

She let it play out with all the drama and patriotic fanfare she could muster, and when she felt like she'd done enough theater, she closed the poll.

"The people have spoken, and our path is clear," she

delivered gravely. "I will do what is necessary to preserve our sovereignty and freedom. Our enemies will try to stop us, but I will stay the course. They will not deter us from doing what is right."

Nefarius ended the transmission. Now that her followers were mollified, it was time to claim the last piece of magic she needed for her plan to finally succeed. She drifted through the atmosphere, over the part of the jungle where the magic was hiding.

It tried to disguise itself, of course, and any mortal attempting to find it would wander the jungle aimlessly. Nefarius possessed both *fire* and *spirit*, thanks to Krox, which meant the cloak was trivial to pierce. She could see Shivan's mind there, under the jungle.

What the people below now called the goddess Shi.

Eradicating a religion was normally very tricky stuff, but to a people as traumatized as humanity had been, it was simple matter to convince them that it was for the best. Individuals would protest, of course, but would they stand up to their government? Would they protest?

Not many. And those who did? She'd see that no news of them spread. They would die forgotten, while she pushed the narrative she needed them to believe.

Their support was vital. She was powerful in this new body, but Xal couldn't be underestimated. She needed as much strength as possible, and worship from billions of faithful would go a long way to bolstering her.

She pressed down into the atmosphere, descending toward the jungle. In the distance she spotted a godling, one of the humans who contained a surprising amount of *fire* magic. Had she needed *fire* she'd have devoured him, but he wasn't what she'd come for.

She needed *dream*.

Nefarius landed on the jungle, crushing thousand-year-old arboreal giants and fledgling settlements alike. Tens of thousands died in the initial landing, a trial number in her estimation, and not her followers in any case.

Nefarius burrowed into the earth until her claws found magic, pure glorious *dream*. She scooped earth away as fast as possible, until she could jam her face directly into the magic.

A glorious orb of purple-pink brilliance blazed before her. It represented all the knowledge that Shivan had accumulated, in addition to being powerful *dream* magic in its own right. Once she'd devoured both the knowledge and the magic, she would know everything Shivan had known, as she already knew everything Krox had known.

In a way, that would change her. Her personality would become a blending of all three, but only to a small extent. She was the dominant influence, and set the terms of their consciousness. What remained of Krox was quite pleased with the arrangement, not that she cared.

She'd caged him, and muted him in the process. It was possible he might offer valuable counsel someday, but for now he was a mana battery bolted onto a database.

Nefarius plunged her face into the magic and devoured it greedily. Glorious pulse after glorious pulse flowed down her gullet, fueling her magnificent body. Magic flowed down each component ship, what had become her bones, filling their magical repositories and offering her a new source of power to draw from.

There was so much! So much power. So much knowledge. Nefarius took it all, every scrap. She drank and drank, until there was no more. Then the Wyrm-goddess kicked off the planet, using it to propel her back into orbit.

Her exit crushed a continent, and sent enough dust and

debris into the air that the planet would face a nuclear winter for years. That would effectively doom her enemies, so she paid the world no more mind as she rose back into orbit.

Xal would arrive soon. And she would be ready.

52

ACT OF WAR

Davidson had been working around the clock for six days now, with never more than three-hour naps. He was used to grueling hours, often filled with physical exertion, bad food, and worse conditions.

This was infinitely more challenging.

Davidson had to be a hero.

He attended press conferences. He helped prepare broadcasts detailing key battles, and shook hands, and kissed babies, and attended state dinners. Bhatia had a never-ending parade of tasks, but she insisted this was how he could be the most useful.

They needed people to believe in Aran. In Voria. In the Confederacy, and what it had stood for before it disintegrated. They needed to resurrect it, and people's spirits with it.

Unfortunately, they'd been swimming upstream, so to speak. Nefarius had returned Ternus, along with all its industrial might. Overnight, New Texas's position had been changed, from the strongest remaining military position, to once again being subservient to Ternus.

It chafed a lot of people, and Davidson was one of them.

Ding dong ding. The apartment's three tone doorbell sounded, and Davidson rose from the couch and trudged to the door. He had ninety minutes before the next conference and had been planning to sleep for eighty of them.

His door opened before he reached it, and Governor Bhatia let herself in. She looked less polished in person, her mahogany face less perfect. She also looked far more approachable.

"Good lord." She rushed to him and placed a hand against his forehead. "Well, you're not sick at least. But you look like death warmed over. Clearly we've been pushing you too hard."

"I can sleep when I'm dead." Davidson retraced his steps, and sagged back onto the couch. "This is brutal, but necessary. We're making progress, right? This is helping?"

"That's why I'm here." She sat down on the couch next to him, and placed a hand over his in a motherly way. "It's working on New Texas. People here love you, and they're responding to your reports and the documentary. They're firmly in Voria and Aran's corner, and they're not going to accept Ternus labeling them traitors."

"But?" Davidson asked.

"But, that's as far as it goes." She removed her hand and now she was the one who looked like she needed to be comforted. "The NEF-1 unit was given full access to our defense mainframes, codes, surveillance apparatus, you name it. Austin gave her the full keys, and she's used them. All media has been sanitized for weeks. Nothing is making it off world. Ternus hasn't heard a word of what we've been saying."

"Even if they did, what could we say?" Davidson scrubbed his fingers through his beard. "Nefarius is a weapon we created, so far as they're concerned. We need a way to shake their faith in her."

Bhatia's comm unit vibrated. She looked down and scanned the screen, then met his gaze, all blood draining from her face. "Nefarius has just issued a statement and attacked Yanthara. She's claiming that she's removing their Catalysts to protect them, but...well, see for yourself."

She held her comm up, and showed Nefarius ripping a swathe of the planet away. Tens of thousands were killed immediately, but the debris from ripping a hunk of purple crystal from the world would trigger a nuclear winter that would likely kill millions.

"Yanthara is an ally. This is an act of war." Davidson shot to his feet. "Governor, this is the mistake we've been waiting for. If we can show people that Nefarius is going too far, and that Aran is trying to protect our allies, then maybe we can swing this around."

"That might work on New Texas, but there's no way for us to get access to the Quantum network." Bhatia gave a frustrated sigh. "You remove whatever countermeasures Nefarius has running that are preventing us from transferring data, and then we're in business. We're short on hackers good enough to take on a god, unfortunately. I have my best people on it and it is...not promising."

They needed a miracle, but Voria was busy, and who knew where Aran even was.

53

I LIVE

Aran closed his eyes, and welded his intent and resolve into an unbreakable alloy. He kept his eyes closed, and tuned out everything but his own heartbeat and the song that lay beyond it.

The song of the void.

He reached for that void, and found that it extended far beyond him now. It connected to the vast organism that was Xal, which had been permeated by the same magic for untold epochs.

Aran became one with that void. He gave himself over fully to it, and it to him, until there was no longer any difference. When he opened his eyes he was no longer Aran.

He was Xal.

Xal looked about the lightless system where the very pantheon he had founded had feasted on his still dying body. He could feel his limbs, or most of them anyway. They stirred, but sluggishly.

His jaw worked and he attempted to speak. A low subsonic rumble rippled out into the system, but no intelligible words.

Aran returned to his body with a gasp, and found himself coated in sweat. His chest was heaving, and he looked around wildly until the cockpit came into focus.

"Are you all right?" Nara asked, her voice muffled.

"Fine." Aran blinked rapidly, then focused on Nara. "Did you hear Xal?"

Kazon nodded over in his command couch. "Yes, brother, a great roar."

"Why did you stop the test?" Nara asked, her concern evident.

"I don't know...I guess I felt like I was dying," Aran realized aloud. His mouth tightened into a determined line. "Let's do it again."

Aran inhaled, then closed his eyes and relaxed against the command couch again. He pushed away the thought that he'd have to fight Nefarius soon, and focused on Xal. He tuned out everything but his heartbeat.

This time when he opened his eyes it was easier. He was less Xal and more Aran, more aware of his surroundings and who he was.

Aran extended one of Xal's clawed hands and flexed it. He flapped the wings and rolled the ankle on the one remaining foot. The god's titanic limbs responded far more quickly than they had any right to. An object of that size should have been sluggish and required enormous energy to move.

Somehow Xal had infused it all with *void* magic, and made a planet-sized elder god as nimble as an unaugmented human. That would be vital during the battle with Nefarius, and removed at least some of Aran's anxiety.

"I livvve," Aran rumbled through Xal's mouth. "Soon, we ride to war, my children. The goddess responsible for my death has risen once more. Our vengeance is at hand."

That sounded suitably ominous, Aran hoped. How to convey what he needed from them?

"Our strength comes from unity," Xal rumbled, "We are one nation. One people. Together, we will destroy our enemies. Pray, my children, pray for vengeance. Think of your enemies on distant homes, of us being there, slaughtering them. Pray for this, and I will make it so."

Aran released Xal and returned to his body, panting, and once again covered in sweat. He blinked a few times, then Nara's concerned face came into focus. "It was much easier that time."

The golden orb blazed into sudden brilliance, and Aran raised a hand to shield his eyes. Warm pulses flowed in, oscillating between brilliant and tolerable.

"What is happening?" Kazon called over the thrum of the orb.

"I called for worship," Aran yelled back. "I think this is result. We'll need it to translocate to Yanthara, right?"

"I don't see another way to move something this large," Nara called, barely audible over the thrum of the orb. "I imagine Xal must have some sort of reservoirs to store worship. I wish we understood more of how it worked. Enoch could tell us, if we had time."

As if summoned by the word 'time', a discordant chirping sounded from Kazon's breast pocket. He looked down with an embarrassed smile and plucked out his comm. "Oh, my." He tapped the screen. "Hello, sister."

A tiny hologram of Voria sprang up over the screen, arms folded and looking very concerned. "I hope I'm not interrupting anything vital."

"You aren't," Kazon assured her. "We just conducted the first field test of Xal, and it went well."

"That's good news, because we're out of time." Voria

began tapping her lip. "Nefarius has come to Yanthara. I just spoke to Crewes. It was all I could do to prevent him from attacking Nefarius alone."

"That doesn't track," Aran broke in. "Crewes isn't that reckless."

Voria's image turned to face Aran. "Nefarius conducted a 'poll' about attacking Yanthara, and then acted on the results. She devoured the *dream* Catalyst where Rhea was hidden."

Bile surged in Aran's gut as he thought about the priestesses. One priestess in particular, who'd clearly had feelings for Crewes. No wonder he was ready to fight.

"We're out of time, Aran," Voria pressed. "If you can't get Xal into the fight, and do it now, then I'm going to have to go without you."

Aran looked to Kazon and Nara. "Can you guys think of any reason why we can't go right now?"

Kazon shook his head.

"We should notify the other princes," Nara pointed out, "but I can take care of that if you can get us to Yanthara."

Aran glanced up at the blazing orb, which now brimmed with brilliant magic. "Time to end this, once and for all."

54

WAR

Frit gave Kaho a final squeeze, and then stepped away. He looked so magnificent in his golden robes, though she disliked the stylized dragon on the right shoulder, as she knew that represented Nebiat. The left shoulder held a stylized version of her, though, which she very much liked.

"I have to go, and you know I might not come back." She hated goodbyes, but she forced herself to look him in the eye. "I love you, Kaho."

He smiled down at her, and cupped her chin with one of his massive hands. "You will return, my love. I believe in you. As does our whole world. Today, you ride to victory. Know that we are with you."

It meant everything to her. She smiled, and then teleported aboard the *Spellship*, on the bridge where Voria stood with Ikadra. Voria was on a missive with Aran and his bushy-bearded friend. She caught a brief glance of Nara, and noted that her skin was darker than it had been. Then the missive disconnected.

"I'm ready," Frit said quietly, wanting to advertise her presence so that Voria didn't think she was eavesdropping.

"As am I." Voria turned to Frit, her translucent form no longer strange. "I've prepared my people as best I can, and have verified that Aran will be there momentarily with Xal. We will never have a better opportunity. The Godswar, for good or ill, will be settled in a few hours."

Frit nodded. What else could she say?

"I'm ready too," Ikadra chimed in. "I mean, if anyone cares..." No one answered. "Just leaving me hanging like that? Harsh."

There was a moment of weightlessness, and then they were elsewhere. Voria had translocated the *Spellship* a considerable distance away from Yanthara, and had apparently chosen her position to keep the planet between them and Nefarius.

The bridge's scry-screen zoomed in on the world, where a small fleet of ships had gathered. The Yantharan fleet were preparing to assault Nefarius, who had curled into a black ball and wrapped her wings around her for protection.

"She's still digesting," Voria muttered.

"The *dream* magic?" Frit asked. "How long do we have? Maybe we should strike now."

"Unless that's what she's waiting for," Voria countered. She gave a quick head shake. "No, we wait for Aran to arrive. They'll be here soon."

The *Spellship* moved swiftly toward the Yantharan fleet, but didn't close the gap entirely.

Crewes's face suddenly replaced the view on the scry-screen, with the bridge of the *Talon* behind him. To Frit's immense shock she realized that he was no longer human. The flesh and blood was gone...replaced by flame. Every detail was the same, save that it was sculpted from fire.

Frit blinked a few times and looked away. She'd never much liked Crewes, but he'd suddenly become a great deal more attractive. Certainly there was no harm in looking.

"Major, you are a sight for sore eyes." Crewes gave a fiery smile. "You got eyes on Aran? We sure could use an elder god right about now. I can't keep these Yantharan boys back much longer. They want payback, and the idea that they'll just get wiped out doesn't seem to dissuade them any."

"Let them know that if they wait," Voria explained, "we'll have help shortly."

"Will do." Crewes's expression hardened. "It's personal now, Major. For all of us. We won't let you down."

Then Crewes saluted, and Voria returned it. It had all the finality of a funeral, and Frit wondered just how powerful the being they'd come to kill was.

55

ELDER GODS

Nefarius was aware of many things. She monitored the communications flowing over Quantum, while also measuring the rate of magic absorption. If her calculations were correct, and they always were, then she'd complete ingestion just as Xal arrived.

Which would occur any moment now.

She watched his meager pantheon gather. There was a handful of conventional ships, but in their midst were two notable exceptions. The first she recognized. She'd seen the plans for the *Spellship* back when Inura had first conceived of it. The idea that he'd made it a reality was incredible, and she looked forward to prying it from the little *life* goddess's hands.

The second ship was smaller, a mere cruiser, but it possessed an immense amount of *fire* and *void* magic. She couldn't sense much of what was inside the smaller ship, but guessed there was at least one god of note. Perhaps more than one.

Not worthy of that much note, though, or they wouldn't

need to fly around in little ships. True gods were vessels in their own right.

Nefarius moved to her avatar, just as Talifax arrived in the reactor room, her nerve center, after a fashion. It was located inside the vessel that had once been the *Dragon Skull*, near the back where the armor was most dense.

That armor had a flaw, now, thanks to this Aran and his endless meddling. She looked forward to slaying him, especially knowing he was a Hound of Xal. He wouldn't be the first she'd murdered, though this time she would ensure all the hounds were dead, and that their master could never return.

"Has everything been prepared?" She glided a step closer to Talifax, who dropped into an appropriately subservient crouch. He hadn't bothered to repair his armor, and still bore her hand print on his neck.

"It has, mistress. Xal will be here in moments, with his whole host. If you best him here, he will never return."

"When," she corrected, turning from the sorcerer. "You will not be needed during the battle. Return to Ternus and take charge of the new black fleet. I want it ready for departure when I am finished feasting on Xal."

"Of course, mistress." Talifax bowed even lower, then disappeared.

Nefarius stared hard at the space he'd occupied a moment before. He would betray her, but the question was when? Had he already? Was there some possibility here he'd neglected to mention? Some way she might be defeated?

There would have to be some factor she was unaware of. Some possibility she hadn't seen. That seemed unlikely, but she failed to suppress her unease.

Nefarius returned her consciousness to her full divine

body, and was pleased to see that the absorption had reached 98%. In a few more moments she'd be ready for combat.

Space folded and twisted in the precise area where she'd expected it, far enough from the planet not to be an immediate threat to their gravity, but close enough to reach combat quickly.

The great Xal, the oldest god she'd ever personally met, appeared before her. Nefarius gave a delighted laugh when she saw the deity's condition.

Xal's body was rotted and worn. One leg was missing, and ragged holes dotted both wings. A sharp purple glow shone through a hole in the chest, exposing Xal's heart. This was going to be easier than she thought.

Then her gaze touched Xal's. Two things became immediately clear. This wasn't Xal. She detected none of his ancient wisdom in that awful gaze. What she did detect was resolve and tightly controlled rage. She suspected she was staring into the eyes of this hound she'd heard so very much about.

"So you weren't even able to restore him fully," Nefarius boomed, her voice defying physics as it echoed through the system. "If you were wise you would have run. If you'd gone far enough then you'd have been able to live your life for a few centuries before I found you. I am surprised you've embraced death."

She brandished Worldender in one taloned claw. She didn't need the weapon to best Xal, but it would make the fight easier. Not even Xal's ancient body could withstand such a weapon.

"Have you nothing to say, Xal?" Nefarius crooned, probing this hound's metal. "Will you go silently to your death?"

She deployed ten thousand drones, and allowed them to fan out through the system for additional telemetry, and of course to gather footage she could use later as propaganda. Her followers would be very interested in the outcome of this battle.

They couldn't watch it live, of course. She'd blocked that, because there were too many things she'd have to do that they must not see. Their willingness to attack Yanthara would end if they saw the manner of it, the casual death she'd inflicted. Once the battle was over she would write the history, and it would glorify her, as was proper.

She extended her wings and used *void* to close the distance to Xal. They were approximately the same size, which would make this combat a great deal more fun than nearly every other battle she'd engaged in with another god. Relatively even fights were rare.

Xal had never been a warrior, per se, but he'd built a warrior's body, so she was wary as she approached. Nefarius swung Worldender in a brutal arc designed to cleave Xal from shoulder to groin.

To her mild surprise Xal nimbly slid to the side, allowing the weapon to pass within a kilometer of his shoulder. It whistled harmlessly past, and Xal countered with a vicious roundhouse that she parried with a wing.

Xal vanished.

She vanished as well, appearing a million kilometers away.

Xal reappeared from the teleport, his clawed hands settling over the space where Nefarius neck had been a moment before.

She teleported again, this time behind Xal, and launched her tail like a harpoon. To her shock Xal's right hand shot out and seized the tip. The demonic god pivoted, and his other elbow came back, slamming into her skull.

Nefarius brought Worldender around, and Xal vanished again.

"I am impressed, Xal," she called, hoping that somehow her one-time rival was in there, listening. "Your new puppet can fight. But it won't save you."

56

OPENING GAMBIT

Aran desperately dodged another strike from Worldender, then ported several hundred kilometers away to gain a moment to think. Nefarius was already scanning for them, and would be on them again in moments. Each teleport cost *void*, too, which meant he couldn't use them freely.

"We can't keep doing this forever," Aran said, dimly aware of the cockpit where he sat with Nara and Kazon. "I'm open to suggestions. What do you two have?"

"The mecha is designed to utilize all of us," Kazon said. "When we engage again I can put up a ward."

"This thing works like a matrix," Nara murmured. "I can both counterspell and use offensive magic. Why don't you attack her, and this time Kazon and I will support you?"

Aran focused on the battle, and set himself to receive Nefarius's charge as she streaked across the black. He twisted at the last minute, dodging around Worldender. The tip scraped his shoulder, and that part of Xal's body simply dissolved.

There was no resistance to the blow, and it carried

Nefarius slightly off balance. Aran felt Xal's left arm rise, directed by Nara, and a thick disintegrate shot from the palm, slamming into Nefarius's back.

Scales boiled away into nothingness, exposing the dark metal underneath, which eagerly drank Nara's spell, just as it had Aran's back at the Fist.

"Damn it," Nara cursed. "That isn't going to work. I can still handle the teleports at least."

"Kazon, can you make me a spellshield?" Aran asked as he ducked another slash, and then hopped away from still another.

"Done." Golden sigils burst out from the wrist on Xal's left arm, and quickly resolved into a titanic version of the spellshield he normally wore on his spellarmor.

They suddenly blinked as Worldender hummed through the space they'd just occupied.

"Is a sword pushing it?" Aran asked as he twisted around another blow. Nefarius just wouldn't let up, and he wasn't fast enough to get away. The more they teleported, the more she learned to predict their movement.

"Done!" Golden energy burst from Aran's palm, and flared into a long curved blade that looked a good deal like Narlifex.

"Now we're talking." Aran grinned as he guided Xal into a defensive stance. He snapped the shield down to parry Worldender, but was shocked when the spear's wide, sharp head dissolved the shield as if it had never existed. The weapon continued on, and severed Xal's left forearm, sending the hand spinning away as the rest dissolved.

Aran twisted around the next blow, and brought his golden sword around in a quick chop. Nefarius raised a wing to block, and the sword shattered against it in a spray of sparks.

"Why are we always so outclassed?" Aran ducked another of Nefarius's swings, as Nara teleported them once more.

How were they going to get out of this one? They had no options that he could see. There was no way that Xal could beat Nefarius.

And then it hit him.

Xal couldn't beat Nefarius. Maybe Aran could. Maybe the abilities he'd been given hadn't been to pilot Xal, but to cripple Nefarius some other way. He'd seen the inside of the *Dragon Skull*, which looked pretty damned important.

Theoretically, he could translocate inside. Maybe he could do some damage.

He turned to Nara and Kazon. "I'm about to do something monumentally stupid, but I don't see that we have a choice. Nara, can you take over piloting for a while?"

"Sure, I can run away about as well as you." Nara's eyes glossed over as she eased into control of the god. "Go. Pull off a miracle, and make it snappy."

"Luck, brother." Kazon capped Aran on the shoulder from his couch.

"Thanks." Aran closed his eyes and concentrated on the room where Kezia had died. That area of the ship would be forever burned into his memory.

He appeared to find that all the battle damage they'd inflicted was repaired. The pulsing blue light from the reactor glowed as strongly as ever, and Aran now realized that must be the circulatory system that moved magic between the ships. An artery, basically.

"I had a feeling you'd be back," came a tinny, metallic voice from the shadows. It perfectly mimicked the Ternus drawl.

Footsteps clicked closer as the figure emerged into the

light of the reactor. The android appeared human, and was shorter than him, and slender. Her armor was the same molded black that Skare had worn, but her face was more articulate, though still clearly synthetic.

"Talifax foresaw this possibility." Nefarius extended both hands, and long, slim blades extended from her palms, until she held a pair of dirks. "He realized that you might try to strike the reactor, and thus disable my neural link to the human's Quantum network. If you beat me, godling, then you might be able to tell the sector what's happening here. Your friends on New Texas have been desperately eager to tell your side of the story, but I have been...disinclined to allow them."

A slow, wicked smile spread across her features.

"Are you trying to see if you can make me angry?" He took a step closer to her, and slowly eased Narlifex from his sheath. The blade was much heavier since it had drunk the pool of Xal, heavier and more powerful.

He gripped the hilt in both hands, and adopted a two-handed style to compensate. It would make his blows devastatingly effective, and he had a feeling he was going to need that extra power against her armor.

"Don't you take an opponent's measure upon meeting?" The smile never slipped. "I find it unlikely that Xal's puppet will fall prey to such a basic stratagem, but we can't skip the opening gambit, can we?"

She slowly approached, her blades striking twin rows of sparks along the deck as she closed.

Aran leapt forward and launched a strike at her abdomen. One of her swords flashed up and expertly parried, while the other whipped toward his groin.

He twisted over the second weapon, and released

Narlifex as his body became lightning. Aran crackled into her right eye, trying to get inside the delicate electronics.

The instant he struck the metal he was flung violently backward, and returned to his normal form, landing in a smoking heap.

He struggled to rise as she prowled closer, seemingly in no great rush. "Oh, that won't work, sweetie. You fail to understand—none of my sister's tricks will save you, any more than they did her, before I drank her essence."

57

TEAMWORK

Aran extended a hand and poured immense *void* into Narlifex's form, where it lay on the deck behind Nefarius. He yanked the weapon forward, and increased its mass and velocity as the pointy end pierced the back of Nefarius's armored shoulder.

He twisted out of her way as the momentum from the blow carried her past, then seized the hilt of his sword. Aran flared *fire* within him to increase his strength, and ripped the sword free in an attempt to do as much damage as possible.

Nefarius staggered a few steps away, sparks crackling from a gash in her shoulder. She rolled the shoulder experimentally and grinned at him once more. "I must say I am impressed with my younger brother's handiwork. This body is marvelous. You'd have taken an arm if I were a hatchling."

Then she was on him. Aran desperately parried, but Nefarius's blades were smaller and faster. She slipped a dirk past his defenses, and it punched into his side, loosing a flow of dark blood. It flowed more sluggishly than it should have, and the wound didn't hurt nearly as much as he'd have expected.

"I can see Xal has also crafted an impressive body." She yanked her dirk out with a grunt, and kicked him backward with a quick roundhouse.

Aran fed himself more *fire*, and charged. He knew this strategy wasn't working, but Nefarius seemed to enjoy toying with him and he needed time to think.

We cannot best her, Narlifex snarled, his thoughts clotted with rage. *We must retreat. Flee, master.*

"Retreat is not an option," he snarled under his breath as he hopped away from another one of Nefarius's endless slashes.

How the depths could he beat someone faster, stronger, and immune to all the damage you could inflict? None of the tricks he'd used in previous fights would work, and he hadn't picked up any new ones.

He wasn't even wearing spellarmor, because he hadn't expected to go hand to hand. He thought he'd be piloting a god.

Nefarius lashed out with a fist suddenly, and he'd been expecting a slash. Aran wasn't able to dodge and her metal fist connected with demonically hardened jaw. His jaw lost. Blood and teeth scattered across the deck as he was knocked prone a dozen meters away.

Aran tried to struggle to his feet, knowing he only had seconds.

"Take your time," Nefarius called magnanimously. "I'm in no rush. While you're failing in here, I'm also pursuing Xal, slowly exhausting his supply of *void* as he runs. At the same time I'm cutting together some wonderful footage of the battle so I can show my heroic victory on behalf of the mighty Terran Imperium. That has a nice ring to it. Much nicer than Ternus. What does that even stand for, anyway?"

Aran considered and discarded a dozen plans. None would do more than stall, and he needed something to get him on the offensive. He needed help.

That was it.

Aran focused on his link to Nara and Kazon. *I need a missive to Crewes, now. Tell him to get back to the site where we lost Kez, now, or we're all dead.*

Nefarius peered past his head as if studying something only she could see. "Interesting. You seem lucid. Do you really think summoning one of your godlings will influence the outcome? If you do I'd be happy to wait for them to arrive."

She stalked backwards a bit, watching him warily, then smiled again. "I am truly enjoying myself for the first time in...I can't even remember how long. You are an amusing adversary, Hound. Xal impresses me once again. When I devour your essence I'll enjoy seeing your perspective on things, and understanding exactly how Xal crammed so much combat knowledge into your head in such a short span of time. But then he always was the craftsman."

Aran rose slowly to his feet, shocked that she was giving him a chance to recover. To think...it seemed such an unnecessary risk, unless she really was so confident of victory that nothing he did mattered.

He considered his plan, glancing over at the reactor. It was rough at best, but if he pulled it off he'd get a shot at the reactor uninterrupted, maybe long enough to do some real damage.

"So, Nefarius," he panted, holding in his own innards with his free hand as he limped in her direction. He tried to look pitiful, which didn't take much, since right now he was.

"What do you get out of all this? Everyone has painted you as this mindless villain, but there's got to be a reason you're devouring all the magic. Is it about power?"

He figured keeping her talking would buy time for Crewes to arrive, in case she changed her mind about letting him recover.

She cocked her head and studied him. "I realize you're trying to delay me, but you also seem genuinely interested."

"Why wouldn't I be?" Aran paused a few meters away. He sank Narlifex's tip into the deck, and leaned on the weapon for support. "You're willing to destroy the sector in pursuit of your goals, and I have to believe that's just the beginning. So what's your endgame? You're going to kill me anyway, right? Not a lot of risk in telling me."

She gave a shrug, and flicked some of his blood from the end of her sword. "I guess not, is there? You know, if I'd had a century, a decade even, I could have turned you into an unstoppable killing machine. If I trusted Xal any more than I did Talifax I might even take you for a consort."

"I feel like you're avoiding my question." Aran released his wound, and realized that the trickle of blood had stopped. In fact, the wound appeared to be slowly healing. Must be a gift from Xal, one he hoped didn't come with strings.

"A little," Nefarius admitted. "I want to believe you are no spy, and that your question is genuine, but I must assume you are working with them, and that this is an effort to ferret out information."

"Uh, okay." Aran pulled Narlifex from the ground and stood under his own power. It was easier than it had been even a minute ago. "So you think I'm a spy for someone, or something, and clearly you fear whatever this is."

"All gods, those wise enough to remember those who

lurk beneath, are wise enough to fear them." Her robotic eyes whirred as they narrowed. "My patience is wearing thin. But, your friends are about to arrive. You may attack me whenever you are ready."

She stood there calmly, her swords drooping casually against the deck. The hubris floored him, and he wished he could think of any way to take advantage of it.

A sound louder than the thunder of the gods drowned out everything in the room, and a moment later a blast of debris shot through the room as the *Talon*'s pointed hull punched into the room.

Crewes exploded through the membrane in a ball of flame, followed by a more tame Bord, which suggested that Rhea must be flying the thing.

"You have no idea how good it is to see you," Aran called to his friend, who'd changed just as much as Aran had. "The whole fire thing is a good look for you."

"Yeah, I'll explain all about it after we kick this bitch's ass." Crewes's eyes narrowed, and he focused on Nefarius. "You killed Serala, and half a continent, lady. You're bad news, and we're gonna put you down."

Aran advanced on Nefarius's left, drawing her attention. "Crewes, follow my lead."

"Always, sir."

Bord prowled around the edge of the fight, keeping his distance, but ready to dart in when needed. Aran studiously avoided looking at him, in case Nefarius was unaware. It seemed unlikely, but nothing was lost in the attempt.

Aran reached for his magic in what he was coming to think of as a divine way. It worked like true magic, but all it required was thinking about what he wanted to accomplish.

"Give her something to think about, Crewes." Aran

waited as Crewes advanced, a towering inferno of white flames growing around his armor as he moved.

Nefarius shifted her stance to take in both of them, but her primary attention was focused on Crewes. Aran reached for his *void* magic, and opened a Fissure directly behind her.

He sprinted forward, and used *void* to increase his mass a thousand fold. Aran slammed into Nefarius's armored body, and launched her back through the Fissure. She screamed in wordless anger, and cast her blades aside as she seized the edges.

"Crewes," Aran yelled, trying to use his magic to force the Fissure to close, "blaze like the sun, man. Close the Fissure."

"This is for Serala, bitch!" Crewes gave a roar, and the inferno around him rose in height and intensity. It kept growing, and the Fissure began to crumble. "Yeah!"

Void rippled out from Nefarius, and the portal began to stabilize. Her hands yanked, and the Fissure began to widen.

"No!" Aran yelled, and focused all his will on closing the Fissure. It closed a half meter, but then stopped, and refused to shut entirely.

The portal began opening again, this time faster than before.

"You think mortals don't matter," Bord screamed from the far wall. "You think you can trample us, and hurt us... and kill us. Well, you can't. We matter. And today I'm getting revenge for my lady. This is for Kez!"

To Aran's immense shock, Bord fell to his knees, clasped his hands, and began to pray, "Oh, lady of light, I call upon you to lend me your aid. Help me fight the darkness. Grant me your light, and your strength."

Clean, white brilliance exploded from Bord, the same

clean glow that Voria herself shed whenever Aran had seen her. Crewes's fire had dimmed the Fissure, but when the light met it that was when it really began to crumble.

Nefarius's fingers lost their grip, and the Fissure snapped shut in her wake.

58

SECOND WIND

Aran spun to face the reactor the instant the Fissure winked out. He reached for his hound ability, and focused on the magic flowing through this node. A tremendous river of *void*, on par with what he had taken from Xal, flowed into him almost immediately, but the tide didn't stop.

Nefarius had already accumulated an immense amount of power, and Aran could only take so much. But he had to make that amount as large as possible.

"Captain Aran," Rhea's calm voice came over the *Talon*'s speakers, "you're about to have company. A flying android just appeared at the planet's umbral shadow and is heading in your direction. Fast."

"What do you want us to do, sir?" Crewes asked, hefting his spellcannon onto his shoulder. The heat coming off him would have cooked a normal man standing that close, but Aran was no longer a normal man.

"Get Bord onto the *Talon*, and get out of here," Aran ordered, certain he was making the right decision. It was a long shot, but it might work. "Go! I need to start doing some real damage."

Bord and Crewes sprinted back up the *Talon*'s ramp, and the ship began to retract out the hole it had entered through.

Aran turned back to the reactor, and drew upon some of the magic he'd been siphoning. He gave a low, angry smile. "Time for a little payback."

He focused an immense amount of gravity, the kind of gravity at the center of a black hole, right where the base of the reactor met the tech.

A tortured screaming of metal began, and critical systems and components were ripped loose from walls and sucked into the growing singularity.

"What. Have. You. DONE?!?" Nefarius roared, zooming into the room on a wave of *void*. "I will do worse than kill you for this. I will eradicate you!"

"Gotta catch me first." Aran shot her the rudest wink he could manage, and then teleported back to his command couch inside Xal. His last view of her expression made all the bullshit he'd been through recently worth it.

"Aran?" Nara called, seemingly from a great distance away. He realized that his head was swimming.

"Too much." He cradled his head in his hands.

"You have to dump the magic, Aran," Nara was saying somewhere in the distance.

The pain mounted, a living thing directly behind his eyes. Aran forced himself to open them, and to stare at the golden orb. "Kazon...can...you...moderate...magic...flow."

Aran didn't wait for an answer. He poured the *void* he'd taken from Nefarius into the orb, which began to discolor and darken. Vast swathes of magic poured through it, funneled throughout Xal's body by the network of golden neurons the ship had grown.

Xal's body grew stronger. Faster. More resilient.

Aran poured more magic. More. Still more. Every scrap of what he'd taken went into Xal, strengthening their god. Just in time, too.

Nefarius's gaze had settled on them, and her dragon form was coming. It would be on them in moments, and it still held Worldender, poised to strike.

59

CAN'T STOP THE SIGNAL

Davidson took another sip of his coffee and watched the battle playing out at Yanthara. He winced when Nefarius tore loose a hunk of the planet, and hated himself for being grateful that he got to sit this one out.

Next to him Governor Bhatia deftly edited footage, adding the atrocity they'd just seen to the news reel she'd prepared. Davidson had seen the entire thing, and if the rest of the sector did, there'd be no way they could follow Nefarius any longer.

The trouble was, Nefarius had locked down all comm traffic, and they still didn't even know where the primary transmitter was. Presumably that was somewhere in her head, and until it was cut there was no way for them to get their footage onto Quantum.

Davidson winced again when Xal lost a forearm, and his spirit sank when the demonic god turned and fled. Nefarius chased Xal around the system, and it seemed pretty clear how it had to end.

Then Nefarius's head bucked back suddenly, and something shot out like a bullet. The dragon shook its head, and fixed its eyes on Xal again.

Beep. Beep. Beep. Beep. A steady series of tones started coming from Bhatia's tablet.

"Does it have to keep doing that? I'm kind of watching—"

"Lieutenant!" Bhatia shot to her feet, and nearly dropped her tablet. "That's the code I set up to let us know when we have a live connection again. Something in that battle disabled Nefarius's jamming. We can transmit."

She took a moment to adjust her hair, and within seconds looked like she'd spent hours primping. "Are you ready to help save the sector, Davidson?"

Davidson gave a grin. "Let's hope people are ready to listen."

Bhatia tapped a button on her tablet and a drone rose into the air. The camera came on, and then the red transmitting button.

"Greetings, citizens of Ternus," she began, tone warm and motherly. "It is my sincere hope that this message finds you, and finds you with receptive minds. Foul deeds are afoot. We have been lied to. We have been duped. Our heroes have been unfairly besmirched, and at the center of it all lurks an evil that threatens to overwhelm us all. Now I am not a military leader, so I give you one who is. One who survived Marid, and Starn, and New Texas. One who is still standing, despite everything our enemies have thrown at him. Major Davidson, can you tell us why we should be afraid of the NEF-1 unit?"

"I can, Ma'am." He bobbed his head politely, and focused on the camera. "The NEF-1 unit is a Trojan horse, created by the Inurans. They told us it worked for us, but really? It works for them. All that magic it's devouring? The enemies it's protecting us from? It's only killing them so it can eat them, and when it's done it will eat us too."

They'd agreed that using the Inurans as a justified and accurate scapegoat might be better than trying to say a goddess was being resurrected, and Davidson was comfortable with that small lie.

"See for yourself," Davidson continued. He gestured at the space next to him, knowing that the audience would be seeing the same footage playing on the governor's tablet. "This is what NEF-1 did to our ally, Yanthara. If you are a citizen of Ternus, and were recently returned to our reality, then I urge you to play that bit back and watch it again. We doomed their world, people. Nuclear winter, for a thriving colony. It will never recover, and they are our allies. How do we condone something like that? We're still gathering evidence, but we believe the poll was a fraud, and that most people were against this atrocity."

He paused, and waited for Bhatia, as they'd discussed.

She broke in, her eyes shining with tears. "My world was very nearly destroyed. I was in a bunker, and I'd given up. I knew I was going to die, that my world would be nothing but a tomb. Voria and Aran saved us. Voria used her magic to wipe out every corpse at once, and the people of New Texas are alive because of it. Me personally? I wouldn't be alive if Captain Aran's company hadn't held the line."

"That's why we're asking," Davidson picked up smoothly, "that if you trace your lineage back to Texas, and the Texas renews the U.S. program, that you consider who our real friends are. Do you put your trust in the men and women who held the line? In Voria, who won at Marid, and at New Texas? In Aran who helped her win all those battles and more? We need heroes, ladies and gentlemen. I've fought beside Aran and Voria. They're exactly the kind of heroes we need. Now I know a lot of you keep to the old ways. If you do, and if you pray, I want you to think of Aran and Voria as a kind of saint. Pray to them, like you would to the Lord Almighty, or one of his saints. Pray that they'll have the strength to protect us from that."

The footage now showed a simulation of Nefarius dismembering Ternus, and then New Texas, and then Colony 3.

"NEF-1 and the Inurans are not our allies," Bhatia picked up smoothly. "Aran and Voria have never given us cause to doubt them, and they were the only ones brave enough to speak out about the Inurans. We can't let them die unsupported. Lend them your prayers, and together we can help them ensure victory. I know this will sound strange to many of you, but there is strength in prayer, whatever you believe personally. I know we can do this together."

The recording light winked out, and Davidson turned to face the governor. "Do you think it will do any good?"

"Let's hope so, Major. Congratulations on your promotion." She shot him a sidelong look. "Don't protest or we'll make it colonel. We need officers."

Davidson scrubbed his fingers through his beard. Part of him had wondered what would happen if Aran won and stopped the bad guys, but he'd never really believed it was possible.

He'd always assumed mankind would go quietly into the night. Defeatist, maybe, but when one had seen as many worlds destroyed as he had, it tended to negatively affect one's outlook.

"Then you've got me." Davidson smiled. "I'll do my part."

Bhatia laughed warmly. "Our part may already be done. Now we wait, and see if the sector comes to our aid."

60

ENDGAME

Aran dodged yet another blow from Worldender, and wished he had a weapon to counterattack with. Nefarius was noticeably slower after he'd drained some of her magic, and they were noticeably faster, but sooner or later she was going to connect and they were going to lose something vital.

"Kazon, what do you have for me, buddy? I need a weapon, man." Aran couldn't afford to split his focus, and missed whatever the reply might have been. He was staying ahead of Nefarius, but just barely.

"Shinura!" Kazon intoned, loud enough that Aran nearly missed a parry.

"I don't think praying to—"

"No, no, he's here." Kazon sounded excited.

"I cannot believe I am risking discovery," Inura's familiar voice came from somewhere to Aran's left, inside the cockpit, and he wished he could split his focus long enough to see what was going on. He couldn't.

Aran dodged another swipe. The next would have hit

him, but Nara teleported at the last moment, and they dodged.

They were not so lucky with the next one. Worldender punched through Xal's abdomen, and Aran winced sympathetically when he realized many demon villages had just been obliterated.

The spear left a gaping dissolved hole as it tore free, but thankfully the wound hadn't damaged anything vital.

"If you've got a god in here," Aran growled, "then give me a gods-damned weapon I can fight with."

"We already gave you one," Shinura snapped, close enough that it distracted Aran, and he lost the other leg.

"Damn it." He gritted his teeth, and elbowed Nefarius in the face, then teleported away. "No riddles. Fix this."

"Your sword. Draw your sword," Shinura explained. "Quickly—shove it in the damned orb. How you didn't already figure this out I will never know. Did you not think the bloody blood memory of a bloody god was important? What did you think that pool was for, anyway?"

Nara teleported them several times in rapid succession, buying time. "Do it, Aran. Quickly."

Aran yanked Narlifex from his sheath, and rammed the blade into the golden orb. He'd been wanting to do that for some time, ever since the first tendril, and it felt good.

The orb began to vibrate, and the dense black genetic material the sword had absorbed began flowing into the orb. It pulsed outwards through Xal, across the golden neurons, through the god.

Most focused on the remaining arm, and began pooling in the fist. The liquid began to grow, and lengthened into a blade. A curved blade.

Narlifex, the blade thundered in Aran's mind, *is strong now. We kill Nefarius.*

The dragon-deity had finally caught up, and she was charging with Worldender braced before her like a lance. Aran studied her approach, then instinctively swung the god-sized Narlifex.

He braced himself for the weapon to shatter, as the golden sword had, but Worldender clanged off his blade. Aran rammed Xal's severed stump into Nefarius's mouth, then brought Narlifex down on the arm holding the spear.

God-forged blood metal met Inuran forged alloy, and won. Narlifex sliced cleanly through Nefarius's arm, and the spear tumbled free.

Nefarius responded with a vicious kick, and tore off a hunk of his bloody stump, which she wolfed down ghoulishly. She seized Worldender with one of her feet, and flapped several hundred kilometers away, only a small gap when dealing with beings their size.

"I've underestimated you, but that ends now." Her eyes narrowed, and flared purple. "You've stolen enough of my magic to prolong this, but not to beat me. I don't care if you can parry now. I was the finest swordsman in this sector hundreds of millennia before your species learned speech. Xal has accomplished a minor miracle with you, and that is laudable, but you are not equal to the task—"

As she monologued, the golden orb began to pulse. The black that Narlifex had added was quickly overwhelmed by a brilliant white. Not the gold of *life* magic. This was different.

"It's worship," Nara whispered, leaning closer with a bemused smile. "Where is it coming from?"

"Who cares?" Kazon barked a laugh. "How can we use it?"

"To heal Xal." A grim, evil smile grew on Aran's face. "Nefarius is right. Let's end this."

Aran swung Narlifex one handed, and parried Worldender as Nefarius made another attempt. She twisted around, and breathed a cloud of black tendrils.

"There they are," Nara said. "Sooner or later they were going to deploy those tendrils. Good thing we're ready."

Nara used what was left of Xal's stump to fire disintegrates at the tendrils, quickly reducing the mass. She ported Xal backwards, kiting Nefarius as the Wyrm struggled to close the gap. Every passing second more of Xal's body healed. It began with the wound in his side, and then the chest cavity, and then his missing legs. Worship, brilliant glorious worship, rebuilt Xal's body. Strengthened it. Quickened it.

The demons dwelling in the newly healed areas were absorbed, tens of thousands joining Xal as both their bodies and minds were welded into the god's. It was grisly and horrifying, and necessary if he wanted to win.

Aran finally went on the offensive. He darted forward and brought Narlifex down in a tight arc, which knocked Worldender away and allowed him to get close. Aran jabbed into Nefarius's midsection over and over and over. He jammed Narlifex in, each stab ripping out another chunk.

Nefarius reared back and prepared to breathe another cloud of tendrils. Aran responded with a head butt, but knew it only bought a moment. "You guys got something?"

"Oh, I got something," Crewes's voice came over the comm as the *Talon* streaked into view, "and scaly ain't gonna like it."

A river of liquid star-fire shot from the *Talon*'s spellcannon, and slammed into Nefarius's mouth. At first the tendrils eagerly drank the flame, but they quickly shriveled, and then burned away entirely.

"Yeah, that's right, bitch. You think I'm a damned side-kick? I don't think so."

Aran grappled with the dragon, which became easier when Xal's stump grew into a functional hand once more. At first he struggled, and Nefarius pushed Xal's arms back.

More worship poured in. More.

Now they were pushing Nefarius back. She teleported, and Aran spun as he sought her location.

"You think you're winning?"

She was below him! Nara teleported, but not soon enough. Worldender slammed into their thigh, burning away flesh and bone. It regrew almost as quickly, worship flowing in to fill the gaps the ancient weapon had left.

A pair of immensely powerful beings appeared in the sky, and Aran very nearly panicked and shifted to fight them too. It was Frit and Voria.

Voria was now a towering goddess, about as tall as Xal's knee. She held the *Spellship*, with its blazing blades twirling before her. "I do think we're winning. We outnumber you. And we out-worship you. The sector sees you for the threat you are, and now we are going to put you down."

Aran charged, and swiped at Nefarius's face with Narlifex. The dragon fell back, allowing Voria a free shot at her back. She slashed into the metal with the *Spellship*, and a gaping hole appeared. It wasn't catastrophic damage, but the dragon roared in anger.

Frit blazed an angry orange-white, then shot toward the dragon. Her body punched through the tail, and the end began to glow a dull angry orange. The glow continued to intensify, though there was no sign of Frit. Until the end of the tail exploded, sending the jagged barb at the end spinning away off into space.

Aran slashed again, and again. He kept Nefarius on the

defensive, which allowed his allies to whittle her down. She was losing now, and she knew it.

Now it really was time to end this. In the distance he spied Yanthara's moon. He felt a little bad, but better the moon than the planet.

Aran summoned as much of Xal's *void* as he could pull, which was far, far more than he was expecting. He centered the gravity on Nefarius's foot, which still clutched the mighty spear.

That foot tore loose with a mighty pop, and the spear flew into Xal's grasp. Aran took it up in Xal's newly regrown hand, and charged with both Worldender and Narlifex.

Nefarius desperately parried the sword with a wing, but that left her open. Aran hopped backwards, and hurled the spear. It caught Nefarius full in the chest and carried her into Yanthara's moon, shattering both dragon and planet in the process.

The part of Nefarius's chest that was touched by the spear ceased to exist, but her limbs, and her wings, were flung off in all directions, shattered by the force of the explosion.

"No, I will not poison our sector," Aran roared. He became Xal fully, and focused on Xal's immense reserves of *void*. He used it to gather the fragments, then pulled them into a growing singularity.

Aran collected every last remaining bit of Nefarius he could find, and sucked it all into the black hole. Only when the last scrap had disappeared did he release the singularity. He extended Xal's free hand, and Worldender flew back into it.

They won. Somehow they'd won.

"This isn't victory," Shinura said. Or Inura maybe. Aran had no idea which this was, as the white-haired Wyrms looked identical. He thought he'd seen the god die, but the way Shinura spoke sounded a lot more haughty than the shade he'd first met. "If even a single scrap of Nefarius survived that, then she will be back."

"Besides," Nara pointed out, her eyes going hard. "We still haven't dealt with Talifax, and it isn't over as long as that bastard is still out there."

"Do as you will," Shinura said. "My part is done, and I plan to get far from this sector."

And then he was gone. For good, Aran imagined.

61

PLANNED FOR EVERYTHING

Talifax's laughter echoed throughout the mausoleum as he stared down at the pool, which showed Nefarius's draconic body devastating Yanthara's moon. Several tons of tainted material escaped Xal's purge. Bits of black ship, and worse, would eventually land on some unsuspecting world.

That would take millennia, of course, but those were merely seeds. The true goal had been the removal of the greater pantheon, which had taken Talifax over a hundred thousand years to achieve.

There would be neither reward nor thanks, but such things were trivial. Talifax had spent millennia contemplating the whispers of those who lurked beneath, and understood what they were seeking.

Creation was flawed. You could keep a flawed system running, for a while at least. But eventually you needed to build a better system. Before that system could be built, the old would need to be removed. Fortunately, there was nothing in this reality worth saving, himself included.

He passed a thick palm over the pool and the dark liquid

went still. Talifax rose from his knees, and stretched. Such a simple physical luxury, one that he treasured. He walked up the broad stairs, and out of the viewing chamber, into the fortress proper.

A black fortress on a black world two dozen sectors away from the war he had so carefully orchestrated. His sanctuary, and one of the few monuments to Those Who Came Before. He stared at the ruined world, visible only because of the constellations of tombs in the sky, each glowing with a sickly green light.

Talifax raised a deft hand and sketched a quick trio of *void* sigils. Hard casting was another luxury, like stretching. One didn't precisely need either, but that didn't mean they couldn't be indulged now and then.

The Fissure cracked open, exposing darkness beyond. Something writhed there, imperceptible without more light. Eyes cultured above those tentacles, but it was impossible to count them in the dark.

Talifax dropped to his knees and genuflected. "All is as you have instructed, master."

No, a voice thrummed in his mind. *It is not. You were instructed to remove the pantheon.*

"And I have done so. Nefarius was the last," he protested, though he didn't look up. His masters could be...touchy. "There is—"

You fool. You have failed, the voice thundered.

The Fissure cracked shut of its own accord.

Talifax climbed to his feet, an unfamiliar emotion bubbling up within. Panic. It wasn't fear, or even terror. Those were reactions of the mind and could be controlled with discipline. Panic was the absolute lack of options.

What did his masters mean? How had he failed?

"You know," a very smug voice came from behind him,

"this is not at all how I'd choose to decorate my world, but I do have to admit it fits the tone of what's about to happen to you. Grim."

A human, small compared to Talifax, stood before him. That human had the dusky-dark skin of a demon-blooded, and wore an all too familiar sword belted to his hip. He had no spellarmor, but Talifax could feel the violence in the man. No, the god. Aran didn't need spellarmor, his walk said, as he ambled toward Talifax.

"How did you find me?" Talifax cocked his head as he folded his arms. His panic was gone, at least. This was a problem he could solve. Nor did he fear Aran, as he could translocate away before the god could do anything.

And, since Aran had already translocated, he would not be able to follow. Talifax had run from gods before, and would again, if needed. This was manageable.

"Turns out," Aran began as he eased the blade from its sheath; power wafted from the dark blade, drawing Talifax's eye, "that Neith was willing to take an apprentice."

Talifax blinked a few times. "You can say her name. You've overpowered the geas."

"Yeah, well, I'm not a mindwiped recruit anymore, Talifax." The tip of his adversary's dark blade scraped along the stone as he approached. "We fought your best, and beat them, and unless I'm missing something...there's no way you can take me in a straight fight."

"You're right about that." Talifax smiled beneath his helmet. "But I don't need to fight. Good day, Captain."

He translocated to a small shipping facility he'd acquired on one of Colony 3's moons, on a deserted part of the planet. It had been used by the booming mining industry, but was utterly worthless once the ore played out.

That made it perfect. Isolated, but in a system teaming

with life, which helped to hide magical signatures like his. It, combined with many other magical safeguards, would make predicting his movements all but impossible.

He'd appeared inside the facility's lowest level, which lay beneath three kilometers of the planet's dense iron crust, another layer of protection.

The best protection, though, was getting away from this place as quickly as possible. He'd need about fifteen minutes before he could translocate again, which would mean that...

A tiny red dot appeared on his breastplate, right over his upper left heart. Talifax pulled open a void pocket and his hand settled around the dragonbone wand's ivory haft. His armor would protect him from the first spell, but he needed to locate his assailant, and respond with something lethal.

The muzzle of a rifle flared black, and a ball of pulsating purple streaked toward Talifax. It stopped just short of his armor, and then pulled itself into a tiny marble. Enormous gravity washed over Talifax, and to his horror he realized his armor couldn't protect him.

The titanic gravitational forces could only be generated by one thing, and that thing was one of the few eventualities he'd not prepared for.

"That's right," came a vaguely familiar voice. Feminine. Human. "It's over, Talifax."

Nara sauntered into the light, her long dark hair bound in a tight braid down the back of her form-fitting body armor. None of that commanded his attention, however. The rifle she held did.

"By the nameless ones," he whispered, blinking at it, "you've recovered Shakti. How did I not foresee this?"

She was one of only a handful of weapons that could kill

him, and the only one anywhere near this sector and timeline.

Talifax thought he'd planned for everything. He'd predicted that assailants might follow him here, and that he might be ambushed without being able to translocate. He still had teleports, and even if his enemy countered those, his armor should have stopped any attack.

He'd prepared for very nearly anything. Very nearly.

One could not stop a growing singularity with any magical object or spell. The best one could hope for was slowing it, or if you were a titan, perhaps, escaping it. Talifax gritted his flat teeth and focused on his reserves of *void*. They were truly vast, and he was able to constrain the singularity's growth. Momentarily at least.

"How?" he managed. His armor grew cold, and a thick layer of frost accumulated, then that frost was ripped into the singularity.

"Frit? Come take a bow," Nara called, and gestured theatrically as the Ifrit sauntered into view.

The Ifrit wore a truly predatory smile as she approached, though she was careful to stop well away from the singularity's threshold. Her flaming hair danced around her, framing a wicked grin.

"You think you're so clever, and that we're so dumb." Frit's eyes narrowed. "We knew that no matter what happened you'd try to run. So my role in the final battle was to figure out where you would run to, and what you would do."

She produced a jagged shard of glass, one that glowed with immense, ancient power. "I used this, and the temporal matrix, and I asked Nara a whole bunch of 'what if' questions. What if Talifax betrays Nefarius? What if Talifax translocates away? What happens if you shoot him the chest with say, a black hole?"

The singularity crept out another millimeter, and its gravity increased to match. Talifax's armor gave an audible groan.

"No," he snarled, ripping his helmet off to expose his trunk and his tusks. He would die with his face exposed. Talifax hurled his helmet toward the ground, but of course the singularity caught it and sucked it in. "I don't believe it. There is no way that this was orchestrated by mortals. I was not bested by mortals!"

Nara's eyes flared a deep violet, and the penetrating voice that issued from her mouth was not her own. "You are partially right, little sorcerer. The mortals have done well, and have become the pantheon I need them to be, one unassailable from without. But it was my hand that guided them."

Talifax had a million questions, but only one came. "Xal?"

"Indeed." The vessel, Nara, gave something approaching a smile. Ancient magic glittered in her eyes. "I have distributed my consciousness among all my followers. Ironically, it was you who gave the idea to Nefarius, who in turn shared it with me. Instead of using the blood to enslave...I became the blood. I manifest in whomever I choose, wherever my magic is found. I drew the trio of vessels to the light. I forged them into weapons all in service of this day. All so that I could look you in the eye, sorcerer, and tell your masters, through you, that they have lost. They sought to eradicate the pantheon in our sector, to weaken us for their inevitable invasion. Instead I have forged a powerful, diverse pantheon. Demons, humans, Ifrit, Wyrms, Shayans,

Inurans...all have a reason to work together now. I have united them."

The singularity crept closer, and Talifax's breastplate buckled. A heart exploded, and he clutched his chest, though the other three were compensating.

"I know you can hear me," Xal continued, through his vessel. "You lurk in darkness, always seeking to spread it. To snuff the stars themselves until everything outside the Great Cycle is darkness. And I am here to tell you that we will not allow it. I will go to other sectors, and I will prepare them too. I will unite this galaxy, and we will stand against you."

Talifax opened his mouth to speak again, but the singularity advanced, and his body, which had survived rigors that many gods could not, was suddenly and violently ripped into its component atoms.

62

CHOICES

Crewes stared up at the *Talon*'s scry-screen as the kid trudged his way up the wide redwood limb and into his new life. For the first time since Nefarius had killed Serala, something eased in him. It was time to start the healing, for those that could be healed.

Not all of them could. He sure couldn't. He was like a wounded animal, disemboweled, and trying to cling to life somehow. There just wasn't fixing the kind of wounds he'd taken. Crewes hadn't realized just how much she'd meant to him until she was gone.

That wasn't all of it though. He'd spent several hours watching footage of Yanthara after the battle. So many casualties. Thankfully, Voria had used her magic to stabilize the weather, and the planet was already recovering. It would take much longer for the survivors.

"Where will we go now, sir?" Rhea asked from the neighboring matrix. "And, more importantly, how will we get there?"

Crewes turned from the screen, and blinked at the Outrider. He wasn't used to being the one who answered questions, and he already hated it. Was he really going to have to explain every little thing he did? Guess maybe so. At least he'd had good examples to draw from.

"Virkon." Crewes rested his flaming hands against the *Talon*'s command couch, and was thankful that the ship seemed impervious to his new body.

So was Neeko, who'd curled up and was sleeping directly underneath him, no doubt.

Rhea raised a raven eyebrow. "You're going to try to recruit?"

"You don't approve?" Crewes asked, already self conscious. He thought it was a pretty good plan.

"I do." Rhea paused thoughtfully, cocking her head and staring at a point over Crewes's head for a moment. Then she looked down at him again. "I'm trying to be diplomatic. If we're going to recruit, why wouldn't you start with Bord? He's a fine soldier and a gifted mage. We need him to open Fissures."

"Nah." Crewes patted the stabilizing ring affectionately. "See, it occurred to me. The *Talon* opened a Fissure all on his own, once. I bet that he's absorbed enough magic that the ship can handle it. That about right, ship?"

The scry-screen shifted to show the planet's umbral shadow, and a wide purple crack veined across the sky.

"It would appear you were right, sir." Rhea gave him a hard stare, not mean, but a firm no BS kind of look. "That still doesn't answer the question."

"Kid's seen enough war," Crewes supplied easily. He'd given this a lot of thought, and was comfortable with his choice. "I could have asked him to stay, and he'd have stayed. But he ain't like us. He's not a lifer. He's still got a chance to be normal, and maybe claw his way back from the mountain of shit life dumped right on top of him. So I want to give him that shot. If I'm wrong, and the kid ever needs a home, well, he's got one."

Rhea looked away suddenly, but Crewes caught a faint smile. "I see. Excellent choice, Captain."

Crewes leaned back in his couch. "You keep that good mood close, because I have one more call to make."

Rhea stiffened. "My father."

"We can't exactly fly to Virkon without checking in with him." Crewes tapped a *fire* sigil, then another.

The screen shifted, and a moment later the missive was accepted. Kheross's handsome features appeared, an irritated expression marring them slightly. "What do you want, human? Now that Aran has accepted his new role, there is no longer any reason for us to be in contact."

Crewes shifted uncomfortably. He was really bad at this stuff. "I called to offer you a job. I'm rebuilding the Outriders, and we need the best. You're the best." He left off the obligatory 'scaly', as that wasn't going to score him any points.

Normally he wouldn't care, but Serala would have cared. She'd have disapproved, and he couldn't really handle that right now, even knowing she was gone.

Kheross leaned his head back and brushed a lock of white hair from his shoulder. "And how about you, daughter? You're fine with me being aboard the vessel? Not that I've agreed."

"You've been cleansed." Rhea's posture, normally ramrod straight, slumped. "I'm sorry, father, for the way I treated you. You're alive and healed. You're welcome here. We'd benefit from your expertise and experience."

"You've no idea how it warms me to hear that." Kheross's hostility melted, and he beamed a fanged smile at his daughter. "I wish I could join you. Truly. But I have accepted a new role on Virkon. The few remaining Wyrms have agreed to serve as advisors, while the Outriders are taking their place as the rulers of Virkon. We will guide them, but no longer will we rule them."

"Captain's gonna love that." Crewes found himself smiling again. Serala liked cooperation, and so did the major.

"I would like to formally invite you to our world," Kheross offered. He gave Crewes a respectful nod, and you'd have thought he was pulling teeth. "You are welcome to recruit, and I expect you will find exactly what you're looking for. The question is...what then?"

"Man, I don't even know what day it is, scaly." Crewes waved dismissively at Kheross. "What makes you think I've got a plan?"

Kheross leaned his head back and laughed. It wasn't long before Crewes joined in.

63

REMEMBER THE BEER

Bord raised a hand to shade his eyes as the *Talon* lifted off, then jetted toward the upper atmosphere. She was absolutely silent, that great beauty, and larger by the day from the looks of it. Such a terrifying ship, but the food had been second to none. Kez had loved that.

He hefted his pack, and turned from the *Talon*, knowing he wasn't ever going to see it again, except for maybe on the holo when Crewes stomped the faces of whatever next decided to threaten the Confederacy.

That was okay. Bord gave something approaching a smile as he walked off the landing pad, and up the road bisecting the second branch, up near the top of the tree. He walked past groups of Shayan children, mostly, but here and there tiny drifter lads and lasses chased after them, and they seemed to get along splendidly.

"Kez would have loved that, too." Bord stopped, and began to cry. Not the ugly kind that he usually did, but soft, quiet tears.

Tears of remembrance.

"She'd thought that was right proper." Bord kept walking, and didn't fight the tears.

He'd tasted true happiness, which was more than most people would ever get. And he'd helped save the sector, in a small way. He'd mattered more than he ever expected.

Kez would have liked that too.

She'd always wanted to matter, to help make things right. She liked protecting other people, and Bord shared that love, at least. He liked helping people, and protecting them.

But he was done with war. He couldn't fight, not ever again. He'd punished the people who'd killed Kez. He'd smashed Skare's smug face, and watched Nefarius explode into a million, trillion bits. He hadn't seen Talifax die, but he'd heard about that too. Nara and Frit had done for that bastard.

They'd won, and now he could rest.

He hefted the pouch attached to his belt, like some adventurer from that *Relic Hunter* show. It bulged with dragon scales, enough to buy up a branch if he really wanted. And he had two more bags in his pack.

Bord ambled along the branch, passing parks, and gated manors. He finally stopped outside the one he'd picked, which was smaller than its neighbors. Not because he couldn't afford the larger, but because Kez wouldn't have approved.

Too much space, she'd have said. It's more cleaning. We don't need it, even with a wee one. He opened the wrought iron gate, and walked up a soft carpet of redwood needles to the front door.

His front door.

Bord pushed it gently open, and stepped inside. It was ginormous, especially for just one person. He walked through the kitchen to the glass door, and waved a hand in front of it. The glass shimmered out of existence, and he stepped through onto his back deck.

This had been the real reason he'd bought the house. A gazebo sat next to a small pond, and a swinging bench just big enough for two people and a wee one swung in the breeze. It afforded a magnificent view of the fields and mountains stretching into the distance. It was the kind of view no drifter or urchin would ever have had access to a year ago.

Next to the gazebo was something special he'd had fashioned. A life-sized statue of Major Voria, standing tall, with Ikadra held proudly before her. Just how she'd been at the end, stalwart, and ready to defend them all.

The *Spellship* had been designated the flagship of the reborn Confederacy, and she its caretaker. Bord thought that fitting.

He moved to stand before the statue, and snapped a tight salute. "Thank you, ma'am. For everything. For saving us. For helping me to become a man, and for making sure Kez was there to see it. You've given us all so much, and I don't know if anyone's ever told you how much we all appreciate it."

"They have," came a familiar voice from behind him, "but it's still nice to hear. Thank you, Bord."

He turned to see the lady of light herself blazing in the morning sun, magnificent, and beautiful, and divine. She wore a wistful smile, and her hair was in a ponytail for once, instead of a bun.

"Do you remember Marid, Bord?" she asked, staring off into the distance, lost in memory he'd wager.

"Course I do." He grinned, rising from the ground and

dusting off his pants. "You don't forget the planet where you died."

"And you remember how we brought you back?" She was eyeing him sidelong now, and from her expression there was something he was supposed to be getting. But he wasn't getting it.

"Yeah..." He eyed her curiously. "The beer was blessed by Shaya. Super rare stuff, right?"

"Blessed by Shaya, a goddess of life."

"Yeah, so really, really good beer. Why you'd need a goddess to—hold on," he realized aloud. "Are you saying you can bring people back to life?"

"I can." She smiled warmly.

"But I thought there was a time limit, and you needed a body and stuff."

"There are limitations." Voria raised a hand, and it began to glow. "But Kez was a true believer. One of her last acts was praying to me, and when she died, well it turns out that souls congregate around their god or goddess. She came to me, Bord. She's been here, dreaming."

The light became too bright to look at, but in that light Bord saw the outline of a person. A drifter. An outline he'd never, not ever forget.

The light faded, and there Kez stood, as beautiful as she'd ever been. Blond curls spilled down her shoulders, and her cheeks dimpled as she smiled at him.

"I saw everything, Bord." She opened her arms and he dashed forward to seize her in a fierce hug. "You did so good. I'm so proud of you. You're a proper soldier. I love the house."

"Major, I don't even know what to say..." The tears were back, and this time it was going to be one of those ugly cries.

"Shh...it's okay. No one's watching. Just a goddess, that's all." Kezia punched him lightly in the arm.

Ikadra's sapphire pulsed. "Damn, that was cold, Kez. You people are hard core. Welcome back!"

Bord blinked up through the tears. "I can't believe I got my happily ever after."

"I think we all did, Bord." Voria smiled down at him, then turned to pat Ikadra, "Come, on, Ikadra. Let's leave them in peace. We have work to do. Rebuilding the Confederacy is going to take time, and a great deal of work."

"And poo jokes," Ikadra added, helpfully in Bord's opinion.

"You're all right, staff." Bord reached up and awkwardly patted his golden haft. "Don't let those bastards grind you down. You keep them poo jokes coming."

"Oh, I will." Ikadra pulsed mischievously. "Trust me. I will."

64

HOMECOMING

Frit descended slowly from orbit, making as big a production of her arrival as she possibly could. She blazed like a falling star, visible to every follower on this side of the world. Those on the other side could observe through scrying, or a few through the first crop of Ternus tech they'd purchased as part of the treaty.

Warm worship rose up to meet her, fortifying her and filling her with magical strength. She basked in it, and for the first time didn't feel guilty. These were her people.

Her descent took her toward a pyramid that hadn't existed the last time Frit had been here. It towered over Nebiat's draconic statue, a clear statement about their relative places in the hierarchy of this world's pantheon.

She'd never have thought of implications like those, which made it clear that placing Kaho at the head of her temple had been a magnificent decision.

Frit landed in a puff of smoke at the edge of a wide balcony near the top of the pyramid. A dozen very important-looking hatchlings and Ifrit instantly dropped to their knees and bent their necks in respect.

"Rise." Frit strode toward Kaho, who was the first to his feet. Once she'd have protested about the bowing, but more and more she was coming to understand that traditions and appearances were important.

"Mahaya." Kaho smiled down at her with that sea of fangs, a sea she rather adored. "Welcome home. The treaty has been signed?"

She strode over to a throne that she'd only just noticed, a giant obsidian slab. Imposing. Frit sat, and turned to face the man she'd grown to love. "Our sector has a new pantheon. Voria sits at its head. We have peace, for the time being."

"You don't think it will last?" Kaho's wings drooped.

"I pray it will." Frit brushed a lock of flaming hair from her face. "But I wonder how long it will be before Ternus remembers Krox attacking their capital, or before the surviving demons realize that Aran could easily conquer this entire sector, and there's not a damned thing any of us could do to stop him."

"Troubling issues." Kaho sat on the step beneath her throne.

The rest of the advisors each bowed, and quietly scurried away. She gave a wave to acknowledge them, but kept her focus on Kaho.

"There will always be problems, I know." Frit threw a leg up over the throne in a way she thought Nara might have done, but it felt wrong so she returned to a normal sitting position. "You know what, though? I'm just happy we're facing them together. Our world is strong. Our people are united. I'm ready to face the future. With you."

Kaho's grin, the boyish one she'd seen the day she met him, slipped back into place. "There is time for our happily ever after. For the first time I can indulge scholarly pursuits.

Already our earth mages are advancing in their mastery of construction. Instead of war...we'll bring commerce to the sector. We can help people rebuild."

Love swelled in Frit. She already missed Nara, but being a god she could visit her whenever she wished. She wondered what Nara's new demon friends were like. Perhaps she'd have to arrange a visit soon.

EPILOGUE

Aran sat heavily on the bleak throne that Malila had occupied the last time he'd been here. As promised, when the dust had settled she and her followers had left the skull, which was, by right, the property of the Voice. His property.

"Welcome." Aran allowed his gaze to roam among the demon lords. They'd all come, of course. No one was going to miss the first post-Nefarius meeting.

Nara stood at the foot of the throne's steps, the barrel of her rifle resting on her shoulder in a not-so-casual show of support. It also afforded an excellent view of her ass, which Aran was taking full advantage of.

Kazon stood opposite Aran, his left hand sheathed in the Gauntlet of Reevanthara. That gauntlet fit him now. Kazon's beard had grown, and his skin had darkened, which also fit somehow. Aran had seen similar changes in himself.

The other demon lords were much, much less friendly than Kazon and Nara.

Malila and Malazra stood together, inseparable now that

they had a common foe—Aran. Enoch stood off by himself, his expression vacant as if he were somewhere far away. It could have been a ruse. Aran hoped so.

"Thank you for inviting us, mighty Voice of Xal." Malila bowed low. Her sister echoed the gesture, and the others followed suit.

Aran stole a casual glance at Nara as she bent over. It was good to be the king.

"I apologize for requesting this meeting," Malazra broke in, taking a step closer to the throne. Seeing the pair next to each other made the resemblance inescapable. They were very nearly twins. "I feel the urgency warrants it."

"I respect you." Aran rested a hand on Narlifex, a subtle 'I might respect you, but respect doesn't mean fear.' "And I respect your wisdom, especially. You've seen a great deal more than the newer princes. What troubles you, Malazra?"

"Why haven't we attacked the humans?" She cocked her head, genuine confusion plain on her features. "We suffered catastrophic losses during that battle. Our people are angry. They crave vengeance. And we could crush the humans utterly. Easily. I'd say the same of the Wyrms, but let's be honest...they're mostly an afterthought. Why have we not conquered the sector?"

Aran rose from the throne, and walked down the steps. He stood before Malazra, and even having grown a few centimeters from his demonic transformation, she still towered over him.

"It's true that we lost countless demons," Aran admitted, without flinching. "But they were absorbed into Xal, not killed by humans or Wyrms. Attacking a neutral third party because we suffered will only encourage a cycle of war. And I will not allow that, because it's not what Xal wanted."

"But if we do not come for them, then—"

"Then nothing." Aran narrowed his eyes. He hated that he had to do this through force, but reason wasn't something demon lords respected, and like it or not that was exactly what he'd been forced to become. "We get to choose what our people become. When Xal left the Great Cycle he chose to become a builder. A craftsman. He taught his people, us, to be better. To rise above our baser nature, the same nature humans, Wyrms, demons, and likely every other species shares."

Aran paused. That was a critical test when speaking. If you commanded respect, then your audience would wait. If not, though, the opposition would plunge in like a unit exploiting a gap in a line.

No one spoke.

"Xal made his wishes clear," Aran finally continued. He moved to stand next to Nara, and wrapped an arm around her. "We stand united. Not just demons. Not just this sector. Everyone. We don't unite through force. We are not an empire. We are a confederacy. We ask our members to help defend each other, but we do not conquer, or wipe out. We do this, because together we are far stronger. Nefarius's entire goal was to destroy our unity, to leave us shattered and broken so she could gobble up the pieces. We will not allow that to happen."

Nara stepped forward, and Aran gestured at her to indicate she had the floor. She held the rifle casually aloft, for their collective inspection. "Do you see this? This is an artifact of unrivaled power, yes? We can all agree that, at some point, our ancestors had the ability to craft things we can't even comprehend."

She lowered the rifle. "I have asked and Kazon has

graciously agreed to found a university where we will train our people to build and think, not just to fight. We will learn to make artifacts like this, and to create things we cannot even envision yet. Doing that will require more than just demonity, or humanity, or the Wyrms. It will require scholars from all races. They will come here. We will send students there. We will work together, and we will grow together. Because together we will never fall prey to something like this again."

"The alternative," Aran broke in, delivering a grateful nod to Nara, "is endless war. We teach our people to conquer. To destroy. We become Nefarius and beat the sector and then the galaxy into submission. And I won't have that. That is why I have joined the Confederacy. That is why Virkon will use the Crucible to research new ships and tech. That is why we will supply troops to the fleets the humans are turning out. Understanding of our people will turn fear into respect, especially if all races do their part."

Aran reached for the ocean of magic inside him, utterly incalculable in size, and used a bit of *void* to rise into the air, over them all. "But if you disagree with this policy, all you need to do is challenge me. Anyone?"

Kazon looked between Malila and Malazra's scandalized expression, and then laughed. "Ah, brother, at first I was not certain how I would adapt to this new life. I believe I am going to enjoy this."

Aran landed next to Nara. "Thank you for coming, lords, ladies. You are dismissed."

One by one each lord bowed, then translocated away, until Nara and Aran stood alone.

"So," Aran began, fumbling for a smoothness he'd never possessed, "do you have dinner plans? Because afterwards I am totally planning to make a play for second base."

"It's time to celebrate. We earned it." Nara gave him a truly wicked smile. The smile became an eye roll. "We should probably skip dinner, though. By that point I'm sure we'll have another crisis to deal wi—"

Aran stepped in and silenced her with a kiss. She was right. No sense wasting any more time.

NOTE TO THE READER

Thank you for reading The Magitech Chronicles. The adventures really just start here! Other series are on the way, plus the RPG of course.

If you're interested enough to want to know when the next series comes out, pop over to magitechchronicles.com and sign up to the mailing list on the right-hand side of the page.

I'll give you a chance to beta read the next book, work on the roleplaying game, and you'll hear about a small Magitech Chronicles Facebook Group with like-minded readers where we talk about everything from the roleplaying game to what's coming in the next book.

We'd love to have you!

-Chris

Made in the USA
Coppell, TX
05 January 2021